Swift

by
Heather London

Swift

ISBN-13: 978-0615683706

Edited by The Mighty Pen
http://www.mightypenediting.com/

Cover design by Stephanie Mooney
http://www.stephaniemooney.net/

Dedication

For my amazing husband, Ryan, and BFF, Kia.

Chapter One

"Today is not going to be a good day," I mumbled out loud, opening my eyes and glaring out my window. I could see the black, ominous clouds rolling in, casting a dark gloom in my already melancholy bedroom. Maybe I should have taken the color of the sky as a warning, as a sign that I should have put off what I had been procrastinating on for weeks now. I rolled over and looked at my alarm clock, confirming what I already knew: the large green numbers read 6:32 a.m.—way too early to be up on a Saturday morning.

"Just get it over with already," I muttered, throwing the covers off and sighing as the sound of rain began to pound on the roof above me. The smell of coffee and sound of banging dishes told me that Aunt Rose was already downstairs in the kitchen, making breakfast. It would be a miracle if I got out of the house without her seeing me. The last thing I wanted to deal with just then was a pity party from her or her telling me how she didn't want me "doing this alone." I carefully opened my bedroom door, hoping it wouldn't squeak if I opened it just right. I tiptoed to the bathroom, ran a brush through my hair, and after eventually giving up on untangling it, put it up into a ponytail.

After getting dressed and gathering all the gear needed to brave the crappy weather I was ready to make my escape. I reached the end of the staircase and peeked around the corner to see Aunt Rose unloading the dishwasher. As she turned to put away the silverware, I made my move. I could just hear her voice: *Meredith Marie, where do you think you are going? There is a monsoon outside.* And that would just be the beginning.

I rounded the corner of Maple Avenue, relieved I had gotten away without being caught.

The few houses I passed on the way were all still dark on the inside, probably because the people were still fast asleep in their warm, dry beds. Why would any sane person be up so early on a dreary Saturday morning?

I wrapped my arms tightly across my chest, trying to secure the little warmth I had left inside my body. Not that I should have been surprised; this was typical East Coast weather. The weather in Marblehead is so unpredictable, especially at this time of year. The closer I got, the more the smell of salt from the ocean burned my nose with each breath, and with each breath, the memories flooded my head and the sick feeling in the pit of my stomach worsened. I wrapped my arms tighter around myself, hoping it would help ease some of my anxiety and pain.

Finally I approached the black iron gates of Waterside Cemetery. As I stood there staring at the gates, I debated if I wanted to go inside. There is still the option to turn back, I thought. I haven't even stepped foot inside yet. Besides, the rain has caused a thick fog; it's probably not very safe to enter a graveyard when it's foggy. Who knows what could happen? I could trip over a gravestone, break my ankle, and get trapped inside this dreadful place.

Standing there like a coward, I stared deeper into the desolate graveyard filled with nothing but cold, concrete stones: some tall and slender, some wide and short, and some so small you could barely see them over the overgrown grass and fog. A few graves had fresh flowers on them, but most of them were bare. I sighed, realizing that the bare and empty feeling I was having would soon end if I just got what I was there to do over with. For all those bright and sunny days that I had avoided going there, this was the price for my procrastination.

Taking a deep breath, I put one foot forward and began the walk that I'd become accustomed to over the years. The stone path leading to the far edge of the cemetery is always lined with the appropriate foliage for the season. Since it was late May, there were yellow daffodils along the way.

In the far left corner of the cemetery, where there are no trees for shelter and mostly dead grass, there are four graves. They are so small and simple that it is not even proper to call them gravestones. These graves were not my main reason for going there, but over the years, I've made a point to visit them each time I go. You could say I was drawn to them in a way. Most people would probably miss them unless they accidently stepped right on them like I did a few years back. The rectangular plates lay in the ground all side by side, equally spaced apart. They all hold no more information than a single name: *Harper*. They certainly show their age; they are barely legible and worn-looking. I'd always felt pity for the people in the graves because there were no first names to give them each their own personal identity, no words to describe who they each had been as a person—trivial as those things may be after you are gone from this world.

After stopping there for a few moments, I continued on my journey to the real reason for going to the graveyard. Glancing up at the sign, "Angels Passage," I knew that I was getting close.

After a few more steps, I came to the site where both my parents and twin sister are buried. The largest headstone in the cemetery reads my last name: *Martin.* The names of my father, mother, and sister read below, along with all the sentimental beloved and loving stuff. Not that any of that isn't true, but it just doesn't seem right for them. There is so much more to them than those simple words. Those words don't even come close to doing them justice.

There was a reason I came to the cemetery that day: I came to tell my family that I was leaving Marblehead. It felt awful telling them that I would not be able to visit them as often, and saying it out loud hurt more than I thought it would. My mind had been made up for a while now, but I hadn't been able to find the courage to go there and tell them. It's not that I had finally found the courage; it's just that I had finally run out of excuses. Those past few weeks, I had had plenty of them: homework, studying for finals, graduation, and then there was my eighteenth birthday. I had decided that going to the cemetery the day before, the day of, or the day after, would not be a great way to celebrate. But I had turned eighteen three days ago, and now that excuse was way past valid.

I tried my best to explain to them why I was leaving, why I wasn't going to college, and why I wanted nothing more than to get out of this town. It was true; I was the abnormal one in thinking the town was suffocating—once it sucks you in, it never lets you go. There was an overpowering need for me to get out of that place and find the answers I had been looking for my entire life. Maybe the ones I had asked myself a million times since I was eight: Why was I the one to survive the accident? Why had I been given a second chance? I knew that I was meant for something more than being just Meredith Martin, the girl who suffered a tragic loss at a young age. There was nothing I wanted more than to erase that brand bestowed upon me.

While I sat with my back propped up against the cold gravestone, I pulled out pictures from my graduation and flipped through the stack. It took my breath away when I realized how much I looked like my mother. Her longer oval face did not match my rounder heart-shaped face, but her dark green eyes, long brown hair, and pouty lips were exact matches of mine. I hold no resemblance to my dad, but I did inherit his introverted, independent personality. I was what most conformists would call a nonconformist.

After sitting and talking with the three people I loved most in the world, I desperately needed a friend, someone that could actually talk back to me. I called the only other human being that actually understood me … or at least pretended to.

The phone rang six times before he finally picked up.

"Hey, Roger, meet me down at the diner in twenty minutes? My treat," I asked, sounding desperate, hoping he couldn't hear it in my voice.

"Mer, it's Saturday, and you remember that we just graduated a few days ago, right? We are supposed to be using this time to sleep while we still can." He sighed. I could tell by the raspy-ness in his voice that I had awoken him from a deep slumber. "But since I am in withdrawal of your bright and joyful *personalities* … See you there in twenty," he finished in a sarcastic but casual voice.

"You're the best. See you soon." I quickly hung up the phone before he could ask me any more questions. He would probably not like that I was at the cemetery by myself. He always said that I should never go there alone, that it was not good for me.

I told my family goodbye and promised that I would be back a few more times that summer before leaving town. Then I laid the picture of me and Aunt Rose against the gravestone and ran my left hand along the top of it as one last loving gesture before heading out.

The daffodil-lined path was almost dry now; I hadn't even noticed that the rain had stopped. When I looked up, I could see the sun fighting to get through the canopy of trees above me. Every few feet, the sun's rays would push through a thin layer of tree limbs and shine on my face. The feeling of warmth made me smile. It was a content feeling that I had not had in a long time. I had been torturing myself for weeks now to come and talk to them, and now I had done it.

Suddenly my feeling of joy was interrupted by cries of grief echoing throughout the cemetery. I turned my head right and left, searching for the person suffering, when a figure to the right caught my eye. I squinted, trying to see the person more clearly, but she was still too far away. The closer I got, the more I realized I didn't recognize her at all—and I knew everyone in that town, more than I wanted to. Her long, corn-silk blonde hair would have easily stood out in Marblehead, and her long green skirt and white lace blouse were definitely not the style around here. She was kneeling with her hands cupped over her face as if she were trying to hide her tears from someone. But as I scanned the area around her, I realized there was no one there but me. As I got closer, I could see that she was kneeling in front of the four mysterious Harper graves that I had made a point to stop at during each of my visits. She can't be crying because she knows them; those graves are ancient, I thought to myself. The people buried there have been gone for a very, very long time.

I cautiously moved toward her, but soon she noticed my presence. The young woman's head jerked up and her wide-eyed stare stopped me dead in my tracks. In that second, I wished that I could run, run faster than the wind, faster than the speed of light. I wanted nothing more than to get away from the startling green eyes that stared at me as if they had seen a ghost. For the first few seconds, no words passed between us. There was just her cold stare and the adrenaline coursing throughout my body.

As I stood there, frozen, I searched for words to speak. I wanted to say something along the lines of "Sorry for interrupting you" or "Please excuse me," but the words were stuck in my throat. Anything. Just one word?

Finally, as if a bond had been broken, I found my voice again. "Hi," I whispered, swallowing hard. *Hi*? That's all I can say? Here I am staring at this stranger that quite honestly looked like she could have just walked out of the psych ward, and all I can mutter out is *hi*?

But there was no reply, no change in her facial expression.

"Sorry if I scared you. I heard you crying." Stupid. What am I saying? Just leave. Walk away before you make things even more uncomfortable. "Umm … Sorry to have interrupted you." My voice cracked, and I turned to walk in the opposite direction.

Then the girl, who had not spoken one word or even made a move since our eyes met, stood up. "It can't be," she finally muttered under her breath as she slowly backed away from me.

Well, at least she could speak.

"It can't be *what*?" I asked, watching her walk backwards toward the exit of the cemetery.

She was so simple-looking, nothing like the superficial girls covered in makeup I had gone to school with. She looked more like me, plain and simple. She looked to be about my age, maybe even a couple years older. It was her clothes that I couldn't get over. They did not seem like they belonged in this era, maybe not even in this century.

The girl shook her head, turned around, and practically ran toward the entrance. I followed her, keeping my distance, not wanting to intrude more than I already had. I shouldn't have interrupted her; it was none of my business. She glanced back a couple times and each time she did, she got faster and faster. As she exited between the large black gates, she turned left and took one last look at me before disappearing behind the tall stone wall.

Even though I knew I shouldn't, even though I knew it would make me feel like a spy, and even though I would feel awful if she caught me, I couldn't help but look for her as I approached the exit. I tried my best to be subtle, slightly turning my head to the right and reaching my eyes in the same direction as far as they would go. But there was nothing. No sign of her whatsoever. And even though I knew stopping in the middle of the street and scanning it was not so subtle, I couldn't stop myself. But she was still nowhere to be found.

A strange ache pained my heart. I couldn't understand why I cared so much about this girl I didn't even know. And I couldn't explain the strange feeling I had when I saw her, especially when our eyes met. I just hoped that wherever she disappeared to she knew where she was going, because the road back into town was in the opposite direction. All she was going to get up that way was a dead end that forced her to turn left onto the abandoned Estate Lane, the part of town that people in Marblehead rarely visited—actually, absolutely avoided was more like it. The few homes still left standing on that block are creepy at best, and all of them have been condemned by the city. No one steps foot on that street, unless of course they are trying to prove something. But even then, I have seen senior football players too scared to get within a hundred yards of that place. After a long minute of standing there and staring at the vacant street, a single thought sent my heart into spasm: Roger!

Chapter Two

When I had the diner in view, I saw Roger glaring out the window. The glare became focused on me as I walked toward the booth.

"Geez, what's your problem?" I questioned as I flopped down into the black vinyl seat.

"It's Saturday and I'm out of my bed before noon, that's my problem," he responded with a slight grin on his face. I knew that grin meant he was teasing, but I sensed a little irritation in his voice as well.

"Get over it," I joked back, trying to keep my tone light. "Besides, if you had not gotten up to meet me then you would not be able to hear the crazy story I've got to tell you." I tried to sound convincing so he would ease up on the glare he still held on me.

"Sure, you do." He looked skeptical as he glanced down at the menu.

"Quit whining, you big baby. Seriously, once we get some food ordered, I will tell you about the crazy girl I saw crying inside the cemetery," I said, taking a look at the menu as well. Not that either of us needed to look at the menu. The hundred times we had been there over the years, we'd never gotten anything but two double stacks and two glasses of OJ. I pushed the menu toward the end of the table and sat farther back into the booth.

"You went to the cemetery today? Why didn't you call me? I would have gone with you, Mer." He met my eyes with a sincere and sympathetic look on his face.

Sure, he only hears that I went to the cemetery. He doesn't even pay attention to the damsel in distress I just mentioned. Actually, I had not been planning to tell Roger about the cemetery in hopes of avoiding a lecture or pity party from him. But after what happened with the girl, I couldn't not tell him what happened. Roger was my best friend, and I had to tell someone.

"Yeah. Right. If you think this is early on a Saturday morning, then you would have killed me if I called you at 7:00 a.m. And I kinda wanted to go by myself, anyway—you know, be alone with them," I said, shrugging out of my rain jacket, which I had forgotten that I still had on. "It doesn't matter now; what you should be interested in is the *girl.*"

Finally the waitress approached, and we put in our usual order.

"Okay, I'll bite. What happened with this girl you saw?" he asked, rolling his eyes.

I glared up at him but went on because I was excited to tell him even if he would more than likely just shrug it off. "Well, as I was walking out of the cemetery, I heard someone crying—"

"Normal," Roger interrupted. "I have to tell you, Mer, seeing someone crying inside a cemetery is not big news."

I sighed, giving him a pointed look. "Are you going to let me finish or just keep interrupting?" I didn't want to mention anything to Roger about her standing over the Harper graves. He always thought I was a little strange for wanting to visit them every time he went with me to the cemetery.

"Go ahead," he answered, gesturing for me to continue.

I laid out the entire scene for him, but he didn't seem too impressed or think it was half as interesting as I did. Maybe leaving out the part about the Harper graves killed it. "... But the craziest part was that she stared at me like I was some kind of freak, like she had seen a ghost or something." I hoped that adding in a little drama would pique his interest.

"Well, you do look like you just rolled out of bed," he joked, but I had to believe there was some truth behind it.

"Ha. Ha." I scowled up at him.

"So was she young, old? Tall, short?" Roger asked, sounding a little more interested.

This girl was *so* way not his type. I mean, she was blonde, so at least she had that going for her, but she didn't look like a Victoria's Secret model, so she wouldn't have held his attention for long. I mean, she could have been pretty if she tried harder, but she was still a little too plain for Roger's taste.

The waitress came, placing our pancakes and OJ in front of us.

"She looked to be about our age, long blonde hair, not too tall, about my height." I guessed, not knowing how to describe the girl in much more detail. I grabbed the syrup, drowning my pancakes in it, and then passed the bottle across the table to Roger.

"Come on, Meredith, give me details," he pressed, acting impatient with my bland description.

"Honestly, she looked pretty normal except for her clothing," I sighed, annoyed that that was all he cared about.

“Her clothing? That’s boring,” he said as if he was done with the conversation. He took a large bite of his pancakes.

“I don’t know why you would be interested in what she looks like anyway. Aren’t you going to have your hands full *wooing* all the girls in Rockport?” He was going to be spending most of the summer there with his dad.

“You’re right, but I still have a few days left here to woo,” he said, raising his eyebrows. He shoved another large bite into his mouth.

“Ugh, you are such a pig; I don’t know why I talk to you,” I scoffed, shaking my head. I took a bite and quickly realized I’d put on way too much syrup this time.

“Because I’m the only friend you have.”

“Hey, I have Rebecca, too,” I argued defensively.

“Sure, I’ll give you that, but I’m your only *real* friend,” he said, clarifying his previous statement.

That was true. Roger was my one and only true friend. Don’t get me wrong, Rebecca was a great friend, but she was only someone I would hang out with on occasion. If I ever needed girl talk or an excuse to get out of the house every once in a while, she was the one I would call. It sounds selfish, but it’s the truth. Roger was the only one who knew me inside and out, backwards, forwards, and any other direction possible.

There was a long pause between us, and my thoughts went back to the girl in the cemetery. I just couldn't get those startling green eyes out of my head. I sensed Roger staring at me, and I looked toward him, watching as he rubbed his chin with his right hand like he was in deep thought.

"Maybe she's just visiting a relative for the summer … or maybe she was kidnapped and her captors are hiding her out in one of the old haunted estates." He barely got out the last few words while keeping a straight face.

"You should not be making fun, Roger. She could have been in some sort of trouble or recently lost someone she really cared about," I snapped back, annoyed that he would make such light of the situation.

"You're right," he said, trying his hardest to wipe the smirk off his face and failing miserably at it. "Forgive me. I was just trying to make you smile. You seem like you are really beating yourself up about it."

"I'm just worried about her, is all." I couldn't explain it to myself so there was no way to try and explain to Roger the strong connection I felt to the stranger: the way I felt paralyzed with fear the moment her eyes met mine, the unmistakable connection I had with her.

"Well, don't be too hard on yourself; you said she ran away from you, right? What more could you have done?" he said, trying to reassure me.

"Yeah, I guess so. I just hope she's okay," I said, staring out the window.

After eating about half my plate, I pushed it toward the end of the table and saw that Roger had finished each and every last bite.

"You ready to go?" Roger asked me with his I'm-about-to-puke-from-eating-too-much look on his face.

"Sure, let's go. I don't want you to miss out on any more of your beauty sleep." I grabbed my jacket and scooted out of the booth.

"What time should I pick you up tomorrow?" Roger asked as he held the door open for me.

"Pick me up? For what?"

"Uh, only the biggest party ever! Probably the best party or your life." He acted bothered at the fact that I would forget such an important event.

Oh, yeah, I remember. The Graduating Senior's Only party. The one party that most kids at our school started to look forward to on their first day of freshman year.

"Ugh, right. How could I forget?" I moaned. "No one will miss me if I don't show."

"Sure, they will. *I* will miss you." He glanced at me with a sincere expression on his face. "Rebecca is going to be there, too." His voice was full of persuasion.

I turned to glare at him, not knowing if this was just a lie so I would agree to go or if he was actually telling the truth. "How do you know she's going? She did not say anything to me about it."

He smirked before responding, and I knew he was up to something. "I saw Rebecca at the store last night, and she said that she was debating not going to the party. So I mentioned that you were going, and she was sold," he said, looking very satisfied with himself.

"She is so gullible," I said, shaking my head. "You know that you have this power over her, right? She has had a crush on you since first grade."

"Why do you have to be so difficult?" he said, ignoring my previous comment. "It's just a party; it's *supposed* to be fun. You remember fun, right?"

And more than anything, I wished I had the answer. I'm really not this horrible, depressed, introverted person. Well, I guess that depends on who you ask. But really, there's just something about loud music and a hundred people who I don't particularly have anything in common with that makes we want to puke. Roger is an exception. He is and has always been my best friend. He just also happens to be the most popular guy in school, and for some reason he loves me. Not *love* loves me—more like a brother would love a sister.

"I just don't like parties like that. I don't fit in with those people. It will probably just be a bore fest, anyway."

"Mer, you don't fit in with anyone, but that's why I love you. Besides it's going to be the last time you see any of these people for a long time—myself included," he said, trying his hardest to convince me. And as much as I hated to admit it, he had a point. It was probably one of the last times I would have to hang out with him before I left. And not just Roger; Rebecca would be gone soon, too. She was spending the next month riding around in an RV with her family before heading off to Boston University.

"Okay." I sighed, giving in. "I will go to the party, but no promises on how long I will stay."

"Awesome." He grinned smugly, happy with himself that he had just won. "Now that you have already agreed to go, I must tell you that it's a luau-type party, so dress appropriately … maybe a cute beach dress or something." He slowly backed away from me with defensive hands up, ready to protect himself.

"What! You are going to pay for this," I warned.

"Come on, at least try and have a good time and participate. Please?" He frowned.

"Yeah, can't wait," I said sarcastically as I raised my hands up in the air pretending to celebrate.

"What am I going to do without your optimistic, cheerful personality all summer? My world is going to be so dark." He grinned.

"You are going to miss me, and you know it."

His smile grew as he pulled me in for one of his infamous bear hugs.

"Okay, too tight … so full … I am about to—"

He let go before I could finish, anticipating what I was about to say.

"Okay, well, go home and take a nap. You need your beauty sleep more than I do," he said as he began to walk backwards toward his car.

"You are such a jerk," I snapped and then turned around on my heels, waving as I walked off.

"See you tomorrow night. Be ready to party!" he screamed from a distance, and I looked back to see him crouch down into his shiny, blue '69 Mustang.

I never understood why he wanted that car. It must have been horribly uncomfortable for his six-foot-two build. It did make me smile though as I heard the purr of the engine start and grow even louder as he drove away.

Ugh, just thinking of the word *party* made my stomach turn and my skin crawl. As much as it pained me, I couldn't hate Roger for wanting to try and make me happy. He was the only person who actually got me. The weird, introverted, nonconformist loner. He still loved and accepted me all the same. We probably wouldn't be as close as we are if he had not lost his father when he was younger. His dad didn't pass away, like my family; his dad walked out on them, moved to Rockport, and got a new girlfriend when Roger was just seven. I guess we became close because we had the whole parent-abandonment thing in common, even though they were under very different circumstances.

Growing up, I had always envied Roger. He's what I called a dreamer and achiever. He knew what sport he wanted to play in high school, so we practiced all summer before freshman year so he would make varsity. He knew the exact color, make, and model of the car he wanted when he turned sixteen, so he worked double time to make sure he had enough money to buy it. Now he had been accepted to Harvard and would without doubt graduate with honors and continue on to law school. He knew who he was and what he wanted to do with his life. I, on the other hand, could not even tell you what was on my agenda for tomorrow. Well, other than this party I had just agreed to. It was effortless for him to be normal, to want the typical life and be content. It was not as easy for me. For some reason, I felt like there was more out there for me, and if nothing else, I had to at least try and find it.

As I approached the corner of Main and Sycamore, I pressed the crosswalk button and waited. After a few seconds, I looked right and left and saw the street was deserted. Just as I was about to step off the curb, something caught my eye. Or should I say, someone. There on the opposite corner a guy was standing facing me. It was weird, because I could feel the stare that he held on me. My eyes drifted toward him, and when our eyes met, his stare did not waver in the least. A shiver ran down my spine when I realized that I did not recognize him either. He was tall, maybe six feet or so and had blonde hair. His athletic build reminded me of most of our football players at school. I couldn't make out much more detail because of the distance separating us. Our eyes were locked together for a few seconds, only interrupted by the beeping of the crosswalk, letting me know it was my turn to cross. I shook my head as if to wake myself up from a dream, and without thinking twice about it, I stepped off the curb and into the street. And that's when I heard it—the horrible sound of tires screeching, trying their hardest to stop. But by the time I looked to my right, it was too late. I couldn't have moved out of the path of the car even if my frozen legs could've moved—there was just no time. The only thing I could do was shut my eyes tight, hope it would be quick, and pray the pain would be slight. Then everything went totally silent, so silent that I could hear my ears ringing and my heart pounding loud against my chest.

About a second later, a second past when I thought I would be road kill, I slightly opened my right eye and gasped at what I saw. The car was still in front of me, but it was moving in very slow motion. I mean, like molasses coming out of a bottle slow. Everything around me felt weird, different. I looked around, wondering if maybe the car had already hit me and this was just a cruel part of the afterlife or something, making me watch in slow motion how I died.

When I turned and looked to my left, I saw the same guy across the street, still staring right at me. The moment our eyes locked on each other, everything went back to normal. Well somewhat. I looked back in front of me just in time to see the car that I had thought was about to come barreling into me come to a startling halt just inches away from my body. Then I heard someone shouting.

"Meredith! Oh, my god, I'm so sorry. The light turned from green to red in an instant. There was no yellow light or anything. Are you okay?" Mr. Griffin, my old history teacher, hung his head out of his car. He was yelling at me, his voice shaking with each word.

I must have been in shock because I couldn't speak.

"Meredith! Are you hurt?" Mr. Griffin was beside me now. "Do you want me to call an ambulance or something?"

That woke me up out of the daze I was in. "Um—no. That won't be necessary," I said, noticing my voice held the same trembling tone as his.

"Are you sure you're okay? I'm really sorry. I-I swear the light was green and then it just turned red. I tried to stop, but—"

"Fine. I'm fine," I interrupted him. I continued my walk across the street, searching desperately for the guy that had been watching me. Maybe he could help explain what the hell just happened back there, or at least confirm that I wasn't going nuts. But he was nowhere to be found. Something very weird had just happened. The car had been going too fast. It had been going to hit me before something or someone stopped it. It was as if time had stopped or slowed down somehow. I walked home in a daze, trying to convince myself that I was just overreacting. What I thought

I saw back there just couldn't have happened. It just wasn't possible. When I arrived home, I walked right into the barrage of questions I had so masterfully avoided that morning.

Chapter Three

"Meredith, you had me worried sick. Where did you sneak off to this morning?" Aunt Rose asked impatiently, trying to maintain a serious tone as she held her hands on her hips.

Dropping my backpack and purse at the foot of the stairs, I tried to snap myself out of the daze I was still in. The last thing I wanted was to make Aunt Rose worry about me more than she already did. When I looked at her face, I had to press my lips together, trying to make an effort to not smile. I knew how hard it was for her to play the strict guardian role. She was more like an older sister to me than anything.

But to please her, I decided to play along and act like the disobedient child taking her punishment. "Sorry, I should have told you that I was headed out." I exhaled, hanging my head low. "I went to the cemetery." Even though it was a low blow, I knew mentioning it would quiet her. I was just not in the mood for talking or playing that part for very long.

"Oh—well, I just wish you would have told me. I would have gone with you. All you had to do was ask," she said, immediately changing her stance and attitude.

I smiled timidly. "Don't worry about it. I already got the lecture from Roger on going there by myself. But like I told him: I just wanted some time alone with them."

When she smiled back at me, I knew that was the end of that conversation. Then guilt washed over me, and I started to feel bad for throwing out the cemetery card so early on. It was tough looking at her face, seeing her sympathetic eyes staring back at me. Maybe I should've played the disobedient child part a little longer.

Aunt Rose was my guardian, my adult supervision, my answer whenever I was asked who I lived with, but she was not my real aunt. She was actually my mom's best friend; they had grown up together in Marblehead. Since I had had no other family around when my parents passed away, she was the lucky one that got stuck with me. The only name I ever called her growing up was Aunt Rose. She had given up everything for me and never thought twice about it. She had left her apartment and nursing job in Boston and moved into my house, not wanting me to have any more change than I had had already.

"To change the subject, how about we talk about your plans for this summer? You know, just so I can get an idea of your schedule and stuff." She bit her lip, knowing that was a bit of a touchy subject between us.

"Okay, but I already told you most of it. Get a job, save up some money, and then travel a bit when the summer ends. What else do you need to know?" I questioned, hoping she didn't want specifics because I had none.

"Oh, nothing, that's perfect. I just wanted to make sure those plans had not changed. You are so wishy-washy lately." I was not wishy-washy, but before I could defend myself, she began again. "Which brings me to tell you that I have the perfect job for you." Her eyes lit up in excitement.

"Oh, no, please not the hospital. You know I can't stand sick people, blood, or the smell of that place," I complained. My throat went dry with fear and I made my way into the kitchen for a glass of water.

She laughed, following me persistently. "Relax, it's not the hospital. Although I think that would be nice, you know, so we could spend some extra time together. But I wouldn't do that to you."

Aunt Rose was a nurse at our small, local hospital. Even though the town rarely ever saw any action, there were the occasional deep cuts with a kitchen knife, kids jumping on their bed, falling off, and busting their heads open, and lots of gross sick people.

I listened to her as I drank some water, quenching the dryness in my throat.

"Well." She hesitated for a moment. "I kinda ran into Ms. Donaldson today, and she asked about you. I mentioned that you were going to be here this summer, and she said that there was an opening for an assistant."

"Kinda ran into Ms. Donaldson? She asked about me?" I questioned suspiciously. Ms. Donaldson was our town librarian; she must have been close to eighty years old. I had a hard time believing she even remembered her own name.

"She was just trying to make conversation. I thought it was nice. Besides, it sounds like the perfect job for you," she insisted.

I can't lie; it was a little weird that Ms. Donaldson had asked about me. It was weird because I don't think she even knew who I was. She had never acknowledged me by name the few times I had gone to the library. And truth be told, I tried to avoid that place whenever I could. During school, I did most of my research projects online just so I would not have to go down there. The place gave me the creeps. But as the idea resonated, it didn't sound half bad. It would probably be quiet since it was summer and school was out. I had to admit, it sounded a lot better than working as a waitress or a grocery store clerk.

"Uh, thanks for the heads up, Aunt Rose. I will go down there and apply this week," I promised.

"Great! Well, that was easy." She smiled and patted me on the back. "I'm off to work. Someone called in sick, so I will be pulling a double shift, which will leave you on your own for dinner tonight. Call the hospital if you need anything," she shouted while on her way out the door.

"Will do!" I shouted back as I heard the door slam.

On my own for dinner *tonight*? I was on my own for dinner almost every night. When Aunt Rose wasn't working or sleeping, she was usually with her boyfriend Jack. But it was cool because I actually liked being alone, and I liked Jack. By the looks of it, he and Aunt Rose made a strange couple. Aunt Rose was a petite woman with short, blonde hair while Jack towered over her and wore a pony tail down his back. But I guess in their situation, opposites do attract. Jack and Aunt Rose had been dating for a few years now, and he owned a car detail shop in town. The kind of shop that you bring your car in to if you want to turn it into a flashy one. The kind of car that would draw attention in a crowd. That's why I respectfully declined each time he offered to fix mine up if I ever got one. It's not that Aunt Rose didn't try her hardest to buy me a car for my sweet sixteen; it's just that I never wanted one. I lived three blocks from school, six blocks from the town center, and a couple miles from the cemetery. Why would I need a car when I could just walk? But just because I didn't get a car doesn't mean I didn't get my driver's license. It was necessary for emergency's sake and the occasional grocery trip I made.

I headed upstairs, peeled off my clothes, and threw my pajamas from earlier that morning back on. I curled back up in bed, hoping that drowsiness would consume me, but no such luck. So much for beauty sleep, I thought to myself. As I lay there, the thought of the party slowly crept into my head and then panic set in as to what I would wear to the dreadful event. The thought turned me into a crazy person. I got up out of bed and began to tear through my closet to find anything appropriate for the Hawaiian theme—something, anything that would allow me to blend in. Go unseen if at all possible.

But I couldn't find anything appropriate. I spent the rest of the day picking up the mess that I had made, which led into doing laundry, cleaning out from under my bed, and rearranging my entire room. A part of me was annoyed at myself for starting the process, but another part was thankful for the distraction. Since school had ended, I had been having trouble keeping myself busy. I was actually looking forward to getting a job. Maybe this job at the library would be a good thing. Actually, if it was going to help me buy my ticket out of Marblehead, it was a great thing.

Before I knew it, it was dark outside, and after popping a TV dinner into the microwave, I parked myself on the couch for the rest of the night.

The next morning came too soon, and I woke up feeling nauseous. Unfortunately, not in a sick way, more like I had been dreaming about the impending party all night long. There was still the problem of what to wear, so I picked up the phone and dialed the only person I knew who could help. "Rebecca, hey, it's Meredith."

"Hey, what's up?"

"You are going to the party tonight, right?" I asked, hoping Roger was telling the truth and it had not been just some ploy to get me to go.

"Uh, yeah. Roger told me that you wouldn't go unless I went," she said in the shrill voice that would make me cringe if it was not coming from her.

"He said what? That little …" I trailed off, fuming on the inside.

"Huh?" Rebecca asked, sounding confused.

"Oh, nothing, just telling myself to punch Roger later when I see him."

"O-kay. But you are going, right? I mean, I would not feel comfortable without you there," she said, suddenly sounding panicked.

"Why? You know more of those people than I do."

"Yeah, but you are best friends with Roger, the most popular guy in school. I was actually going to call you later to see if we could ride together."

"Well, Roger is picking me up at 9:00 p.m. Do you want us to swing by and get you?" I offered.

"That would be awesome."

"How about us hanging out later, maybe go shopping together? I need some help with what to wear. I'm not very good at these things," I said urgently, my voice breaking from my slight panic.

"You look great in anything, Meredith. Just wear something you are comfortable in and you'll be fine," she replied reassuringly.

How about jeans and a T-shirt? I thought to myself. How would that look at a Hawaiian-themed party?

"Are you free today or not?" I asked, trying not to sound too anxious.

"Really wish I could, but I still have relatives in town from graduation, and if I am going to run off to the party, I have to put in some family time. Sorry."

"No problem." I sighed.

"So, see ya around 9:00 p.m.?" she asked excitedly.

"Yeah, sure."

I hung up the phone, knowing I was on my own with shopping. After eating breakfast, I peeked outside the kitchen window above the sink and saw that the sun was shining. Maybe the day wouldn't be too bad after all. Before I headed out, I left Aunt Rose a note, telling her I was going into town for a while, assuming she would get home from her double shift while I was gone. Even though I was eighteen and a graduate from high school, I guess it was still a nice gesture to tell her where I was going, especially after how she *tried* to overreact yesterday morning.

I looked around for my purse, finally seeing it in the exact spot I had dropped it yesterday, sitting at the bottom of the stairs next to my backpack. I slung it over my chest as I took one last glance in the hallway mirror. My hair was back in a ponytail like yesterday, and I had not even attempted to put on any makeup. Tonight I will try and make myself look decent, I promised the reflection staring back at me. Then I walked out and locked the door behind me.

The last thing I ever wanted to do was shop. It was actually one of my most hated things to do; it qualified as a chore in my book. You could tell this pretty easily with one look in my closet.

The weather was nice and warm, almost too warm for jeans. It was such a drastic change from the miserable weather yesterday. It was a quick, ten-minute walk to the town square, where there were a few clothing shops. I picked out the store I had been in once with Aunt Rose. She dragged me there to buy a dress for one of her friend's weddings. The whole shopping experience was a disaster, and she had never made me wear a dress again or offered to take me shopping.

As I entered the store, the bell dinged above my head, letting the clerk know I had entered. A young girl sat behind the counter flipping through a magazine. "Let me know if you need help finding anything," she said, not even raising her head from the page as I walked past her toward the sale rack.

"Thanks," I responded, glancing toward her. I knew who she was; her name was Riley Shaw. She was Matthew Shaw's little sister. I knew this because Matthew was one of Roger's friends from the basketball team, and she used to have a major crush on Roger, like stalker-type crush. She had left him love notes on his car outside school, stolen his gym shorts, and even had got caught spying on him in the locker room. Roger, of course, thought she was way too young and a little crazy. Plus, Matthew swore he would kill Roger if he came close to her.

I shuffled through the sales rack and picked out three dresses I thought would work for the theme. My choices were nothing over the top, nothing too bright or ostentatious, but they would be perfect for the blending-in style *I* was going for. I tried on the first dress and awkwardly walked to the big mirrors outside the dressing room. If I was going to actually wear a dress, I wanted to be able to see myself from every angle, just to make sure there were no hidden surprises. I turned, facing left and then right, and then strained my neck to check out the back.

The first two dresses were total disasters. The third dress I picked out was actually my favorite even though I had yet to try it on. I hoped it would be the one and my shopping experience would be over. Just as I was zipping up the side, I heard Riley greet a new customer from behind the counter. Great, I really thought I was going to get out of here without anyone seeing me, I thought. Before stepping out into the open space with the big mirror, I slowly opened the door to see if I could spot the unknown shopper. The coast was clear, so I quickly marched out and gave myself a once-over. It was perfect: not too tight or too short, and it would totally work for the theme.

Feeling relieved that I had found something, I exited the dressing room and began my walk to the register. As I fumbled through my purse for my wallet, I regrettably bumped into the mystery shopper. I let out a silent gasp when our eyes met. Those were the same startling green eyes that I had seen in the cemetery yesterday. I apologized, keeping my head down and focusing on getting to the register and out of there as fast as possible. She seems to be doing okay, I thought to myself. She's not dead at least.

"Hi, did you find everything okay?" Riley asked as I approached. "You're Meredith, right?"

"Yes, and you're Riley, Mathew's sister." I did not phrase it as a question.

"That's me, although I would rather not claim him." She rolled her eyes as she began to ring up my dress. "Is this for the party tonight?" Her eyes lit up in excitement.

"Yeah," I responded, not sharing her enthusiasm, trying to fight the nausea at the sound of the word *party*.

"It's a great color for you, goes really well with your hair and complexion."

"Thanks," I smiled timidly. I never felt comfortable when anyone paid me compliments. Not that it happened often.

"Roger is going to be there, right?" Her voice sounded desperate, like it would ruin her day if I answered no.

"Uh, yeah. He is the one who talked me into going," I said, shaking my head at the thought of him lying to both Rebecca and me just to get me to go.

"Awesome." A large grin stretched across her face. "I overheard my brother talking about it. He doesn't know I am going and will probably have a conniption when he sees me there, *graduates–only* rule and all. I mean, it's a party, so the more the merrier, right?" she asked.

"Totally." It's not like I cared if she went or not. I couldn't care less if the whole entire school showed up. I handed her my debit card and watched the grin on her face grow. I wondered what was going on in her head, even though I knew it probably had something to do with Roger. Ha, I thought to myself, realizing that my payback for Roger would be seeing the look on his face when Riley found him. This party may be worth my while after all.

"Here you go. Receipt's in the bag."

"Maybe I will see you later tonight," I said, smiling as I grabbed my bag and headed for the door. The conversation with Riley had distracted me, and for a minute I forgot about the girl I was trying to avoid. The second I approached the door, I saw someone moving in the corner of my eye, and it all came back to me. Keeping my head down, I hurried out the door, hoping to avoid any more uncomfortable run-ins. I had only made it a few steps from the store before I heard the bell from the shop's door ding again.

Chapter Four

"Excuse me," a soft but firm voice from behind me spoke.

I stopped and swallowed hard as I turned and found myself staring straight at the blonde girl's face. The look she held was a mixture of fear and nervousness.

"Hello. I wanted to try and explain myself from yesterday. It was very impolite of me to run off like I did. I am sorry for being so rude," she spoke eloquently and articulated each word.

My mind was trying to register what she had said, and it took me a few seconds to find the right words to say in return. "Really, you have nothing to apologize for. I shouldn't have intruded. It was just, I was worried about you," I confessed, immediately feeling vulnerable that I had just admitted that to her.

"That is very sweet of you. I was a little distressed yesterday and not myself. I am Abigail Harper, by the way—but most people call me Abby," she finished, holding out her right hand.

She must have thought I was crazy because I just stood there, shocked and confused. But my mind had gone blank when she said her last name was Harper. It could have been just a strange coincidence, but that was the same name on the four graves I had seen her standing over at the cemetery. The same four graves that I stopped at every time I visited my family, and the same graves that looked to be a couple hundred years old. My heart began to beat hard against my chest, and I quickly snapped myself back to reality. Must have been her great-great-grandfather, I tried to tell myself.

"I'm Meredith. It's—nice to meet you," I stuttered as I extended my hand to meet hers. I had always felt something when I was near the Harper graves, some energy or force that I could never describe, not to anyone, not even myself. The energy was even more overwhelming when I stood that close to Abby and made contact with her hand. It took me a few seconds to come back into the present moment, and I jerked my hand back to my side. As I looked into her eyes, I could tell that she had felt something as well.

"You must be new to town," I said urgently, trying to distract myself from the strange energy running through me.

"You could say that. We are just here for the summer. My family and I are staying in one of the older estates, trying to restore it," she said.

"Oh" was the only word that escaped my mouth. Well, that solved part of the mystery. Now I knew why she had been heading toward Estate Lane, but it did not explain how she disappeared so quickly and why she had been visiting the graves.

"Welcome to Marblehead," I said, shrugging, unsure of what else to say.

"Thank you." She smiled. "I'm sure we will see each other around, it being a small town and all."

"Right. Um, well, I really have to be going," I mumbled, looking in the direction of my house. There was no way to explain why I was acting so nervous or why I was in such a rush to get away from her. It wasn't like I was short on time. The party was still hours away, but the energy between us was becoming unbearable. It was as if I was in my own personal tug of war. Some force was pulling us to one another, but there was also something trying to keep us apart.

“Of course. It was a great pleasure to meet you, Meredith Martin.” She smiled as she slowly backed away from me, similar to her movements from yesterday, minus the crazed stare.

When I got home, I dropped my purse and the bag with my new dress near the stairs and wandered into the kitchen. The note I had left for Aunt Rose was still lying in the same spot, but it had been modified with a new one.

Thanks for the note but you didn’t have to leave one. Sorry we missed each other. Taking a nap before working the night shift again. See you when I wake up.

AR

After eating some lunch, I went ahead and jumped in the shower. Not that I needed two hours to get ready, I just wanted something to distract me from the thoughts running through my head. It was difficult to ignore the weird feeling I had had when I was near Abby and how her last name matched the one on the mysterious graves, the same four graves that looked to be hundreds of years old. Not to mention the weirdness that was still on my mind from yesterday: the way I almost got run over by Mr. Griffin before his car miraculously went into slow motion mode before hitting me. I chalked them both up to just strange coincidences. What else could they be?

Then as I stepped out of the shower and was drying off, something about earlier struck me. Before Abby and I had parted ways, she'd said, "It was nice to meet you, Meredith Martin." I didn't remember introducing myself with my full name. I never introduced myself using my full name. Or at least, I didn't think I did. I shook it off, thinking that I must have; otherwise, how would she have known?

It took me no time at all to get ready. I was an hour ahead of schedule and aggravated at myself for being ready so early. It just gave me that much more time to sit and think about what I was about to endure. When I finally heard the purr of Roger's Mustang on my street, I took a deep breath and tried my hardest to put a smile on my face, pretending to be excited for his sake.

I opened the door before he even knocked, hoping not to wake Aunt Rose, who was still sleeping before her night shift.

He whistled as he approached the door. "Wow, Meredith, you look great."

I rolled my eyes. "Ugh, stop. I'm just trying to blend in. I figured my T-shirt and jeans would stand out too much." I turned to scan the living room for my purse and saw it resting near the bottom of the stairs.

"Sorry to disappoint you, but you are definitely going to stand out. You're a knockout," he said, looking me up and down.

I looked down, examining myself, not understanding what was so great about a lilac-colored dress with a few flowers on it. "Okay, seriously, no more. You're creeping me out."

"You're just lucky that everyone thinks of you as my little sister, so no one will touch you."

"That's a relief. Let's just go and get this over with," I gritted the words through my teeth as I slung my purse over my shoulder, totally giving up on pretending to be excited.

"Oh, hang on, forgot something." I stopped just before locking the door. I ran back to the kitchen and grabbed the pen, adding a new note below Aunt Rose's last one:

Going to the seniors-only party ... won't be out too late. Have a good shift.

Fortunately, it was a short trip to Rebecca's house. I was eager to see what she was wearing and prayed that I was on the right track with my outfit. We stopped out front, and before I could even get out of the car to get her, I saw her racing toward us, exhilaration spread all over her face. Her brown hair was curled and it bounced up and down with each step she took. I breathed a sigh of relief when I noticed her dress was somewhat similar to mine.

She jumped in back and immediately started ranting about her day. "Oh. My. Gawd! I thought 9:00 would never come. I love my grandparents and all, but if I had to listen to one more cutesy story about me when I was a child, I think my head would have exploded. I don't know how I'm going to survive with them in a confined space."

Roger and I looked at each other and started to laugh. The laughter felt nice, allowing some of the anxiety I had been keeping dammed up to flow out of me.

"Well, hello, Rebecca. How was your day? You seem tense," Roger said sarcastically while looking in the rearview mirror at her. Then we all laughed as we drove to what would probably be one of their most memorable nights and one of my most miserable ones.

As we turned onto Ocean Avenue, I could already hear the loud music coming from Devereux Beach.

"Wow, hear that?" Roger asked excitedly. "Patrick brought his stereo from home and set it all up … with a few extra speakers, of course. Pretty cool, huh?"

"Yeah, cool," I answered, trying not to sound too sarcastic but knowing he'd read right through it.

"Totally awesome," Rebecca replied excitedly from the backseat.

"Come on, Meredith. You can't already be a downer; you haven't even gotten to the party yet. Just try and have a good time, okay?" He glanced over at me with a pleading look on his face.

"I will do my best." I smiled genuinely, not wanting to ruin his fun with my miserable attitude.

As we got closer to the beach, I could see the glow from the large bonfires spread out over the stretch of sand. The actual party may not be my cup of tea, but I must say, it was beautifully done. My stomach began to knot as we turned into the makeshift gravel parking lot a few blocks down. Great, the lot is already completely full, I thought. It looked like we were one of the last to show as we were relegated to park on the grass at the very end.

"Here we go," Roger said as he put the car in park.

"Don't leave me alone, okay?" Rebecca said as we began to walk down the gravel path toward the beach.

"Deal," I said, sounding relieved, knowing I would have at least one person by my side all night.

As we approached the first group of people, everyone screamed Roger's name, and he was immediately surrounded. Rebecca and I were left standing there alone and looking very uncomfortable.

“Rebecca!” I heard a voice shout.

“Rebecca! Hey over here!” the voice shouted again.

She scanned the crowd and found the mysterious voice. It was Sarah Morris, the head cheerleader. Rebecca turned to me with an agonizing expression, like she was asking my permission if she could go. “Come on, let’s go see what they want,” she said eagerly.

“No, you go for it,” I responded. “I’m fine, really.”

“You sure?”

“Totally.”

“Cool, I will come find you in a little while.” She hurried off, waving to the small group of girls as she approached them.

“So much for sticking together,” I muttered under my breath.

I couldn’t say I was surprised; this had been just what I had envisioned happening—Roger being bombarded the second we arrived, Rebecca finding her little group to hang with, and me being left alone. With a roll of my eyes, I walked off, annoyed at myself for agreeing to go to the stupid party. Just try and have a good time, I repeated to myself as I walked toward the first large bonfire.

The next hour or so was spent mingling with a few people I knew from class, mainly talking to them about what college classes they were taking in the fall and how nervous, excited, or scared they were to be leaving the comforts of Marblehead. I played along, nodding in agreement, but I was really screaming on the inside. Most people would probably think I was insane if they knew how much I really loathed this place. Of course there was no way I could blame the people who loved Marblehead so much. It was a beautiful seaport town, with beautiful beaches and a serene landscape. A person should be committed to hate it so much, right? I guess the town itself was great, except for the complete feeling of suffocation I felt when I was there.

After making a few rounds, I decided to exit the party quietly. My mission for coming there was complete; I'd kept my word to Roger and said my goodbyes to the few people I'd wanted to from school. The next time a popular song blasted over the loud speakers and everyone screamed in excitement, I made my exit. I didn't tell anyone I was leaving and hoped Roger would understand. There was no doubt that I would have to explain myself in the morning, but it was worth the price to get out of there. No one noticed as I walked into the darkness, away from the light of the bonfires. Just as I left the perimeter of the party, I remembered my revenge on Roger. Darn. I guessed I would just have to settle with hearing it all secondhand from him, knowing that he would leave out all the juicy details on when Riley showed up.

As I turned the corner from Beach Street onto Orchard Drive, memories began to flood my mind—the good times that occurred before I lost my family, when I was still a somewhat normal person. I realized then I might actually miss the place when I left.

Then somewhere nearby, I couldn't be sure exactly where, loud voices interrupted my thoughts. I tried to cancel them out and return to my memories, but the voices were too loud. It was difficult to see where they were coming from since the area around me was covered in darkness. All I could make out was a girl and a guy arguing over something, and by their tones, I could tell it was not just some silly argument. The guy's voice was getting louder and louder with each word. I tried not to be an eavesdropper, but it was not like I could hide or turn another direction. This was the only street back to my side of town.

"We need to act quickly," the girl spoke sternly.

"We can't do anything yet. We don't know anything about her. We don't even know if we can trust her. This could all be some sort of trap," the guy responded, his voice becoming angrier with each word.

"What do you suggest we do, then? We have to do something. Just sitting around waiting for something to happen to her or to us is not an option," the girl snapped back.

Then there was silence for a moment until I heard the guy's voice speak up once more, his voice much more calm. "I'm working on it. Let's be patient and spend some time evaluating the situation. We will figure something out, I promise."

After a few seconds of hearing nothing but my deep, slow breaths, I continued walking but at a much faster pace, quickly realizing that it had not been the best idea to walk back home by myself. Not that anything bad ever happened in the town, but the irrational thoughts that were flooding my head were going to give me a heart attack. Plus the argument I had just heard sounded like one that the people would not want anyone else to hear.

"Meredith?" A voice from the darkness in front of me spoke.

Both my breathing and heart stopped simultaneously as I came to a halt and stood there, motionless. My eyes searched the area around me, but all I could see was darkness. After a few seconds, the little voice in the back of my head told me to speak up, and I listened to it. "Hello? Who-who's there?" I stuttered out.

As I stared down the dark street, two figures slowly drifted into view, stopping just a few feet in front of me. It was still very dark, but as they approached, I could tell one was Abby Harper and the other was the stranger who I'd seen in town yesterday, the same guy who I'd caught staring me down at the crosswalk.

"Hello, Meredith," Abby spoke.

I put my hand to my chest, trying to secure my heart from jumping out of it as I strained to see them through the blackness of the night.

"Sorry if we scared you, and *really* sorry if you heard our little dispute. We were just having a little brother-and-sister quarrel."

I couldn't be sure, but it looked like her lips formed a straight line, as if she were embarrassed. "No worries," I choked out, still gripping my chest.

I made eye contact with Abby, and then my eyes were drawn to the person standing beside her. He looked at me with the same gaze that drew me to him yesterday at the crosswalk. For a moment, there was nothing else I wanted to do but try and take in every inch of his face. The darkness made it difficult, but I squinted, determined to see him more clearly. When my eyes finally found his, I could do nothing to avert their gaze. It was just like yesterday, right before I walked out into the street and was almost killed. Suddenly, a sound distracted me, and I realized it was Abby clearing her throat. My eyes shot back to her large, almond-shaped ones. It was difficult for me to make out the startling green color I had noticed before, as it was still too dark to notice those types of details.

"Meredith, this is my brother Blake." She grinned as she turned to look at the guy standing beside her. "Blake, this is *Meredith*, the girl I told you about."

I couldn't ignore the way she said my name, making it into three syllables. It also made me curious as to why she had even mentioned me at all … especially to him.

The looks they exchanged were very odd, as if they were talking to one another in silence. I wondered what they could be saying.

And as if I had no control over my own body, my eyes moved themselves back toward Blake. I stood there staring at him as he and his sister gave each other the longest stare down I had ever witnessed. Deep down I knew I needed to pull my gaze away, to look anywhere else but directly at him, but I couldn't find the strength. The energy I had felt earlier with Abby had returned, but now the feeling was magnified as I stared at him. Just as I was beginning to lose myself in his face, taking in his square jaw, full lips, and beautifully thick hair, he quickly snapped his head in my direction, giving me a killer stare that made me gulp loudly. My heart raced, my mouth ran dry, and I searched for the words. Speak. I have to speak. He was expecting me to say something. The words I so badly wanted to say were stuck in my throat. I reached my hand up to my neck to massage it, hoping it would help the constricting muscles and let my words flow smoothly. But before I could find them, he took in a deep breath, looked back toward Abby, appeared to scream something with his eyes, and stormed off.

It took me a few seconds to come back to reality and before I could analyze what had just happened, he was gone.

"Sorry … I don't know what happened," I said, suddenly feeling dizzy as I looked back at Abby.

"You will have to excuse him. He is angry with me and taking it out on you. I'm afraid we are not making the best first impression on you, are we?" She frowned, looking at the ground as she spoke.

"Um, it's fine. I really have to be getting home now," I muttered, walking past her and leaving her standing dumbfounded, thinking I was a freak for sure.

Something was going on with me. Nothing like that had ever happened to me before. I had never experienced weird connections with strangers, nor had I ever become mute in front of them. It had felt like I was about to burst out of my own skin if I stood there any longer. Maybe I was going through some young life crisis. Maybe turning eighteen and the reality of knowing that life was about to take a huge turn was getting to me.

Chapter Five

Finally home was in sight, and I was so thankful that my weird day was finally coming to an end. After a long, hot shower, I dressed in my pajamas and sat down alone for a bowl of cereal at the kitchen table. I tried hard not to think about the weirdness between Abby, Blake, and me, but it consumed me. There was the possibility that I was reading too much into it, that I really hadn't made a total fool of myself. But unfortunately, I didn't think I was that lucky—I had seen how they'd looked at me. The thought that really threw me off was that I cared so much.

When I finished eating, I rinsed my bowl and spoon then marched upstairs to my room. I flopped down on my bed, turned on the TV, and hoped some good trash television would be a distraction.

But as I flipped through the channels, the things I had pondered over my bowl of cereal kept haunting me. It was so frustrating because I had never cared so much about what two people thought of me. What does it matter anyway? They're just here for the summer, I thought, and I won't ever see them again after that. All I have to do is avoid them for a couple months. Should be easy enough.

Finally I found a crime show that stole my concentration. About halfway through the show, drowsiness began to eek its way in. I tried to fight it off, wanting to make sure the perp was caught, even though I knew he never got away. Just when I felt my eyes falling closed, I heard a loud crash downstairs and they shot wide-open. My first thought was that Aunt Rose must have come home, but then I remembered her note: She was working the night shift that night. Maybe it's Roger coming to yell at me for leaving the party early? I guessed, trying to fight off the other potential situations creeping into my head. Chills covered my body, and I slowly rose from my bed, picking up the pace as I made my way to the window. As I glanced out of it, my heart stopped, seeing that Aunt Rose's Jeep Grand Cherokee was not in the driveway, and there was no Mustang on the curb where Roger usually parked.

I bent down, retrieving the baseball bat from under my bed, the one Aunt Rose had given me solely for situations like this one. I stopped at the top of the stairs and listened, but there was no sound other than my heart pounding in my ears and the tick-tock of the grandfather clock at the bottom of the stairs, almost on beat with one another. I slithered down the steps and flicked on the light switch as I reached the bottom. But there was nothing. Everything seemed to be in its place, and it was quiet. Too quiet. I swallowed hard and continued on to the kitchen. I had my baseball bat ready to strike, and I checked to my right and left with each step. I flicked on the light switch in the kitchen, fully prepared to deal with whatever or whomever I was about to see. Still nothing.

I exhaled, realizing I had been holding my breath the entire time. It must have just been the TV, I told myself. It had been a long day, and I could have just exaggerated the noise. After taking in a couple deep breaths, I shook off my nervousness and pulled some milk from the fridge with one hand and a glass from the cabinet with the other. My heartbeat was just returning to a normal rate when I heard another large crashing noise just outside the back door. Losing all control, I dropped what I was holding and watched in slow motion as the milk carton and glass fell toward the floor. The next thing I heard was the glass shattering at my feet. The milk oozed out of its carton onto the tile. As much as I wanted to run, I was stuck there, frozen. My mind was overwhelmed with fear, not sure of what to do next. Scream? Run? I had to do something; just standing there and waiting to be attacked was not an option.

Then out of nowhere, there was laughter. It sounded like little girls laughing, and it was coming from the backyard. Was this some sort of prank or sick joke? I pulled myself together and walked to the window above the sink, trying to avoid the milk and broken glass beneath my bare feet.

"No way," I whispered under my breath. It wasn't possible. I leaned forward to see the two girls more clearly, and my pounding heart stopped the second I confirmed what I thought I had seen. It was my sister and me playing hide-and-go seek back when we were kids. Charlotte was wearing her favorite green shirt that we had gotten from our trip to Disneyland, a blue jean mini-skirt, and her favorite purple tennis shoes. My heart ached as my mind flashed back to the day of the accident, seeing her sitting next to me in the car in that exact outfit. That's it, the hallucinations have started. I have officially lost it. I stood there in a daze and couldn't do anything other than stare in shock and disbelief.

“No fair, Meredith. You peeked,” Charlotte whined as I caught her red-handed, hiding behind the shed.

Stretching up on my tiptoes, I leaned farther over the sink in order to see the image of myself running away and laughing. As crazy as it was, I remembered that day. It was not just some random, crazy vision. That was the last day of my old life, the last day my parents and sister were alive. That was the first time I’d seen a vision like that. Nothing like that had ever happened before.

Almost touching my face to the glass, I leaned even farther, desperate to see another glimpse of Charlotte alive and talking. Just as I watched Charlotte run to the other side of the yard, I looked in my peripheral vision and swallowed hard when I saw two strange men standing in the shadows near the tree line. It was difficult to make out their faces. They were not familiar to me. Even with the dark shadows, I could tell their lips were moving. My eyes were stuck on them, and it sent a chill down my spine when the face of the older one on the left broke into an evil smile.

“Meredith, you can’t go into the woods. Mom and Dad said it’s not allowed!” Charlotte shouted to me as I watched the image of myself blur into the forest, toward the two strangers.

Now there were loud screams coming from the forest. My screams.

"Meredith, Meredith!" A voice far away called out to me, and I searched for it, wanting to quiet the terror in its tone. I stood at the kitchen counter, still trying to hang onto the image of my sister, but the image was slowly retreating until it was finally gone, all black. The next thing I knew I was being shaken. I could feel someone gripping my shoulders as they shouted at me.

"Meredith, Meredith, please wake up!" the strangled voice yelled.

"Charlotte," I gasped as my eyes popped open. It took me a few seconds to realize that I was staring at my bedroom ceiling, not standing at the kitchen sink like I had thought.

"Meredith, oh my god, you scared me half to death!" Aunt Rose screamed as she clutched her chest. "When I got home, I heard you up here screaming. I thought … I can't even tell you what I thought." She inhaled and exhaled heavily, trying to catch her breath.

I couldn't speak. I just looked at her and then stared back at the ceiling. A dream? That was a dream? But it was so real.

"Just a dream," I murmured as I began to pull myself up into a sitting position.

The second I got into an upright position, I immediately put my hand on the back of my head. It was pounding as if someone had knocked *me* with a baseball bat.

"You okay?" Aunt Rose questioned.

"Yeah, just a headache." That was an understatement. "Sorry if I scared you. I guess I was just dreaming," I mumbled, still rubbing the back of my head.

"*Dreaming?* You were having some kind of horrible nightmare. Did you fall asleep watching a scary movie again?" she asked, shaking her head, trying to hide her smile.

Fall asleep? This was all so surreal; it seemed like just a few seconds ago that I had gotten in bed and was watching TV. It didn't even seem possible that I could have fallen asleep and really dreamt all of that.

"What time is it?" I asked, still trying to wrap my head around the images I had just seen.

"It's 7:30. I just got home from the hospital," she said as she stood up and began to walk toward the door.

The last time I looked at my clock, it had been just after midnight. Over seven hours ago? It only felt like it had been a few seconds. No way did it seem like it had been all night.

"Well, I am off to bed now. If you go back to sleep, please no more nightmares. I would like to live to see my fortieth birthday." She covered her yawn as she walked out, pulling my door closed behind her.

I fell back down on my pillow and began to relive the dream-nightmare I had just lived through.

Later that morning I tried to call Roger. I wanted to apologize about ditching him at the party. But there was no answer. I hoped he was just sleeping and not avoiding my phone calls. My next call was to Rebecca. I wanted to feel her out, too. I was hoping she was not upset with me, either.

"Hey, Rebecca."

"Meredith! Wasn't the party so great? Where were you all night? I tried to find you."

"Oh, I bailed out early. Wasn't really in the partying mood." At least she did not sound mad at me. "Hey, did you catch a ride home with Roger?" I decided to get straight to the point, my real reason for calling.

"No, he was still there when I left. I got a ride from Sarah."

"Oh, okay. He must still be sleeping, or maybe he's packing for Rockport," I said, biting my lip, thinking maybe I had really pissed him off. All he had wanted was for me to have fun, and I had promised him that I would try. Maybe I should've told him I was leaving—that would have been the right thing to do.

"Speaking of packing, I'm just about done, and I *have* to see you before I head out. Want to meet up for lunch later?"

There was a long pause.

"Um, hello … Meredith, are you there?" Rebecca questioned.

"Yeah, sounds great," I replied, sounding distracted. Not even sure what I had just agreed to.

"Perfect, how 'bout Omega's Pizza at 1:00?" she asked.

"Sure, see you there."

When I got downstairs, I opened the medicine cabinet and took out some aspirin and a bottle of water from the fridge. The horrible headache I had woken up with was still there, lingering in the back of my head. After popping two aspirin into my mouth, I took a large drink of water. And just as I closed my eyes and tilted my head back to help the aspirin slide down my throat, the images from the nightmare began to come back to me. I have to admit, it was nice to see my sister alive and running around, creepy as it was. So even though I knew it was unhealthy to be enjoying this, I just smiled and watched.

Then the images flashed to the two men standing in the forest, and my head began to pound so hard that I hunched over and gripped the counter for support. I winced in pain, unable to open my eyes and get rid of the horrible faces. The two men stood there, the evil one smiling the same evil smile, his lips curling upward as they both stared after my younger self where I had just entered the forest.

What. Was. Happening. To. Me?

After a few seconds, I forced my eyes open, despite the pain, and the images were gone. I was finally able to stand upright. My head was still pounding, but the pain was not crippling at least. Something was wrong. Way wrong. In the back of my mind, I knew the smart thing to do would be to race upstairs and tell Aunt Rose all about what was happening—the car that had moved in slow motion and stopped just inches from killing me, the way I had felt and acted around Abby and Blake, and most of all, I should tell her about the headache and nightmare. That would be the smart thing—the right thing—to do. But I knew myself well enough to know that I would tell her nothing, not wanting to cause her to worry more than she already did. Maybe Roger would be a good person to tell if he ever decides to talk to me again, I thought. At least he already knows I'm nuts and will probably just laugh it off. But at least I could tell someone.

After breakfast and my second failed attempt to call Roger, I got dressed and headed out to the library like I had promised Aunt Rose I would. On my way, I thought about what I would say if Ms. Donaldson asked me about previous work experience. I had never had a job. My parents had left me a little bit of money, so as long as I did my chores, I received an allowance, which only went right back into my get-out-of-Marblehead account, anyway. But if the whole exploring-the-world thing didn't work out, then I would definitely need some back-up cash.

Chapter Six

The library was in view, and it's exactly what you would picture if you imagined a small-town library: a very predictable, two-story, redbrick-with-white-trim building. It stood in between our post office and city hall, looking very small in comparison. I don't know what it is about the place, but the few times I had been inside, I would get an eerie feeling. Also, Ms. Donaldson was not the most welcoming person in town. She had never married, never had any children, and mostly kept to herself. Even weirder, she lived in the attic of the library after converting it to a small apartment. And there was the bizarre stare she would give me each time I walked in the place.

My nerves worsened the closer I got to the large glass doors. As I approached them, I took in a deep breath. I walked in, looking to my left where I knew the librarian's desk would be and where I knew I would see Ms. Donaldson sitting, reading a book. I knew this because the few times I had been there, that is exactly where she sat and that is exactly what she was doing. The door screeched loudly as it shut behind me, the sound making my nerves hit their peak.

"He-llo, Ms. Donaldson," I said, trying to keep my voice from cracking too much.

"Oh, hello," she responded, a smile spreading across her face.

"I wanted to apply for the assistant librarian position. Is it still available?" I asked anxiously, hoping she couldn't hear the unevenness in my voice. I was not sure why I was so nervous. It must have had something to do with first-job jitters or the fact that she was smiling at me. She never smiled at me.

"Why, yes, dear, it's still open. Sit down, and we'll talk." She motioned to the old orange-and-brown plaid chair in front of her desk. Wow, she was being nice. Too nice.

"How have you been? I have not seen you around here lately, but I guess you wouldn't be here unless it was for school, and you have graduated now. So why would you be hanging around here, am I right?" she rambled nervously. I wondered why she would be so nervous.

I continued to smile as I took my seat and got comfortable. "I've been good, thanks. I'm just looking for a job for the summer to save up some extra money before I leave town."

"Leaving? Your aunt did not mention that to me." She paused, looking at me mystified. "But why would she? It's none of my business. Well, I know it's not a glamorous job, and I'm afraid I can only pay you minimum wage, but the job is yours if you would like it."

"Really, that easy?" I asked, surprised.

She laughed. "That easy. I mostly wanted to hire someone for company; it gets so lonely around here in the summer, and I have a few odd jobs that I've needed to get done. Plus, I've had the job posted for a few weeks now, and you're the only applicant. Beggars can't be choosers nowadays."

I couldn't turn it down. Sure, there were definite drawbacks to working there. It was hard to put my finger on the one thing that freaked me out the most. Maybe it was the age of the building and how it looked like it hadn't been updated since it was built. Or, maybe it was how the main room of the library was dank and had a horrible musty smell. It had been a long time since I had been there, and I didn't remember just how unnerving the place actually was. But it was quiet, and it would be so much better than waitressing somewhere. I accepted the job, and we planned out my work schedule. I would start the next day.

After I left the library, I headed straight to Omega's to meet up with Rebecca. As I walked, the afternoon sun glared down on me, and I couldn't wait to get into some air-conditioning and have a nice, cold drink. Just that one thought made me pick up my pace, eager to quench my thirst. As I walked, I couldn't shake the feeling that there was someone behind me, following just a few steps back. Finally, when I couldn't stand it anymore, I whipped around to face the person and demand that they back off. But I stood there facing nothing but empty air. Must just be the heat getting to me or something, I thought. Or maybe I can add paranoia to my growing list of disorders.

I walked in and scanned the restaurant, but there was no sign of her. The restaurant was packed, and only a few free tables remained. The last booth in the corner was still available, so I took it. A few minutes passed, and the door to the restaurant opened again. I raised my head from the menu, fully expecting to see Rebecca strolling in, looking all frazzled because she was five minutes late. She hated being late. But my heart stopped when I saw it was Blake walking in. He immediately began scanning the restaurant as if he was looking for someone in particular. He seemed to find who he was looking when his bright blue eyes met mine. I shot my eyes back down toward the menu, scanning it but not actually reading anything that it said. Things had been awkward between us last night, and I wasn't sure how to act. After a long minute, I felt brave enough to glance up through my eyelashes and scan the room for him. But after a few sweeps, I came up empty.

"Hey, sorry I'm late," Rebecca groaned as she scooted into the booth across from me.

I flinched, startled by her presence. I didn't even notice her approach. "No problem," I responded, greeting her with a smile once I regained my composure.

"So, I am all ready to go, and I must say I am terrified. I don't know how I'm supposed to survive with my family in such a confined space. I mean, we are going to be together twenty-four hours a day for an entire month. How is this supposed to be a bonding experience? I seriously think my mom is losing it. She must think this is going to be fun, right?"

And even though I heard her talking, knowing that she finished her rambling with a question and I was supposed to answer, I couldn't concentrate on anything except for finding

Blake. My eyes wandered around, sweeping the crowded restaurant over and over again.

"Are you looking for someone in particular? I thought it was just going to be the two of us." Her voice sounded a little annoyed and hurt.

It stung me, and I immediately realized what I had done. "No, sorry. I just thought I saw someone I knew. Really, I'm all yours," I said, feeling remorseful.

She continued on as if nothing had happened. "Anyway, I was just thinking of how much I was going to miss you. I'm going to be gone most of the summer, and then I come back just to pack up and leave again." She sighed.

"I'm going to miss you, too. It will be lonely here this summer without you. And don't worry too much about the road trip. Things may not be as bad as they seem. You may even have fun. Just think of all the great memories you will make and new places you will see," I said, trying to reassure her.

"I guess so," she said bitterly.

I decided it best to change the subject in order to distract her from her depressing thoughts and me from thinking of Blake. "I just got a job at the library, so you can't say you're going to have the most boring summer. I think I have that one won, hands down."

"Oh, that does sound awful. I think I would take my little brother over Ms. Donaldson any day." She laughed.

"Yeah, that's what I thought, but she's not *that* bad, actually. I talked to her for a little while today, and she seems really nice."

"Yeah, nice and *boring*," she added, and I couldn't help but smile. At least Rebecca wasn't still dwelling on how horrible of a summer she was going to have.

"Woah, hottie at three o'clock is checking you out." She said, leaning in closer to me.

"What, who?" I asked, trying not to look around the room and give myself away. And as silly as it sounds, I could feel the stare that she was describing. It was similar to the stare I had felt the afternoon that Mr. Griffin almost made me a permanent mark on Main Street and the stare I felt last night when I ran into Abby and Blake after the party. The stare felt as if two lasers were boring into me, drilling some crazy feeling inside me.

"Really, Meredith, I don't know how you are so oblivious to your gorgeousness. I'm actually kind of glad that there will be one less bombshell to compete with me next year at BU."

I shook my head, trying to play it off as I glanced in the direction she said—and saw Blake sitting in the booth directly to my right. Could he have been there the whole time? How could I have missed him? As our eyes met, everything in the room stopped: no noisy chatter from the other guests, no sound of banging dishes, nothing but silence. His blues eyes pierced me, causing my breathing to pick up speed.

"Meredith, don't be so obvious," I heard Rebecca mumble, sounding appalled.

"What? Oh, sorry." I shook my head, embarrassed that I had been caught staring at him.

"He is super cute but based on his build he is probably just some stupid football jock. But you could at least try and play hard to get." She laughed. "Unfortunately, he's probably just a tourist; he will be gone in no time. That is one thing I won't miss about the summers here, the tourist season is miserable. Ugh, it gets so claustrophobic in this town."

"No, he and his family actually just moved here for the summer. I met him yesterday."

"So, you know him? Well, introduce me, *please*," she squealed in excitement.

"Uh, it's not like that. Let's just change the subject to something else."

"Fine, not like it's going to do me any good now. Leaving town and all." She shrugged.

Rebecca was like most other girls our age in the sense that all she cared about was boys, hair, and clothes, but she was also the most loyal, sweetest person I knew. The rest of lunch we spent talking about old times and how much we were going to miss one another when she left. The feeling like I was being watched eventually faded, and the next time I glanced toward the booth where Blake had been sitting, he was gone.

As Rebecca and I hugged goodbye, I felt like I was losing a part of myself.

"Call me when you get back, and maybe we can meet up before you leave for Boston." I sighed as we squeezed each other tightly.

"Promise," her voice cracked, and I hoped she would not turn the moment into a sob fest. I was not good at dealing with those types of situations.

As she walked away, I felt an ache of sadness in my heart. It was at that moment that I knew my life was about to change, that all I ever knew was fading away, and soon I would be leaving, too. I still had not heard from Roger, and it was starting to annoy me that he was mad at me for something so stupid. I had warned him I hated parties and all the stupid crap that went along with them. He shouldn't have pushed me so hard to go.

When I got home, Aunt Rose was still sleeping, so I decided to take advantage of the day and do some grocery shopping. Before I left for the grocery store, I left Aunt Rose a note, telling her I had borrowed her car and I would be back by six. I knew her shift started at eight, so I would have to have dinner ready to go pretty quickly after I got home.

The grocery store was not packed, making it easier for me to get through my list more quickly. As I walked the aisles, I constantly looked over my shoulder, feeling as though someone was right behind me. It can't be the heat now, I thought. I'm in the meat department, and my arms are covered in goose bumps. Could just be my nerves, I figured. With the nightmare from last night still fresh on my mind, I guess there is a reason to be a little jumpy.

Then it occurred to me that I was making a lot of excuses. It was not in my nature to avoid things like this. I realized I should probably talk to Aunt Rose that night. The paranoia-thing combined with the nightmares and seeing cars move in slow motion was probably a really bad sign. For all I knew, it could have been something serious, like a brain tumor or something.

The house was still quiet when I got home, so I started on dinner. Soon the house was filled with the aroma of basil and garlic, making it feel like a home again—a feeling I rarely had anymore. It was even rarer that either Aunt Rose or I prepared a full meal. I usually survived on cereal or TV dinners, but there were the occasions where I craved a home-cooked meal, like my mother used to make almost every night.

Aunt Rose woke and got fully dressed for her shift at work just as I was finishing up making the side salads for us. I placed the lasagna I had made down in the center of the table, and we both took our seats. It felt nice to have someone sitting across from me at the table. Too many nights, I was there alone. But tonight was a perfect night to have dinner together, since I had so much to tell her. Over our salads, I filled her in on the party, and she looked pleased that I had ventured out of my comfort zone and had given it a try. I told her about my quick and easy interview with Ms. Donaldson, and she promised to take me to lunch to celebrate my first job.

Then it came time to dive into the complicated stuff, the stuff about me finally losing it. I hoped she would react nicely and not have me committed or something. "Aunt

Rose." I swallowed hard. "I—um, have been… How are things at work?" I totally panicked and chickened out.

"Do you really want me to tell you about the staple I had to remove from Mr. Clary's forehead last night? Some men should never be allowed to handle tools." She shook her head, pulling a piece of lasagna from the dish. "Here, give me your plate, and I will cut you a piece," she offered.

The tomato sauce oozed out, pooling at the bottom of the dish where Aunt Rose's piece of lasagna used to be, just as I pictured Aunt Rose pulling out a staple from Mr. Clary's head and the blood that followed. I lost my appetite. "No, thanks. The salad filled me up. Maybe I'll have a piece later." I looked away and fidgeted with my fork.

"You okay? You look like there's something on your mind." She gave me a puzzled look.

"Fine." I answered too quickly. "I guess I'm just a little nervous about my starting work tomorrow."

"Don't worry, you are going to be great." She smiled.

After Aunt Rose finished dinner, she thanked me and left for work. I cleaned the kitchen, putting half of the uneaten lasagna in the freezer and the rest in the refrigerator. Then the house was quiet and lonely again. I tried Roger once more, but he was still not answering. It seemed weird that he was avoiding me like this; he had never stayed mad at me for this long. When it was time for bed, I lay there, trying to stay up as long as possible. There was a part of me that was scared to close my eyes, scared of what I would see if I had another dream.

I woke the next morning to the loud buzzing of my alarm clock. It had been a dreamless night, and I felt refreshed and ready for my first day at work. I got ready quickly and had plenty of time to spare before I was supposed to report to work at 9:00 a.m. After eating a bowl of cereal for breakfast, I packed myself a lunch, not knowing if I would get a break long enough to walk somewhere. The morning air was brisk, but I enjoyed how the cool air felt on my face. I arrived at the library about fifteen minutes early, and the lights were still off. Peering through the glass door, I tried to see if Ms. Donaldson was there, but she was nowhere in sight.

Standing outside, I pondered what I should do. Then I remembered the spare key she had given me before I had left the day before. Still I stood there, hesitating about whether or not I should use it. Eventually, I decided to take charge and let myself in. The door creaked closed, and I stood in the entrance, feeling like I had just committed a crime or something. I had a key, so it wasn't like breaking and entering, but I certainly felt like a criminal standing there in the darkness. The time seemed to drift by slowly, and I checked my cell phone for the time: It was ten till 9:00. I wavered over what to do next, not sure on how comfortable I should make myself; it was still my first day after all. Just as I was about to walk over and knock on the door marked "Private," I heard footsteps coming down the stairs on the other side of it.

"Good morning." Ms. Donaldson smiled as she opened the door and saw me standing near the entrance.

"Good morning. Hope you don't mind that I let myself in."

"Not at all. That's why I gave you the spare key, dear." She smiled, shutting and locking the door behind her.

I returned the smile, suddenly feeling a little more at ease. Glancing around, I searched for a place to put my purse and backpack.

"Here, let's put your things under the counter over there." She motioned me to follow her as she made her way across the room toward the checkout counter.

We spent the first part of the day going over the computer system and how to check books in and out. Thankfully, the system was very user-friendly, and I was confident that I could use it without any major issues. Before I knew it, it was lunchtime, and Ms. Donaldson went upstairs to her apartment for the hour, leaving me to run things downstairs. She told me to just holler if I needed anything. Before eating my lunch, I brought the overnight drop box back to the checkout counter and decided to multitask as I ate.

Just as I was about to pull out my sandwich, I heard the front door squeak closed. I looked up to see our next patron. It was just the same as the first time our eyes met that afternoon at the crosswalk, that evening after the party, and that afternoon at Omega's. Breaking our shared gaze, Blake walked further into the library, and I tried my hardest not to stare at him as he made his way to the reference section toward the back of the room. But it was out of my control; I couldn't help it. My eyes followed his every step as he pulled down two books and walked to the table nearest the window.

Chapter Seven

A large thudding sound broke my concentration on Blake. I flinched, my heart picking up speed as my eyes turned back to the person standing at the counter in front of me. I apologized to Ms. Brownlee for not noticing her sooner as I picked up the large stack of books she had thrown down.

"Uh, let's see here. Do you have your library card?" I asked, trying to juggle both the stack of books and the scanner as I walked over to the computer. I'm not sure if it was my nerves from being startled or if I was just having a klutzy moment, but my hand started to lose balance with the books. Before I knew it, they were toppling over and falling toward the ground, each of them making a loud crashing sound as they hit, creating what felt like a never-ending echo in the previously silent library. My face began to heat up, and I could feel my color changing to a bright red.

I muttered a lot of expletives in my head, but luckily the word that came out was not one of them: "Crap." Bending over, I quickly gathered the books back up. I made two trips to the computer instead that time.

I glanced back at Ms. Brownlee, who was still thumbing through a large stack of cards that she had pulled from her purse. It was unclear if she had just missed my episode of clumsiness or if she was just trying to be nice and not stare. I assumed it was the latter. When I reached out to take the bright yellow card marked *Marblehead Public Library* she handed me, my hand was still shaking from humiliation. I scanned each book and then handed the card back to her, making sure to remind her of the due date, hoping she would think I was somewhat capable of doing my job. She forced a smile as she took the books and walked out. After that embarrassing display of awkwardness, it took me a few minutes to gather myself, allowing my face to return from the crimson color I knew it was back to normal.

What is happening to me? I asked myself as I held up my trembling hands and stared at them like they were some foreign objects needing to be sent back to wherever they'd come from. Where was my cool, confident, laid-back self?

Things were definitely weird with me; there was no denying that something was going on. All those years that I had kept my feelings bottled up inside must have been compounding. It felt like I was coming apart at the seams, slowly but surely. After a few deep breaths, I found the courage to search the library for Blake, but he was gone. He probably had snuck out when he saw my perfect display of gracefulness. How embarrassing, I thought, feeling the crimson color returning to my face.

The dreadful day finally ended, and when I got home, I was relieved to see a note that Aunt Rose had left me:

Roger called. He lost his cell phone at the party and couldn't remember your cell number. He gave up and called the house. He's at his dad's and will call you on Sunday. See you tonight. BTW, Jack is coming over later and he's bringing dinner.

AR

In Rockport already? I hadn't thought Roger would be leaving so soon. I probably wouldn't have bailed early on the party. It did make me feel better, knowing that he was not mad at me and that he would call in just a few days. Maybe then I could unload all the weird stuff that was happening to me.

That evening Jack, Aunt Rose, and I inhaled the large pizza that he brought over. I sat and talked with him, catching him up on the newest events in my life, which only took a couple minutes.

"So, kid … where do you think you will travel to when summer ends? I know you don't have any definite plans, but you have to have an idea, right?" He looked at me anxiously.

It was weird that he had asked this question, because Jack was never that inquisitive. I was skeptical that Aunt Rose had put him up to it.

"Well, um, I have an *idea*. I mean, I have a starting point, since I will eventually have to buy a plane ticket." I paused, taking in a deep breath before continuing. Only Roger knew my tentative plan, and I was not sure how Aunt Rose would react to it. "I was thinking about going to London first. My mom's side of the family was from that area, and even though I've never met any of them, I think it would be kinda cool to see where I come from," I said, shrugging.

I was hoping that it didn't hurt Aunt Rose's feelings. She loved my mother, but I knew she took a certain amount of pride in being my guardian, and I didn't want to take that away from her.

"Oh, well, that's something." He shot a quick glance at Aunt Rose, and she turned and gave me a nervous smile. My suspicions had been correct: He definitely had been put up to it.

Before he could ask any more questions, I stretched out and began a fake yawn, but then a real yawn took over, making it that much easier to make my exit. "'Night, guys," I yelled as I got up from the table and trudged up the stairs and into my room. I changed into my pajamas, took out a CD, and popped it in my CD player. It was not long before I started to feel relaxed. I stretched out on my bed and stared at the ceiling, trying to drown out everything but the music.

As I lay there, I could feel myself drifting off to sleep, knowing in a way that I was beginning to dream. But this was no nightmare like I had had the other night. This was a good dream. The place I saw was familiar to me: My family and I were in our favorite spot on the beach with a clear view of the lighthouse in the distance. My mother and father were laughing and talking as they cooked over the portable grill that we had brought with us from home. My sister and I were building sandcastles ten feet from them.

I knew that all I had to do was open my eyes and the dream would disappear. But it seemed so real, so clear and distinct, as if I was living it in the present. I wanted to see it.

Hell, I *needed* to see it. It had been too long since I'd seen my mom and dad happy and smiling or remembered my sister and I innocently playing at the beach on a warm, sunny day. I never wanted to open my eyes.

Just as it looked like dinner was prepared, all perfectly placed on the blanket my mother had spread out along the beach, something stole her attention. Without anyone noticing, not even my father, my mother turned and looked out into the ocean. She stood there for a few seconds, looking out into the water. Suddenly, her head snapped back toward my sister and I. The look on her face was terrifying. As she approached my father and whispered into his ear, his blissful face turned bleak, and all the color drained out of it.

"Girls, gather up your things. We need to go now. There's a storm coming," he spoke sternly.

"What storm?" Charlotte pouted as she looked up toward the bright, blue, sun-filled sky.

"Don't argue with your father, Charlotte. Now get your things and let's go," my mother demanded, raising her voice, something she rarely did.

"Fine." Charlotte stomped over to our plastic sandcastle molds and began to gather them up. "Come on, Meredith. Dad said you had to help, too," she whined as I saw the image of me kneeling down to help her. I glanced back and saw my mom and dad whispering to one another as they gathered the rest of the gear, both looking frantic.

"Come on, girls, we need to go now! Leave everything that you don't have ready to go," my dad yelled. His face was impatient and his hands were full with items we needed to leave with.

Charlotte huffed as she stood up and began to obey him, then yelled at me, "Meredith, you heard him, let's go!"

I stood and obediently followed my family off the beach.

"Faster!" My father yelled as he looked back toward my sister and me. We picked up our pace, running faster and faster in the sand. I struggled, my hands full and my legs feeling heavy, not knowing how much longer I could balance everything I was holding. Soon enough, the running in the sand with my hands full proved to be too difficult. I tripped over my own feet, and the plastic sandcastle molds went flying along with me as I landed face down in the sand. When I hit the ground, my mouth filled with the coarse, dry powder. I coughed, trying to breath, trying to get the sand out of my mouth.

Then something woke me up from my vision. I realized that *I* couldn't breathe. I sat up in bed, coughing uncontrollably, drenched in sweat. I swallowed and took in a few deep breaths as I looked toward the clock. It was 5:30 in the morning. And the headache I had woken up with a couple days ago was back, pounding in the same spot as it had before.

I fell back on the bed and sighed, thinking of the dream, remembering it so clearly, wishing more than anything that I could have that day back. I had always treasured that day at the beach, remembered it fondly. That was the last happy time we had had as a family before the accident.

Everything after that day had been weird at home, and my parents had begun to act … different. We no longer laughed as a family, no longer ate dinner together, barely even spent time with each other. My parents spent most of their time having hushed conversations, always with a panicked look on their faces. My sister and I were asked to go outside and play a lot more than usual, and we were never allowed to leave the boundaries my mom had set for us.

But why all of a sudden was I having these dreams of the past? The dreams I had had the past few nights were not random they were actual memories of my family and me. I couldn't help but wonder if these dreams were trying to show me something.

After a few minutes, it was clear to me that I was not going to fall back to sleep. The possibility that something could be wrong with me haunted my every thought. I was not sure what the dreams meant, but they had to be a sign that something was wrong with me. It could have something to do with the ten-year anniversary of their deaths, I guessed. Regardless, the irrational thoughts crept into my head and the idea of me having some crazy disease took over. I rubbed my eyes with the heels of my hands then threw the covers off, deciding there was only one way to really calm my fears. I got up and planted my butt in front of the computer, opened up a search engine, and typed in "brain tumor."

After a couple hours of research, I felt no more secure about what possible condition I may or may not have had than I did before I had started. Giving up on research, I walked back to my bed and buried myself underneath the covers. Who was I kidding? There was no way I was going to be able to go back to sleep.

After pulling myself out of bed, I took a shower and tried to push all the negative thoughts out of my head. All of my concentration would be needed at work (I had proved yesterday that I couldn't handle carrying a stack of books without making a total fool out of myself). My morning routine started out the same as the previous day: a quick breakfast followed up by packing myself a sandwich for lunch then out the door and off to work.

Work was different that day. Slower. Way slower. Too slow. The day dragged by, and each time I looked at the clock, hoping the little hand was close to the five, it had barely moved since the last time I'd checked. Also, the day was different because Blake didn't show up. Even though I hated admitting it to myself, I wanted him to. I wanted to see him again. I yearned for it, but I wasn't sure why. He was incredibly good-looking, mysterious, and maybe just a little bit arrogant, but he seemed to have another side to him. Not that it mattered, because he never showed. Not the next day, or the next.

The rest of the week at work went by with no major events. But I shouldn't have been surprised—I was working at the library in Marblehead after all. There were also no more nightmares or headaches, so no need to worry Aunt Rose about it. I was cured.

Saturday morning came and I woke early. I tried to cover my head with my pillow in order to block out the sun in hopes of getting another hour of sleep, but it didn't work.

Aunt Rose was up, reading the paper and sipping her coffee, when I walked downstairs to the kitchen. "Good morning. You're up early. There's more coffee, if you'd like some." She pointed with her free hand toward the half-empty carafe.

“Thanks,” I responded as I reached for a cup and poured myself some coffee.

“Hey, it’s my day off and I have a few errands to run. Would you like to join me? We haven’t been able to spend a lot of time together lately. Things have been so hectic at the hospital. And I still owe you a congratulatory lunch, remember?” She looked at me with a hopeful expression, and I couldn’t resist. Not that I had had anything else to do that day.

“Yeah, sounds great,” I answered, pulling out a spoon and stirring some cream into my cup.

After drinking two cups of coffee, I felt reenergized … and that was a good thing, because I needed it. Aunt Rose was not kidding when she had said she had a few errands. We went to the dry cleaners, pharmacy, and nail salon. She begged me to get a mani-pedi with her, but I politely declined and just sat and talked with her while her nails were filed and polished. Then there was my congratulatory lunch. From the moment we got there, she probed me with questions about my travels at the end of the summer. Honestly, I had thought after revealing the information to Jack the other night that she would let up a bit, but it seemed to have had the opposite effect. She quizzed me on specific people I wanted to research, where I planned on staying, how long I was going to be there, and many other topics. I assured her that, before I left, she would have a detailed schedule of all the when's, where's, and who's. I was still not a 100 percent sure on it all. After a few more questions, she seemed satisfied with my answers … for the moment, anyway. For a congratulatory lunch, it felt more like an interrogation.

After a few more errands, we headed back home. "Oh crap," Aunt Rose muttered as we turned onto Maple Avenue.

"What'd you forget?" I guessed.

"I was supposed to stop by the hardware store and pick up a new part for the toilet. The toilet in my bathroom has been leaking, and Jack told me he would fix it as long as I got the part. Do you mind if we go back? Should only take a minute."

"Sure." I shrugged. It's not like I had anything pressing to do at home.

Aunt Rose pulled over, making a U-turn to head back into town. When we arrived at the hardware store, we parted ways. I aimlessly walked the aisles as Aunt Rose explained her toilet problem to the store associate.

"Meredith?" someone from behind me called anxiously. "It's such a coincidence that I would bump into you here, the hardware store out of all places."

I turned around and saw two familiar green eyes on a smiling face. "Abby?" I asked, shocked, giving her a once-over. Her look had changed drastically since the last time I had seen her. She was ... beautiful, and much more up-to-date-looking, if that even describes her transformation. She was wearing an emerald-colored sundress, one that I would see a model wearing in a magazine. Her hair was still the same corn-silk blonde, but it was styled as if she had just walked out of a salon. I couldn't help but look her up and down again, admiring her new clothes and style. Before, she had been so simple and plain-looking. Not that she had overdone it, but suddenly I felt like I paled in comparison, where before I had felt like somewhat of an equal.

"What brings you to the hardware store?" I questioned, trying my best to strike up a conversation in order to distract myself from staring at her amazing makeover.

"I mentioned that we are restoring one of the older estates, right?"

"Uh, yeah, I remember you saying something about that," I answered, trying hard to maintain eye contact. I still had not forgotten the weirdness between us the evening after the party: the things she and Blake had said to one another and the way they had acted when I had accidently interrupted them.

"Well, I'm just here getting some paint samples for the interior of the house." She lifted the basket in her arms to show me. It was filled with tiny cans and a handful of small paintbrushes.

"Oh, cool," I responded, not knowing what else to say.

"Would you—" She started to ask but then shook her head and stared at the ground. "Never mind, I just had a silly idea, but I'm sure you're too busy."

"What is it?" I insisted, regretting the words the moment I said them.

"Well, I was going to ask, if you are not too busy of course, if you would help me decide on some paint colors. You know, come over and help me choose the right ones."

"I don't think I would be much help. I don't really have any experience in that department," I confessed.

"Neither do I. Honestly, this is my first go-around with all of this. And my mom and dad are *so* outdated, and well, my brother couldn't care less about what color blue should go on the living room walls. But I'm sure you're too busy."

As I looked at her, contemplating how I should answer, I swear that she was purposely making a pouty-face at me.

But then my mind drifted to her brothers blue eyes and my yearning to see him again answered for me. It was a weird feeling, one that I was not sure how to describe. We had not really even spoken to one another, but I felt the need to see him again and maybe prove to him that I wasn't a head case. Or maybe I wanted to prove it to myself. The few times I had been in his presence, I had practically killed myself by walking out in front of a car, become mute when we were introduced, acted like a crazed person looking for him at Omega's, and played a klutzy idiot at the library. Yes, I definitely had to prove it to myself that I was not totally losing it.

"Sure, I'll try my best," I said. "But I really don't know if I'll be much help."

"Really?" Her face lit up in excitement.

"I'm with my aunt right now, but I could come by—"

"Tomorrow," she said, cutting me off and finishing my sentence. "That will actually work out perfectly. It will give me more time to prepare; you know, clean up the rooms and put some plastic down," she rambled happily.

I was not sure why she was so oddly excited; it was just an afternoon of choosing paint colors. Maybe she's just missing having a friend, I concluded.

"How's noon?" she questioned, her voice high with excitement.

"Noon is good." I nodded, already starting to feel a little uneasy about agreeing to it.

"Are you familiar with the estates on the edge of town?"

"Yeah, I know the area," I answered. Then I realized what I had just agreed to: I had just voluntarily agreed to enter one of the houses that everyone I ever knew avoided like the plague.

"Great. Well, it's the third house on your left, 12 Estate Lane to be exact. See you tomorrow." She bounced off happily, and I couldn't help but think about how much her attitude had majorly transformed as well. It was possibly even a more dramatic change than her physical one. The first day we had met, she had looked at me like I was the nut; all the while it appears she was the one who looked to be insane.

I met Aunt Rose at the register with an uneasy look on my face.

"You feeling okay?" she asked as I approached her.

"Yeah, fine," I answered automatically, knowing deep down I truly wasn't.

"Who was that girl you were talking to? Someone from school?"

"Oh, no, that was Abby," I responded, glancing out the window to see her disappear around the corner. "She and her family are new to town—well, they are only here for the summer. They are restoring one of the houses on Estate Lane," I explained further.

“That’s nice,” she remarked.

“Yeah, it should be neat to see how it turns out. She wanted some help with paint colors, so I’m going to help her choose tomorrow.”

“That should be fun. You know, your mom always loved those houses. When we were kids she was never scared to go into them like the rest of us,” she said, probably not even realizing what she was actually saying. It was rare for Aunt Rose to speak about my mother. It hurt us both to talk about her as much as it hurt to hear about her.

“Really? I didn’t know that,” I said. Just picturing my mom’s face made my heart ache.

We headed back to the house and ate some leftover lasagna before I retired to my room for the evening. I was not really tired, but I was craving some alone time. The remark Aunt Rose had made about my mother had put me in a depressed mood. I’m sure she didn’t even realize it when she said it, and normally a comment like that wouldn’t stick with me like it did just then; but since I’d spent the past few nights seeing my family in my dreams, I was more sensitive than usual. Especially the dream from the other night, where we were all still happy, made me miss them even more. I lay on my bed and actually wished for another dream like that, wanting it so badly that I began to think about the last day they were alive.

Chapter Eight

It started off like the first nightmare I had had just a few days ago: my sister and I playing hide-and-go-seek in the backyard, totally unaware of the terrible accident that lay ahead. After I had ventured into the woods and Charlotte called after me, my mom had burst out the back door before I could step two feet into the thickness of the trees. She called after me, screaming my name, yelling for me to come back toward the house. The panic in her voice stopped me. I turned around quickly; jumping back toward the grass, back to the boundary line my mom had set and told my sister and I not to cross. When she finally got to me, she took me by the hand and dragged me back toward the house, the entire time scolding me about disobeying her strict orders. I had never heard my mom speak like that, especially not to my sister or me. Her voice was full of anger, panic, and sadness … if a voice could hold all those emotions at once. I remember asking myself as I was being dragged on what the big deal was. It was just the woods, the same woods where my sister and I had gone many times. Why were they suddenly off limits? Why was I being scolded for something that had seemed so trivial before?

Once we were back inside, my mother sent my sister and I up to our rooms while her and my dad continued their hushed conversation in the living room. I remember trying to hold in the tears until I was alone and could hopefully block some of the noise with my pillow. The entire time I was being dragged and scolded, Charlotte followed silently behind us, not saying a word. Before I shut my bedroom door, Charlotte stopped and looked at me with sympathetic eyes, trying to apologize for getting me into trouble; it had been her yelling that had caused my mom to rush out of the house and grab me. But my stare must have been unforgiving, because she continued to her room with the same sorrowful look on her face. After shutting my door, I ran to my bed and leaped onto it, not able to hold back the tears anymore.

It was later that night that my dad had rushed into my bedroom, telling me to get up and get dressed. I remember being confused; it made no sense to me. It took me a few seconds to recall the events that had taken place earlier in the day. Then I remembered: I had gone into the woods, been reprimanded, and then sent to my room. I remembered crying for hours after that, and then I must have fallen asleep. As I sat there trying to get my bearings after my dad woke me, something told me that it was not yet morning. I still felt tired and groggy. I looked down and realized that I was fully clothed, never having changed after being sent to my room. As I got out of bed, I heard my dad giving Charlotte the same instructions that he had given me just seconds before. I stood in the hallway, still dazed and not sure of what was happening. Then Charlotte stumbled out of her bedroom in a confused stupor as well. She too was still dressed in the blue-jean skirt and Disneyland shirt that she had on while playing in the backyard, her favorite purple tennis shoes in hand. I looked down and saw that I had never taken my shoes off. Our eyes met and fear must have crossed both of our faces at the same time. We walked toward one another and held hands, not knowing or fully understanding what all was going on.

My mother called for us to join her downstairs in the kitchen. We walked down the stairs and entered the hallway. I could see my mom hunched over the counter, scribbling something on a piece of paper. She finished and placed the note in the cabinet where we kept our spices. She turned back around and smiled at us, then embraced us in a big hug. It should have been a comforting feeling, but it wasn't. It just added more to my confusion. I could see the same reaction on Charlotte's face, too. Then my dad's voice was behind us, telling us it was time to go.

Time to go? Go where? It was the middle of the night. My mother grabbed each of our hands and walked us outside to the car. Neither Charlotte nor I asked any questions, in fear of what would happen if we did. It did seem like my mother and father were somewhat back to normal. Well, except for the waking-us-up-in-the-middle-of-the-night-and-making-us-get-in-the-car thing. But they acted sweet and loving, the way my sister and I were used to. Those past few weeks they had been distant toward us. They had been much more concerned with having hushed conversations we were never meant to hear. My mother and father joined us in the car, and we began to back out of our driveway. Charlotte put on her shoes, and then we held hands as we drove into the quiet night. That was all I remembered from that night.

The accident happened just a few minutes later on the outside of town. I don't remember many of the details. In the hospital, the police tried their hardest to get any information out of me as to why we were out driving so late or what made my dad swerve the way he did. But I couldn't remember anything except the sounds of the tires screeching along the pavement, the glass bursting as our car flipped and went flying through the air, and my family's screams. That was it. The next thing I remember was waking up in the hospital with Aunt Rose at my side.

Finally, I opened my eyes, not wanting to go any farther down memory lane. Hot tears rolled down my cheeks. Even though I could feel them, I had to touch them to really believe they were real. It had been years since I had cried, years since I had shown any type of emotion in that sense. I rolled over and saw that it was close to midnight. It was imperative that I get to bed. Tomorrow I would be going to the Harpers', and I wanted to be fully alert. I was hoping not to make any more of a fool out of myself than I already had.

After a full night's rest, I woke early and spent the morning picking which outfit to wear over to the Harpers'. After trying on a few different options, I opted for the most comfortable one, my usual uniform of T-shirt and jeans, realizing that showing up wearing anything else would not go with the purpose of the day: choosing paint colors.

"Well, the butterfly has finally come out of her cocoon," Jack shouted from the living room as I walked down the stairs.

"Ha, ha."

"Whatcha been doing up there all morning? I heard you stomping around."

"Oh, sorry, I was just trying on a few outfits for the day."

"You? Trying on outfits? I thought all graduation partying was over?" he asked jokingly.

I rolled my eyes, trying to ignore his remarks. Apparently, I had woken up with the same sad and cranky mood that I had gone to bed with.

"What are you doing here so early?" I asked, hoping it would take the focus off of me.

"I'm here to fix the toilet," he stated matter-of-factly. "Hey, I brought your favorite. They're in the kitchen."

"Donuts?" I opened my eyes wide. I turned and headed toward the kitchen. Comfort food sounded perfect right about then.

"Yep, an entire dozen—half glazed, half chocolate." He followed close behind me. I guess he had been waiting on me to take first dibs.

“So where’s Aunt Rose?” I questioned, lifting the lid off the box, inhaling the sweet smell of sugar and chocolate.

“She’s finishing up getting ready so I can get in there and start working.”

I nodded, my mouth too full of donut to speak.

“Where are you all dressed up to go, anyway?” he asked, raising his left eyebrow in curiosity.

I looked down, inspecting myself and wondering how on earth he got “dressed up” from just jeans and a T-shirt. I swallowed my mouthful before asking, “What are you talking about?” It came out sounding harsher than I’d intended.

“Well, your hair is not in a ponytail and you’re wearing makeup. Wasn’t trying to offend you. You look nice. I was just curious to know where you were headed, that’s all.” He shrugged, clearly regretting that he had even asked.

Guilt washed over me. It was not Jack’s fault that I had spent the last night reliving the worst night of my life. “Actually, I’m helping out the new family that moved into one of the older estates. They’re restoring it and asked for some help in choosing paint colors.” I tried to be conversational, hoping to show him that I really was not out on the attack.

“Oh, yeah. I met the son the other day in town. Blake, is it? Seems like a nice kid. Real polite.”

Polite? Ha. Not from what I’d seen. Even though he had made my heart flutter and just may have been the sole reason for me agreeing to go over there that afternoon, he had been anything but polite to me.

“Well, I better start making my way over there,” I said, grabbing another chocolate donut before heading out. “Thanks for the donuts. Tell Aunt Rose I said bye,” I yelled as I headed toward the door, wanting to get out of there before he could ask me any more questions.

“Sure thing, kid,” he called out just before the door slammed shut.

On the way to the other side of town, I tried to prepare myself for what I was about to do. It was difficult for my mind to process that I had willingly agreed to enter one of the homes I had heard scary stories about my entire life. Of course, the stories had gotten more and more ridiculous with each passing year, but I had to believe that they held some truth, right? Supposedly, those homes had belonged to witches back in the early 1900s, and apparently they were cursed and still housed spirits. Not that I believed in any of that or ever paid too much attention to the gossip, but as I was about to get up close and personal with one of those houses, I began to wonder a little more.

I pulled out my cell phone, checking the time; it was 11:00. There was still an entire hour before I was supposed to be at the Harpers'. There was a reason I had left the house early. A part of me had wanted to visit my family on the way. It would be a shame not to take advantage of the coincidence. I would be passing right by the cemetery on the way to Estate Lane. But the other part of me didn't know what a visit would do to me just then. My thoughts from the night before were still too fresh on my mind, and I was not sure if the tears would find their way back out again.

As I walked, I continued to debate whether or not I should make the stop. But the closer I got, the more it occurred to me that it would be best to wait until after the Harpers' house. It was foolish to even entertain going there before. Plus, I would have an excuse to leave early—I could tell them I had an errand to run, if an excuse was necessary. I was hoping that the process would be quick, easy, and painless. I mean, how hard could it be to pick out a few paint colors?

I turned onto Shore Drive, and the familiar smell of salt grew stronger and stronger with each step. The cemetery appeared on my left, and as much as I tried to fight it, the sickening pain in the pit of my stomach came with it. A few deep breaths and my continued march right past the gates helped ease the pain, and it nearly disappeared as I approached Estate Lane. As I turned the corner, I bumped into someone. It felt like bumping into a large object, something similar to a brick wall, which stopped me and pushed me backwards. I stumbled back, thinking it was just a matter of seconds before my head hit the concrete, when a hand reached for me and pulled me back up to a standing position.

I gasped, shocked at the person I saw in front of me. He towered over me, standing at least six feet tall.

"Sorry," I muttered, hoping the words actually made it out of my mouth that time.

"No, my fault. I should watch where I am going," Blake spoke in a soft, deep voice as his eyes found mine.

Oh, no, it's happening again … I'm speechless, I thought. Please no, not again. I almost screamed out loud. Speak, all you have to do is open your mouth and let the words out!

But before I could convince myself to speak, he began. "Were you on your way to my house?"

I nodded and smiled, apparently still having the issue thinking of something to say.

"Would you like me to walk you? It's not too far up the road," he offered with a longing on his face that sent my heart into a flurry.

"Sure," I muttered, relieved to hear that I could speak again.

We began our walk in silence, but after a few moments, I opened my mouth, praying that the words would actually come out.

"Um, I think I'm a little early," I began. "Abby asked me to come over around noon, and it's only 11:30. I had planned to make a stop on the way over here because the stop I needed to make was in the neighborhood, but then I decided to just do it on the way home so that's why I'm early, and—" I shut up, realizing that I had just rambled on like a babbling idiot.

Great, at first it was that I couldn't get any words out, and now I couldn't shut up. My stomach began to knot up, and I felt my face flush. I was annoying myself, so I couldn't imagine what Blake was thinking. Actually I knew what he was thinking … He's thinking that I'm a mute, klutzy, fumbling, rambling idiot, I concluded to myself. Why would he think anything else? The last few times I had been around him, I certainly acted in those heinous ways.

I swore I heard him chuckle, but when I glanced over in his direction, his face showed no amusement. "Don't worry. I'm sure Abby will be thrilled at the idea of you being early." He turned, catching my gaze. For a number of moments, I can't be exactly sure how long, I gazed at him and took in his deep blue eyes, his chiseled jaw line, the dimple on the left side of his face that I hadn't noticed until then, and every other perfect feature he held. Just like Abby, he had changed from the first night I had seen him after the senior's party. Not a drastic change like hers, but still there was a difference. His blonde hair was still long and wavy, but a few inches had been cut. I didn't remember him having any facial hair before, but now he looked like he hadn't shaved in a few days and stubble was forming on his face.

I swallowed hard and stopped walking, noticing that I had been just following his lead. He stopped in front of what from the corner of my eye looked like a large piece of wood. I looked up and saw that we were standing in front of the largest wooden gate I had ever seen. It looked like it belonged in front of a fortress, not protecting some home in small-town Marblehead. It must have been at least fifteen feet high and thirty feet wide, I guessed. A trace scent of fresh paint hit my nose.

"Here, allow me," Blake began as he reached for the door, unlatching the lock and pushing the gate open. "I just finished painting it, and I don't know how dry it is."

When the gate swung open, it revealed the largest, most grandiose, intricately detailed home I had ever seen. I stood there in shock as my eyes swept from left to right, trying to take it all in. The old white paint was still peeling away from the brick it had once clung to, and the black shutters were in major need of re-staining. A large porch stretched across the entire length of the house, and a stone staircase led to the large red door. It was so bright red that it must have been recently painted.

"I wanted to say sorry for my behavior the first night we met," Blake said, breaking my focus on the house and calling my attention back to him.

He looked intently at me, and I couldn't deny that my face felt twisted with shock. Never in a million years did I think he would actually apologize for that. There was no reason to. "No big deal. Everyone is entitled to an off day, right?" I responded, hoping that he would chalk up all of my peculiar incidences to just a bunch of off days.

"Well, you girls have fun." He smiled, revealing the dimple on his left cheek again and sending my stomach into full-on summersaults. His eyes retreated from mine back toward the house.

When I followed his gaze, I saw Abby bouncing down the stone staircase, making her way down the long, curved driveway toward us. “Hi, Meredith. You’re early!” She smiled as she approached. She truly sounded excited about my being there, just like Blake had said she would be.

“Yeah, sorry, I had planned to—”

“Oh, don’t worry about it,” she cheerfully cut me off. “I’m actually glad you’re early. I had everything all set up this morning, so we can get started *right now*.” She turned to Blake, giving him a pointed look. “If you’re ready of course.” She smiled, turning back to me. And I couldn’t help but wonder if they were having another brother-and-sister quarrel.

“Sure, I’m ready.” That was my main reason for coming there, right? And as much as I tried, there was no way to lie, especially not to myself. I knew why I had really accepted Abby’s invitation: it had been to see Blake. There was no way of explaining why I wanted to see him so badly. Why I felt a certain way when I was in his presence. But I tried to look on the bright side: we had spoken a few words and I had proved somewhat that I was not a total weirdo … or at least, I hoped I had.

Abby turned on her heels and headed back toward the large house. I followed, but not before looking at Blake once more. When our eyes met, he gave me a delicate smile before turning around himself and walking in the opposite direction. I couldn't help but wish he wasn't going.

Chapter Nine

I walked quickly, trying to catch up to Abby with her light and bubbly bounce. She flew up the stairs, and I hesitated before placing my foot on the first stone step. I couldn't describe what was happening, but a strange feeling came over me when I was a few feet shy of the staircase. There was some energy in the air that I couldn't quite explain, but it gave me a gut instinct that something weird was going on. I shook it off, thinking it was just all in my head. It had not been the best idea to think about all the scary stories I'd heard as a child on the way over. I began the walk up, trying to fight off my nerves with each step. When I reached the top, I looked forward to the open door and saw Abby standing in the foyer waiting for me.

"You coming?" she asked, a puzzled look crossing her face.

I nodded and continued to make my way across the wide porch and through the doorway.

"Wow," I gasped when I entered the marble foyer. I stood there in awe, looking up at the winding staircase that continued as far as I could see. In my imagination, these homes had been dark and drab on the inside, all covered with dark wood paneling, cobwebs, and dust—just what you would picture a haunted house to look like. This house was not even close to dark and drab. There was sunlight spilling in from windows in every direction I looked.

There was a large room on my left that must have been the dining room. The huge glass chandelier hanging in it looked to be about the same size as our refrigerator at home. It was full of clear crystals, cascading down and making a point at the end. It was perfectly centered over what looked to be a table underneath a lot of plastic, stretching the entire length of the room. That must be one of the rooms we're going to paint samples in, I thought to myself.

To my right was another large room that must have been the living room, or at least one of them. There was a lot of white furniture, all Victorian-style couches and chairs pushed to the middle of the room, but there was no plastic protecting it. I did notice a lot of plastic beneath a large blank wall. It was opposite a stone wall that held the largest fireplace I had ever seen. All the walls I could see were stark white, as if they had been stripped of all paint or wallpaper, leaving a fresh clean slate. She had not been joking when she had said she needed help in picking out paint colors.

"Follow me. I'll give you a quick tour before we get started," she said as she began to walk down the long hallway directly in front of us.

Still feeling a little uneasy, I followed closely behind her, looking around constantly and marveling over every inch of the amazing home. I never had enough time to take in a room before moving onto the next. We entered the kitchen, and I was taken aback by its size. I swore that the entire first floor of our house would have fit in that one single room. A large island sat in the middle; it was a beautiful white marble, with thin black veins shooting through it, almost giving it an overall grey color. The countertops matched the island, and the tall cabinets that towered over them had been stripped of their paint. There was no table in what looked to be the breakfast area, but I did see a large sheet of plastic covering the ground with a few sample paint cans laying on top. I realized that this was not going to be a quick and easy task; this was going to be a long process.

From the kitchen, we made our way back down the long hallway that led to the front door. We took a sharp turn before entering the foyer, leading us up the stairs to the second floor. The upstairs was quite a different atmosphere from the downstairs. It was exactly what you would expect if you pictured a haunted house. Most of the doors were closed, leaving the hallway dark and feeling very isolating.

There was one door opened at the far end of the hallway on the left. I could see the natural light glowing from the inside of the room. "This is my room," Abby said as we approached the opened doorway. We walked into the pinkest room I had ever seen. It looked like someone had thrown up pink all over the walls, bedspread, and accessories. The only non-pink color I could see was the hardwood floors beneath our feet.

"It's ... nice," I said, hoping it came out sounding fairly believable. "You must like pink."

She laughed. "No, I actually hate the dreadful color. Since we have only been here for a few weeks, we decided to get started on the downstairs first. But as soon as we finish with that, my room is next in line. I don't know what was going on inside the person's head that decorated this room." She shook her head and then gestured toward the hallway. "Shall we?"

I nodded and followed her out. As we made our way back down the long, dark hallway toward the stairs, I noticed a door that had been closed was now open. As we passed, I foolishly peered inside and saw Blake lying on his bed, reading a book. We made eye contact, but I quickly averted my gaze and looked back down the hallway, angry with myself for even looking. It was clear to me that there was something between us, even if I was the only one who felt it. Every time I saw him, my heart fluttered and my stomach did weird flip-flops. Just at the sight of him. I had never felt anything like it before. It was frustrating to me that the first time I felt any interest in someone, he was a tourist who showed up a couple months before I planned to leave town. Just my luck.

"So I figured something bright and cheery for the kitchen. Maybe a sunny yellow or sky blue?" Abby said as we got back downstairs and started heading down the long hallway toward the kitchen. Upon entering the brightly lit room, she bent down and lifted the top off the sample paint cans. She revealed two yellow shades and two shades of blue. She handed me a paintbrush and began to instruct me on what to do.

When she finished her explanation, she said, "I thought you could paint the blue samples and I could paint the yellow. Is that okay with you?"

"Sure," I answered, taking the paintbrush from her hands and bending down to dip it in the lighter shade of blue on the left. I began to paint a large square on the white wall in front of me. The smell of paint made my stomach turn a little, but I ignored it and continued to paint the outline of my square. After we finished painting the four squares, we moved on to the next room, allowing the paint to dry before we made our final decisions. We continued the process in each room that she had set up with paint samples, which was pretty much every room downstairs except the one with its door shut.

Finally we made our way into the amazing living room, the room where the large stone fireplace took up the entire back wall. I followed Abby, and we came to a stop at the large empty wall with the wad of plastic beneath it. She lifted off the lids to each of the sample paint cans, like she had done in each room before. These colors were much different than the ones we had been experimenting with in the other rooms. These colors were all dark shades of blues, teals, and browns. She handed me a fresh paintbrush, and I started with the sample nearest to me. It was a beautiful, dark blue steel color. I picked up the brush and began to paint the outline of my square.

"So you live with your aunt?" Abby asked, totally catching me off guard.

I wondered how she had known, but then I remembered mentioning my aunt at the hardware store the day before. It would be easy enough to put together, I guessed. "Uh, yeah. Well, she's not really my aunt … I've just called her that since I was little."

"Oh." She looked as if she wanted to dig deeper into the topic, but she refrained. "Well, what are your plans after this summer? You did just graduate from high school, right?"

"Yeah, just a couple weeks ago. I'm planning on traveling a bit after I get some money saved up, but it's all still up in the air right now."

She nodded.

If she was going to ask personal questions, then I thought that was my chance to ask one, too. "So do you and your brother live in this big house all alone, or do you have parents?"

She laughed. "Of course we have parents. They went into town but should be home any second now. They have actually wanted to meet you since we arrived here." She paused, looking apprehensive, as if she had just said too much.

Just then the front door opened behind us. When I turned around, I found two people staring at me wide-eyed.

"Mother, Father," Abby spoke up. "This is Meredith, the girl I met in town a few days ago."

There was an uncomfortable silence for a moment. They gave me the same weird feeling as Abby and Blake had when I first saw each of them.

"Of course!" Abby's father spoke as he began walking toward me with a smile on his face. He crossed the room quickly and held out his hand. "I'm Samuel Harper. It's a pleasure to meet you, Meredith."

"It's nice to meet you, too. You have a beautiful home. It's amazing what you've done with the place." When I looked into his eyes, I saw an older rendition of Blake, except for his hair that was beginning to grey. There was no mistaking they were father and son.

"Well, thank you. But I must say it's mostly Abby's doing. She has been working around the clock since we got here." He looked toward Abby, giving her a proud glance.

Just then Abby's mother came to stand beside Samuel. "Hello, I'm Annette Harper. Sorry, I was just taken aback for a moment. You reminded me of someone I used to know. It took me by surprise."

She looked to be a little nervous, but there was something sweet and caring about her. Or maybe the correct description was *motherly*. The moment I looked into her eyes, I knew where Abby got the startling green color of hers. Her hair was a dark auburn color and it was pinned back into what looked like a low bun. She was dressed very conservative but it seemed to suit her.

"It's nice to meet you." I smiled.

"Well, we will not delay you two any longer. Your mother and I will be out back, should you need us for anything," Samuel said to Abby.

When he finished, his eyes met mine. "It is a pleasure to meet you, Meredith." He smiled.

The way they spoke. It was so eloquent and refined-sounding, much like Abby had spoken to me the day outside the dress shop. It made me feel intimidated.

"You too, sir." *Sir?* I don't think I'd ever called anyone *sir* before.

They both turned and exited the room.

"Sorry, that was a little awkward. They are very sweet, but so out-of-date," Abby said as she turned back toward the wall, picking up her paintbrush and continuing to paint the sample square she had been working on.

"They seem nice," I said.

After seeing Abby's parents, I missed my family more than ever. I missed calling someone Mom and Dad, and I missed my parents looking at me like Samuel had just looked at Abby. It was clear her parents loved her very much. Suddenly, I was extremely envious of the girl standing beside me.

Turning back around, I continued with my painting, but just as I put my brush to the wall, my head began to pound. The pain was in the same location as when I had gotten the past few headaches after my dreams. I grabbed the back of my head with my left hand, trying to ease some of the throbbing by rubbing it, but the pain consumed me, forcing me to drop the brush out of my right hand so I could use it to steady myself against the wall. Through the pain, I saw the brush hit the ground, splattering paint all over me and the floor.

"Meredith, are you okay?" I could hear the panic in Abby's voice, but I wasn't able to focus on her face.

The large room became blurry and began to spin. *Oh, no, not here*. That was the only thought that crossed my mind. It was one thing to deal with this in my bedroom, somewhere where no one could see me, but not there. Not in front of Abby, or even worse, Blake. I saw the vision of a man. The man was familiar to me: it was one of the men that had haunted my dreams the other night, the same man that stood near the tree line while my sister and I played in the backyard. As my vision tunneled, I began to see his surroundings more clearly. He looked to be in a small, dark area, in between two brick buildings, maybe. I could see dumpsters, graffiti on the walls, and street lamps in the distance. The exact location was not recognizable, but his face was all too clear. His eyes were as dark as coal and were a perfect match to his jet black hair. He was smiling the same evil smile, seemingly happy, admiring something as he glanced downward. Then I gasped out loud. The man was holding someone in his grasp, and that someone was me.

Suddenly the vision was gone, and the pain in my head began to diminish. My heart sank as I realized that something was very, very wrong with me. Apparently these attacks, or whatever they were, were coming whenever they felt like it. The vision had scared me to the point that I had forgotten where I was until I heard Abby's frantic voice. "Meredith, talk to me. Are you okay?"

"Bathroom?" I choked out, hoping she was able to understand my mumbling.

“Here, let me help you.” She grabbed my arm, guiding me down the hall and stopping at the opened door on the right.

“I’ll take it from here,” I stuttered, walking in and shutting the door behind me.

The room was pitch-black, so I began touching the wall in order to find the light. I flipped on the switch and made my way over the sink. I turned the knob, blasting the cold water and splashing it on my face and around the back of my neck, hoping it would help stop the room from spinning. I was still not sure what had happened out there. The headache had felt the same as the ones that had accompanied my dreams. But that was exactly why it was so strange; I only got the headaches after my dreams, not during the day when I was awake and functioning. Or at least trying to function.

How am I going to explain myself to Abby? She’s probably out there thinking I’m some sort of crazy person. The only choice I had had was to lie. What else could I do? Tell her the truth? I would tell Abby that the paint fumes had gotten to me. I mean, it could happen right? Hell, it was better than telling her that I was a freak that had weird visions and horrible headaches at a moment’s notice.

But I knew the truth; I knew that the paint fumes hadn’t caused this. I just didn’t know what to do about it. Maybe it was time to tell Aunt Rose, even if she would make me take a thousand tests and—even scarier—go see a therapist.

After taking in a few deep breaths and splashing some more water on my face, I felt strong enough to go and face what was on the other side of the door. As much as I wanted to stay in that bathroom for the rest of my life, I knew I couldn't. Maybe some fresh air would do me good. And it would play well with the whole toxic-paint-fumes excuse I was planning on using.

Chapter Ten

I opened the bathroom door and saw Abby standing outside of it, wide-eyed, with a concerned look on her face. "Are you okay?"

"Fine." I swallowed hard. "I think the paint fumes got to me, that's all. I just need some fresh air."

I turned to walk back down the long hallway that emptied into the living room and eventually the front door. Then something distracted my train of thought. In front of me, Blake was leaning up against the entrance to the living room, staring right at me, his arms crossed. Nice. I had been hoping to get out of there without him witnessing me like that.

Abby trailed close behind me. "Meredith, I'm so sorry. Can I walk you home? Or get you some water?"

“No, just fresh air,” I answered, trying to calm the worry in her voice while still walking fast down the hallway.

As I passed Blake, I held my head high, trying my hardest not to let on how embarrassed I actually was. And even though I didn’t look at him directly, I could feel his eyes on me, burning into me like only his stare could. Somehow I made it to the front door, and I flung it open, gasping for the fresh, clean air. I stumbled to the steps and sat, resting my head against the large white pillar on my right. Abby sat beside me and continued to ask how I was doing and if I needed anything. And I continued to tell her that I would be all right after a few minutes, hoping she’d believe me so I wouldn’t feel any more embarrassed than I already did. The fresh air did wonders, and after a few minutes had passed, I began to feel better. I glanced to my left and saw Abby’s same wide-eyed stare.

“I’m really sorry for the mess I made in the living room. And sorry that I was not much help today. I guess I’m more sensitive to paint fumes than I realized,” I said.

“No, you were a great help. I loved the steel blue color in the living room, and now we know it goes well with the hardwoods.” She chuckled, trying to make me feel better. “I’m just sorry you got sick. I should’ve taken better care of you.”

I wondered what she meant by taking care of me, but I figured she meant because I was a guest in her house or something.

"Please, let me at least walk you home. I want to make sure you get home okay," she begged me.

"I'll walk her home." Blake's deep voice spoke up from behind me. "I think you've done enough, *Abby*." The bitter tone was not even directed toward me, but I felt the sting of it. I looked toward Abby and saw her frowning, looking out into the front yard.

Turning my head, I peered over my shoulder and saw Blake standing in the doorway. Even though I had known it was Blake before seeing him, my heart did not want to believe that he could say something so callous and hateful to his sister. Anger coiled inside me, and I felt an overpowering need to stick up for Abby.

"She didn't do anything! It was just the paint fumes." My voice was severe. Maybe it was too much, but I was appalled that he would talk to his own sister like that. I stood up, feeling a sudden wave of irritation wash over me.

I said goodbye to Abby, apologizing again for the mess I had made. She smiled a halfhearted smile, and I wished that I could do more to make her feel better. Eager to get out of there and away from Blake, I began the walk back down the stone steps and along the curved drive. It was not long before I sensed someone following me.

When I turned around, I saw Blake just a few steps behind, staring at me intensely. I rolled my eyes and began to walk more quickly, hoping he would get the hint and just leave me alone. To think that I actually came over here wanting to see him! I thought. What was I thinking? I mean, what a jerk. About a minute had passed, and I couldn't resist the urge to see if he was still back there. But when I turned around, he was nowhere to be seen. Probably just as well.

I exited the large wooden gates and made my way back down Estate Lane. When I turned the corner onto Shore Drive, I came to a sudden halt. There in front of me, just twenty or so feet away, Blake stood, leaning against the stone wall. He was looking straight at me like he'd known exactly when I would round the corner. How did he get there so fast? There was no way he could've walked past me, and there was no other way onto Shore Drive. Well, not that I knew of, anyway. He propelled himself forward off the wall and began walking toward me. I pulled my shoulders back, preparing myself for any snide remarks he was about to say. He approached, and I continued to stare directly in his eyes, not wavering one tiny bit, hoping to show him that I was not intimidated by his rudeness.

But as he got closer, I could tell the look on his face was not meant to be cruel or hateful. His face was full of regret. I relaxed my shoulders and felt the stone-cold face I was wearing disappearing as well.

"I wish you hadn't run off like you did," he said, his eyes searing into mine. "You hardly gave me time to apologize."

It was a deer-stuck-in-the-headlights moment: I couldn't avert his gaze even if I had wanted to. The way he looked at me should be illegal. I swear he possesses some power to seduce with his eyes. It was just not normal for me to be able to forgive anyone so easily.

Then I reminded myself I was not ready to forgive him. It's not like he had personally offended me or anything, but he had been a total jerk to his sister. And I was not up for giving jerks the time of day. As soon as I was able to break his gaze, I continued walking, picking up my pace as I passed him. It seemed childish to just ignore his apology, but it felt like the right thing to do at the time.

"Meredith, please let me explain." I felt my heart pick up speed when he called my name.

"I don't think it's me you should be apologizing to," I suggested, my voice coming out steady and strong.

He was trailing a few steps behind me, but I could tell he was closing the distance between us. A few seconds passed, and he was walking right beside me.

My heart began to flutter when he stopped in front of me, blocking my way. Why was he trying so hard? Why did he care so much what I thought? The guy clearly had a power complex, and he was way too arrogant for my taste.

"You're right." He smiled a half-smile, revealing the dimple on his left cheek. My heart skipped a beat. "I apologized to Abby right after you left. I just didn't like that she let something happen to you." He stopped talking for a moment, and I had a few seconds to analyze what he had just said.

"How did you apologize to Abby and get all the way over here?" I asked. There was no way he could have gone back to apologize and then somehow gotten in front of me unless there were secret tunnels or something. He didn't answer.

Then the second thing he said hit me like a ton of bricks. *He didn't like that she* let *something happen to me?* Who did he think he was? My personal bodyguard or something? I wanted to roll my eyes, but I refrained. Instead, I looked at the ground. "Like I said before, it was just the paint fumes. Nothing else." The lie had come out of my mouth a few times now, and even I was almost starting to believe it, but deep down, I knew it was something more.

"I would really like to walk you home. Just to make sure you get home safely. It was at my house that you risked yourself after all, even if it was just paint fumes."

Knowing it was a mistake to do it, I glanced up. Blake was smiling. When my eyes met his, my heart melted. It was no use. I was weak, and I couldn't resist him any longer. "Well, we are already walking, so I guess it wouldn't hurt if we just kept going," I said.

We walked in silence. I wanted to think of something to say, but my mind drew a blank. I knew a distraction was needed and quick. The cemetery was coming up on our right, and I feared the pain in the pit of my stomach. But it was too late. I tried to be inconspicuous as I wrapped my arms around my waist, gripping my stomach, trying to ease the pain. Just a few more seconds, I told myself, then we will be past the gates and the pain should begin to subside.

In my peripheral vision, I saw his head tilting in my direction, his eyes glancing down toward my waist. "Are you cold?" he asked.

The question threw me off, and I turned to look at him. He was beginning to unbutton the long-sleeved blue shirt he had on, revealing a white undershirt. I couldn't help but notice how tightly the white undershirt clung to his sculpted chest. It was impossible not to stare as he unfastened the buttons one by one. I swallowed hard and knew that I had to stop him. It's not that I didn't want to see more, but his willingness to take his shirt off just then and there made me uncomfortable. Or at least, I think that is the correct description of how I was feeling.

"No—no, not cold at all," I said too loudly. Facing forward again, I let my hair fall around my face, hoping it hid the color I could feel building in my cheeks.

"Oh, wasn't there something you had to do on your way home. An errand?" he questioned. I felt like kicking myself for having such a big mouth.

"It's nothing too important. It can wait."

The pain in the pit of my stomach disappeared as we walked a few steps past the cemetery gates. The rest of the walk was peaceful and actually felt comfortable. As we turned onto Maple Avenue, I started to get anxious about how we would part ways. We had to talk in order to say goodbye. Should I just thank him for walking me home and walk off? Whatever I was planning to say, I had better think quick, as we were only a few houses down from mine.

Just as I was about to stop in front of my house, Blake came to a standstill. I looked up at him, wondering how he had known which house was mine.

"It was a pleasure," he said.

"Yeah, thanks. You know, for making sure I made it home okay." I shrugged.

"Goodbye, then."

A chill ran through me as I stared into his eyes. I swear he got more irresistible each and every time I looked at him.

"Bye," I said, not knowing when I would get to spend time with him again. As much as I hated to admit it, that thought terrified me. What if I didn't?

I turned and began to walk toward the house. It was hard to describe but I felt like there was something different about him that I just couldn't get over—actually there was something different about his entire family. Besides the strange feeling I got when I was around them, they seemed to act strangely in my presence too … like they were uncertain about me somehow.

Fighting myself the entire way to the door, I tried to resist turning around to see if he was still standing there. As I began to open the door, I glanced back around to search for him, but he was gone. There was no way to hide the disappointment on my face.

“Was that the new guy walking you home?” Jack asked as I walked through the door, throwing my train of thought way off.

“New guy?” Aunt Rose echoed as she came around the corner.

Great, this is the last thing I want right now, I thought. “Yes, it was the new kid, and no, there’s nothing to it. He just walked me home because I got a bad headache and almost fainted at his house. Don’t worry, I’m fine.” I finished it all in one breath, not wanting to give them any space to butt in before I was done.

“What happened?” they both asked in perfect unison, and I couldn’t help but laugh.

“The paint fumes got to me. But really, I’m fine,” I said again, hoping they would believe me that time.

Aunt Rose hurried over to me, giving me a typical nurse pat down, and then placed her hand on my forehead, checking for a temperature. “Are you sure you’re okay? You should have called me, Meredith. I would have come and picked you up.”

Yeah, because that’s what I really wanted to happen, I thought to myself. “I’m feeling much better now. The whole thing was really embarrassing, and I would prefer to not dwell on it.”

“Well, I still wish you would have called,” she said, looking at me directly. She appeared satisfied that I would live to see another day.

“How about I make you a deal? The next time I’m over there and I begin to feel faint, I promise to call you,” I joked.

They both tried to contain their laughter, but they couldn’t, and I knew the discussion was over.

But the next question that came out of Aunt Rose’s mouth made me wish for the previous conversation. “Is he cute?” she asked, her eyes lighting up.

I knew the best way to get the discussion over with was to just answer, because if I didn’t, the questions would just keep on coming. “He is all right, I guess. Nothing special,” I lied, not sure who I was trying to convince more, them or me. “He’s not the type that would be interested in someone like me, anyway … not the way you’re thinking, at least,” I admitted, shocked at the disappointment in my voice.

“Don’t sell yourself short, Meredith. You are a very attractive, fun … eccentric kind girl.” I could tell that Aunt Rose had searched for a nicer word than *strange* or *weird.* “Boys love girls that are a little different than the norm. It’s no fun to date someone who acts like every other girl out there.” She gave me a wink as she walked back toward the kitchen. “Dinner should be ready. Hope you all are hungry.”

"Starving," Jack and I answered in unison, and we both laughed as we made our way into the kitchen.

Chapter Eleven

It was Sunday, and work at the library was extra slow. So slow that Ms. Donaldson took time off work to run some errands. I tried not to let the previous day's events at the Harpers' get me down. This was the day that Roger had promised he would call. I could feel the anticipation for hearing from him building inside me. There was so much to tell him! Just as the feeling of excitement began to hit my face, threatening a smile, I heard the front door of the library squeak closed. Internally I sighed, not wanting to have to deal with another patron that afternoon.

But my sulking turned to joy when I realized it was Blake who had walked in. Our eyes met, and he gave me a quick smile. It was so quick that I didn't even have time to return it before he looked away. And again, as hard as I tried, I couldn't take my eyes off of him. He walked straight to the reference section just like he had done before, pulling two books off the shelf and taking a seat at the table near the window.

He flipped open one of the books and glanced up, catching my stare. I looked down, feeling my face heat up to about a thousand degrees and my heart pounding hard against my chest. How embarrassing, I thought to myself.

I was so busy feeling ridiculous that I didn't even realize when he got up and made his way across the room. "Am I doing something wrong?" he questioned, coming to stand on the other side of the counter, just a few inches away from me.

My breath stopped cold, and I looked up toward the deep, soft voice. The left corner of his mouth lifted, resulting in that half-smile that I was beginning to think should be illegal. Meeting his blue eyes, I gradually felt my breathing getting quicker, and I knew that I was approaching hyperventilation. In hopes of avoiding another fainting fit, I looked down and began to shuffle the papers in front of me.

"What would you be doing wrong?" I asked, trying to keep my breathing even.

"The way you are staring, you have me convinced that I'm breaking some library rule or something."

I could hear the smile in his voice. Was he messing with me? The entire time he was standing in front of me, I fought the urge to look him in the eyes. I felt that was the only way to get my breathing back under control. "No, nothing wrong," I said. "I mean you aren't doing it—anything wrong, I mean." Oh. My. God. This was turning into another horrible disaster.

It felt as if there was a giant elephant sitting on my chest, pushing it down and not allowing a breath in or out. *Breathe! Breathe!* I shouted inside my head. Breathe, before you pass out and make an even bigger fool of yourself! At last, I managed a large breath, and I gasped for air, hoping it would help me catch up on the lack of oxygen.

"You okay?" he asked, concern covering his face.

"I'm fine," I responded, sounding annoyed. I was not annoyed at Blake, but annoyed at myself for acting like such an idiot. "Is there something I can help you with?"

"I would like to check this out," he replied, sliding a book to my side of the counter.

History of the 1900s. I glanced at the title and wondered why he would be reading a book like that. It was summer, after all.

"Do you have a library card?" I asked.

"No, afraid not."

"Well, please fill this out, and I will get one made up for you," I said smoothly, handing him the application and a pen and gaining more and more confidence that my normal calm, cool, and relaxed personality was showing itself again.

It was difficult not to stare at him as he was filling the application out on the counter, so I tried to keep myself busy. I did some filing and left the desk to gather books from the front drop box, stealing a glance at him whenever I could.

"All done," he said as I returned back to the desk.

I smiled timidly as I looked over the application, pretending to make sure all the pertinent information was filled out. In reality, he could have written that his name was Abraham Lincoln and he lived at the North Pole, and I wouldn't have noticed. It was too hard to concentrate with him standing so close to me. Something between us had changed since yesterday, but I wasn't sure what it was.

"So, why Marblehead?" I blurted out to dull the pain of the silence as I entered his information into the computer. "I mean, I'm sure there are lots of places with old, historic homes in need of remodeling."

"My family felt like this was the perfect place … You could say that it felt like home the moment we arrived," he said, seeming as though he'd had to come to a decision about saying those last words.

I turned from the computer to hand him his card, sad that I had not drawn out the process a little longer.

"Thank you for the book and for the card," he said, his lips breaking into a gentle smile.

"Just doing my job," I responded, immediately cringing that those words had just come out of my mouth. Ugh, *just doing my job*. Real cool.

"By the way, how are you feeling?"

"Fine—all better," I replied, feeling flattered that he actually cared enough to ask.

"Well, see you around."

"Bye." I smiled, and he turned and walked away.

The last thirty minutes of work were nightmarish. For some reason, all the stupid things I had said in front of Blake were playing over and over in my head. But what bothered me probably more than anything was why I cared so much what he thought about me. I was not sure how much longer I would be able to deny what I was feeling. I mean, it was all laid out for me, staring me right in the face. Practically screaming it: I *liked* him. Then that one thought made my mind go in a thousand different directions. It was not the smartest thing in the world to start liking a guy just a few weeks before skipping town. And even though he had been nice to me the day before and made sure I got home safely, he was still a jerk. Anyone that would talk to his sister that way for something that wasn't even her fault should not be making me feel like this. Even though it was difficult to explain, I knew there was something else to him; he was holding something back.

When work was over, I pulled my purse and backpack out from under the counter, trying to concentrate on the fact that I would talk to Roger that afternoon and be able to spill everything to him soon enough. I turned to tell Ms. Donaldson goodbye, who had just returned from her errands, but when I whirled around, I found her already staring at me.

The words she spoke shocked me. "You look so much like your mother," she said, her voice barely above a whisper. "I hope you don't mind me saying so."

No one had ever told me that before—maybe because they thought of me as some fragile egg that could crack at any moment.

"No, I don't mind," I answered, a smile breaking across my lips. It was weird that she had just mentioned that. Honestly, I had not even been aware that she had known my mother. "Thank you."

I walked out of the library, still smiling at the comment Ms. Donaldson had made. Just then I noticed someone sitting on the bench to my left. It was Blake. When he saw me, he got up and began to walk toward me. My heart fluttered at the sight of him, and I could only stop and watch him as he approached.

He stopped just a few feet from me, his lips parting, about to speak, and then suddenly he turned back around, mumbling something under his breath. I stood there waiting, hoping he would turn back and say what he wanted to say. Finally he turned to face me once again. “I was hoping I could walk you home. Would that be all right with you?”

My fluttering heart began to hammer hard against my chest, and I could feel the excitement all the way in my stomach. “Sure, that would be nice.”

We walked in silence at first, similar to how our walk had begun the day before, but then he asked me a question I was not sure how to answer. “Do you have any brothers or sisters?”

It was a logical enough question. I mean, it should be a good icebreaker for most people, right? But not for me, not when my answer was a very sad one. My heart ached, and I felt a large lump rising in my throat. Just the word *sister* started a domino effect that started with the pain and hurt of losing her and ended with the longing to have her again. I searched for the best way to answer. There was no way I could lie; that would not be fair to Charlotte. Lying about some stuff was necessary, of course, but I couldn't pretend that I had never had a sister, that she never existed. But I had never been asked that question before. Everyone I had ever known before the Harpers' knew what had happened to my family, so there was no reason to ask questions like that.

I knew I had to answer quickly, so the only way to go was to tell the truth. "Yes, I ... had a sister—a twin actually. Her name was Charlotte, but she passed away ten years ago, along with my mother and father." I guessed it would be good to go ahead and get it all out. Best to avoid any more depressing questions.

We continued to walk in silence. He stared at the ground, taking in every last word I had just said as if he was calculating something in his head.

"Sorry," he finally said. "That is terrible."

Not wanting the conversation to get any more depressing, I spoke up again. "It was a long time ago. I hardly remember most things, but I do remember what it was like to have a sister. I miss it very much." Listen to me, here I am opening up my heart to someone I barely know … not even Roger or Aunt Rose get this much out of me. "You're lucky, you know, to have Abby," I added.

He scoffed, but at the same time a small smile broke across his face. “She comes in handy every once in a while, but she’s an annoying little irritant most of the time.”

The walk went quickly, and I was actually sad when I saw my house in view. We parted ways, and my heart ached as I walked away from him. This time I was not strong enough to make it all the way to the door before looking back, checking to see if he was still standing there. About halfway to the door, I turned my head and saw that he was standing in the very spot I had left him. He was watching me. I smiled timidly and continued walking. By the time I reached the door and turned to check again, he was gone.

As I walked in, Aunt Rose was heading out for her night shift. On her way out, she told me that Roger had called a little earlier and that he would try again in a little while. After changing into some more comfortable clothes, I headed downstairs to the kitchen to make a sandwich, hoping to get Blake out of my head. Just as I had pulled the sliced turkey out, the phone rang. I sprinted out of the kitchen and dove onto the couch in the living room, reaching out to answer it.

“Hello?” I gasped as I picked up the phone.

“Man, it’s good to hear your voice,” Roger said on the other end.

"You're not kidding. Can't believe it's only been a week." I paused, taking in a couple deep breaths, trying to steady my breathing. "Sucks not having your best friend to talk to on a daily basis, especially when so much has happened."

"Really? Has Marblehead changed that much in a week? Man, just my luck. When I leave, the most boring town on the planet starts to see some action."

"I wouldn't go that far. It's still just as boring as you left it."

I went on and filled him in on my new job, giving him all the boring details. Then I told him about the Harpers, but decided to leave out my feelings for Blake until I figured them out more myself. Just as I was about to begin to tell him about the nightmares, visions, paranoia, and other strange happenings, I heard someone calling his name on his end of the line.

"Really sorry, but Stephanie just showed up, and we are supposed to be watching a movie in fifteen minutes."

"Stephanie? Is she your flavor of the week?" I asked jokingly.

"More like flavor of the day," he countered.

"Whatever. Blowing me off for some random chick, I see how it is."

"I'll call you later. Promise."

When I hung up the phone, I felt unfulfilled. It probably would have been a good idea to lead with all my weird issues then talk about my boring job and the Harpers afterwards. The funny thing was that Roger didn't even put it together. He did not say anything about the Harpers just moving to Marblehead and the coincidence that they shared the same name as on the gravestones in the cemetery. He had to remember the names on the graves, right? He had visited them with me a hundred times or so. Or maybe he had put it together but was not crazy enough to think they could be connected. Not crazy like me. Even I felt stupid for admitting to myself that the two could be connected. The only logical explanation was that the Harpers were somehow, possibly, related to people buried there, like their descendants or something. Big deal. Even though I knew Roger would be back in just a few weeks' time and I would have my best friend back and things would get better, I knew it would be only temporary. He would be home for just a few days before he was going to pack up and move into the dorms at Harvard. That was his life, his future, his choice.

The rest of my day was crappy. Crappy mood. Crappy everything. I actually looked forward to going to work the next day just to give me something to do. Man, if that didn't prove that I needed a life, I don't know what would. This was pathetic. To get my mind off that topic, I decided to send my thoughts in a different direction. I was supposed to be on a plane out of there in just a few weeks, and I had still had no definite plans as to what I was doing. I wondered if my procrastination was a sign. Maybe it was a sign that I really didn't want to leave Marblehead, my house, my life. Only that was just crazy … There was nothing in this world I wanted more. With that conclusion, I was finally able to put myself to sleep.

My alarm rang, startling me out of a deep sleep. I threw the covers off and marched to the bathroom for a hot shower. Aunt Rose's door was closed, so I assumed that she was home from her shift and still sleeping. After breakfast, I threw together a lunch and headed out for work.

Things at the library were slow, and the day dragged on. Secretly, I hoped that Blake would show his face and brighten my day, but there was no sign of him. It was a strange feeling, the need to see him again. Or maybe it was more of a desire, but it felt all the same to me: an ache in my heart, a yearning to see his face, hear his voice, and feel his presence. But, want or need … it didn't matter what feeling it was, because he never showed.

That night Aunt Rose and I spent the evening cooking and watching chick flicks. It felt nice, and it was exactly what I needed to get my mind off of Blake. After the second movie, I called it a night and headed upstairs to bed.

That was the first night in a couple weeks that I dreamed. It started off normal, pleasant even. I was walking along an unfamiliar beach. The sand was pearl white, and it felt soft as silk on my bare feet. I looked above me and noticed the sky was dark grey, filled with black, ominous clouds, like a bad storm was rolling in. There was not another soul on the beach. There was actually nothing else out there but the water, the sand, and me.

I was conscious that I was dreaming, so I figured the dream must have a point. All the dreams I had had in the past meant something, so this one must have one, too, right? I continued walking on the soft, white-sanded, beach. Even though the sky was grey and my skin was covered in goose bumps, it was peaceful there. After what felt like miles of walking, I looked down at my feet, which were beginning to ache.

My dream took a drastic turn. I was stunned to notice I was walking on black, coarse sand that hurt my feet with each step. Also, I was not alone anymore. I sensed someone behind me. Then I heard a voice. Faint at first, but it began to get louder and louder. Finally I was able to make out what the voice was saying. It was saying my name, calling for me. I stopped walking, listening to the voice, hoping I could pinpoint where and who it was coming from. Spinning around and around, I searched for the person. The voice sounded oddly familiar, and I had to admit that it would have been nice to see a familiar face just then. The next time the voice called my name, it was even louder and more demanding, angry, even. Maybe I didn't want to see whoever was calling me after all.

I opened my eyes, suddenly awake, and I realized that I was not in the comfort of my bed like I should've been.

"Meredith!" A soft, deep voice from behind me shouted again.

I didn't turn around. I ignored the voice, instead focusing on my surroundings. Panic set in, and my whole world began to spin. I felt dizzy the moment I realized that I was outside, and white puffs of light came into my vision. Looking around, I gathered that I was standing in the middle of a dark street, in my pajamas, barefoot.

Then I remembered the voice. It had come from behind me. Spinning around, I found Blake focusing on me with a distraught stare. Then I realized where I was: I was standing in the middle of Estate Lane.

"Blake ..." I swallowed, trying to find more words, but nothing came to mind.

"What are you doing out here so late?" he asked sternly as he approached me, still keeping his distance. He was probably afraid of me or what I might do. Hell, by that point, so was I.

"Um" was all I could find to say. I don't think my heart had ever beaten so fast. I grasped my chest in order to try and calm it down, but it didn't help. Maybe I would go into cardiac arrest, allowing me an easy way out of this embarrassing and confusing situation.

"Are you okay? Do you need to sit down?" he asked again, taking a few steps closer.

I nodded, my wobbly legs falling a few steps backward, finally finding the curb. I collapsed down on it and began to rub my temples using my forefingers.

"Would you like me to get you something to drink, or eat? You don't look so good." His voice sounded frantic in my now ringing ears.

I shook my head. For some reason, the idea of him leaving me scared me more than anything. "No, please don't leave. I will ... be fine. Just give me a sec."

A couple more deep breaths later, I felt that I was able to communicate again. "You scared the crap out of me," I choked out.

"I scared the crap out of *you*? What are you doing out here so late, Meredith?" he demanded, and I could tell that his voice held a bit of anger in it.

In all honesty, I had no idea what I was doing out there. I had no idea how I had just walked almost two miles without fully realizing it. I had been dreaming about walking, but I hadn't realized that I was actually *walking*. The only way to answer his question was to lie; I mean, I didn't want to add "walking zombie" to my grand list of qualities.

"Just ta-taking a walk. Ne-needed to get out of the house for a while," I answered, barely getting out each word. I stared at the ground, in hopes of avoiding any eye contact, knowing that would make the lie easier to pull off.

"Walking late and way out here all alone is probably not a good idea," he said firmly, his tone ripping through my already wounded ego.

"You are out walking—late and by yourself," I said in defense, starting to regain my normal heartbeat.

He chuckled. "That's a very accurate observation."

And when a smile crossed his face, I began to feel more at ease.

"Do you realize that you're wearing just a nightshirt and you're barefoot?" he questioned, trying to suppress his smile.

I nodded. What else could I do? Deny it?

"Would you like me to walk you home?" he asked.

I nodded again.

As I shifted my body to stand, it jarred my vision and my legs began to feel unsteady. Noticing this, Blake reached out, grabbing me and holding me steady.

"You can tell me, you know," Blake said as we began to walk.

My heart sank. "Tell you what?"

"Anything. I just might understand more than you think."

In a weird way, I felt like I could tell him and that he would understand. But I couldn't. How could I possibly explain to him that I had visions of creepy men and weird dreams of the past and that I sleepwalked? That was definitely not the type of conversation I wanted to have with a guy who I was possibly interested in. It actually wasn't a conversation I wanted to have with anyone.

"Okay, when you are ready, then," he said, squeezing my arm, which he was still holding.

Chapter Twelve

The next morning I awoke to the sound of rain. It felt like I hadn't slept in a decade, but that was probably because I hadn't slept much the previous night. It almost seemed like a dream, walking all the way over to Estate Lane and running into Blake. But it hadn't been a dream. The cuts that still lingered on the bottoms of my feet gave me a quick reminder of that the moment they touched the floor. I could also still smell Blake's scent all over me. He had practically carried me the entire way home. Despite the pain my feet were giving me, I got ready quickly, knowing I would have a long and painful walk to work in the rain. It was times like that that I really regretted not having a car.

When I got downstairs, I saw that Aunt Rose had left me a note:

It was raining when I left this morning, so I asked Jack to come and give you a ride to work. He should be here around 8:45 a.m.

AR

I exhaled, knowing that I would be able to avoid the wet and painful walk to work all because I had the best aunt in the world. A part of me did not feel like I deserved someone like Aunt Rose. She was so caring, loving, and sweet. My life would probably not be so difficult if I had just inherited one of those traits. Glancing up at the clock, I realized I still had about ten minutes before Jack would show up. I ate my breakfast slowly, knowing there was no need to rush. Just after rinsing my bowl in the sink, I heard two honks coming from out front. I grabbed my purse and backpack and headed toward the door.

"Hey Meredith, do you think you would be okay alone in the house for a few days?" Jack asked as we pulled up to the stop sign at Maple Avenue.

"Um, sure. I'm alone in the house all the time."

"Yeah, I know, but I'm talking for a few days. Maybe like five or so."

He glanced over at me, I guess to measure my reaction. I really had no reason to care. It was not like being alone for that long would be much different than what I was used to.

More than anything, I was just curious to what he was up to. "Sure, Jack, it's no problem. What's up, though?" I asked, hoping I was not prying too much.

"Well." He paused before continuing. "I'm going to ask Rose to marry me."

My mouth dropped open. I stared at him for a moment in total shock, and then I couldn't help but mirror his smile. *Finally* was the first word that popped into my head. They had been dating for three years by that point and were practically married, except for the whole living-together thing. And I'm guessing that had been for my benefit—Aunt Rose trying to be a good role model and all.

"That's great news! I'm so happy for you guys," I said.

"We'll see. She still has to say yes."

On the inside, I rolled my eyes, knowing that Aunt Rose was probably going to say *yes* before he even finished asking. Scream it, even.

"But I don't understand. Why would you be gone for that many days?" I asked.

"Well, the few times we have talked about marriage, we agreed that we would want a quick and simple ceremony and a really nice honeymoon."

"Sounds like her." I nodded, still not able to wash the smile from my face.

I could barely contain my excitement, knowing that Aunt Rose was about to get the life that she had always deserved. Her entire life had been uprooted the moment she moved into my house to take care of me. Aunt Rose never really had an opportunity to date, get married, and then have a family. And even though she had a choice in taking care of me, there was no doubt that she had sacrificed because of that decision. And recently, there were times where I had felt guilty, knowing that I would be leaving her after that summer and she would be all alone in the house. But now she would have Jack … and who knows? Maybe they would start a family of their own. Butterflies filled my stomach in anticipation of the life that I hoped she would have.

We pulled up to the library. I opened the car door and stepped out, thanking Jack for the ride and wishing him luck with the proposal. It was hard to concentrate at work, given everything that was on my mind. I was preoccupied with the news that Jack had just told me. And I couldn't forget about the events that had happened the night before; they haunted me all day. A part of me wanted everything that had happened the previous night to be a dream. I did not want to believe that I was capable of sleepwalking. I mean, that's for crazy people, right?

I kept thinking about Blake, longing to see him again. All day my eyes were focused on the doors, hoping that Blake would eventually walk through them. But much to my dismay, he never showed. Maybe he is trying to avoid me, I thought. Maybe he realizes that I am some sort of freak and he wants nothing to do with me.

When work ended, I pulled my purse and backpack out from under the counter before telling Ms. Donaldson goodbye.

"Would you like me to drive you home, dear? The sky still looks pretty dark, and I would hate for you to get stuck in the rain."

"No, thanks. I should be fine." The rain had been on-and-off all day. I hoped that it would remain off for just fifteen more minutes so I could get home. My feet still ached from the last night's excursion, but after standing all day I was somewhat used to the pain.

When I walked outside, I turned and saw that I had someone waiting for me on the bench. My heart began to flutter as Blake's eyes met mine and he began to walk toward me. A part of me felt as though I should be embarrassed in front of him, but there were no such feelings. The only feelings I had were anticipation of being close to him again.

"Do you mind if I walk you home? I want to make sure you get there okay and don't end up in the next town or anything." He smiled as he got within a few feet of me.

I glared up at him, but I was also able to appreciate his humor. It was nice to have someone to joke around with since Roger had been gone.

"Sounds great. But where were you this morning? It would have been nice to have my personal bodyguard then, too," I joked.

"But this morning you had a ride to work, right? With Jack?"

I stared at him, shock crossing my face. "How did you know?" I asked.

"Don't get too excited. I'm not a psychic or anything. I came over this morning and had every intention of walking you, but then I saw Jack pull up and you run out."

"Oh." His thoughtful and flattering response threw me. Could he really have cared so much that I made it to work safely?

We began to walk, and it was hard for me not to stare at him. I searched my brain for something to say, but nothing came to mind.

Before I could think of anything, he began asking questions. "So I hear that you are leaving soon?"

I looked at him, shock crossing my face again. How did he know everything?

"Relax. My sister told me." He laughed.

Then I remembered talking with Abby about that when we were painting at their house.

"What do you think you are going to miss most about leaving Marblehead?" he asked.

"My family—my mom, dad and sister, and of course, my aunt," I said, sighing. "I know it seems weird that I will miss my dead parents and sister, because they are not really here—"

"Doesn't seem weird at all," he interrupted.

"I honestly love going and talking to them." I continued to talk, surprising myself at how easily the words flowed out of me when I was with him. "Some people think it's not healthy to go visit them as often as I do, but it really helps to remember. This is embarrassing; I don't know why I'm talking to you about this stuff." I looked down toward the ground, trying to hide the crimson color I felt burning in my cheeks.

"Embarrassed? Why?" he asked. "I just think that proves how much they meant to you when they were here. You should never be ashamed of that."

It's crazy, I thought. I feel like I could tell him anything and he would know just what to say. "This is so strange," I said. "I never open up like this. My best friend and aunt don't even get this much out of me. It's weird how comfortable and safe I feel when I'm around you. I feel like I can tell you anything." It was also crazy that I had just confessed to him what I had just been thinking.

"So, are you saying that I have some sort of hold on you? That could be interesting. I don't think I have ever had a hold on anyone before." I turned to see him grinning, revealing the dimple on his left cheek that I loved so much.

We took the long way home, and I tried to draw out the walk as long as possible. It was near dusk by the time we stopped in front of my house.

"Thanks for walking me and making sure I didn't end up in the ocean, drowning or something," I said.

I was not sure what kind of trouble I was getting myself into. My plan was to leave town in a few weeks. It was not the time to get wrapped up in some guy, especially one who was just going to ditch town in a few weeks, anyway. Why did this mysterious, charming, cute guy have to come into my life now? Why not any other summer?

“You’re welcome. My services are always available,” he replied, smiling. “You are different than I expected. Quite a nice surprise.”

“Same here,” I admitted. And that was the absolute truth. Blake had done a complete 180 degree turnaround from the first time we had met. He did not even seem like the same person who had stared me down at the crosswalk in town or the guy who had glared at me before storming off. Those days seemed so long ago, and yet it had only been a couple weeks.

“I wish the night wasn’t ending,” he said as he looked into my eyes.

It was such a relief to hear him say those words. I didn’t want to admit to myself that I was becoming this clingy, falling-for-a-guy-I-just-met type of person.

“But I guess I better be going,” he said. “I’m sure you can make it the next few steps without getting lost. Or should I stand guard and make sure?” he said in a sarcastic tone.

“Would you like to come inside?” I blurted out, not really sure where that had come from; I’d never invited a guy into my house ... well, except for Roger. I assumed that Aunt Rose was still out with Jack and probably wouldn’t be home for a while. And he seemed harmless; I mean, if he had wanted to hurt me, he had had the perfect opportunity the night before, right? I just didn't want to be away from him.

"Um … I don't know if that would be the best idea," he replied.

I swallowed hard, mad at myself for even asking. I should've known better. "Oh, okay." I shrugged. "I understand."

He nodded. "Well, goodbye."

I turned and began walking toward my house, feeling like something was missing, kind of a hopeless feeling. The desire of wanting him close to me was unbearable.

"Meredith," he called after me.

I smiled at the sound of his voice calling my name. But I tried to hide my enthusiasm as I turned around to face him. "Yes?" I hoped he did not hear the eagerness in my voice, but he would have to have been deaf not to. I was hoping that he had changed his mind and decided to come inside.

"Can I see you tomorrow?"

"That would be great." I would settle for seeing him tomorrow. It was better than nothing. When I turned back around, I couldn't stop the smile from spreading across my face.

"Meredith, is that you?" My aunt's voice called from the kitchen as I walked through the door.

"Yeah, it's me." I wondered what she was doing home. I threw my stuff down on the floor by the stairs and headed toward the kitchen.

"Guess what?" Aunt Rose squealed in excitement the moment I saw her. She looked like a balloon being squeezed to its limits, likely to explode at any moment.

By the tone of her voice, I had guessed that Jack had proposed, and if I had any acting skills, I needed to use them now. "What?" I asked, trying my best to look clueless.

She took in a deep breath before answering. "Jack asked me to marry him!" Then she squealed so loud that it hurt my ears, but I didn't let on that it had in any way. Instead, I screamed in excitement and wrapped my arms around her, telling her congratulations and demanding to see the ring. It gave me goose bumps as I looked into her eyes and saw pure happiness. I had never seen her so happy.

"When did this happen?" I asked, trying my best to act mystified.

"We just finished up dinner, but I couldn't wait to come home and tell you. Now, I know it seems soon, but we're thinking about next week."

"Next week!"

"Well, there's no time like the present." She smiled tentatively. "We just feel like we're ready, and I don't want him moving in until we're married first. How do you feel about that?"

"That doesn't bother me. I don't care if you all live together before marriage."

She laughed. "No silly. I mean what do you think about us getting married next week?"

"Oh. I'm cool with that, too." I mean, it seemed quick but who was I to judge? They had been dating for years, and I knew how badly Aunt Rose wanted it.

"Great. I just wanted to make sure, because I want you to be my maid of honor," she said, trying to keep her voice from reaching its highest pitch.

That would entail wearing a dress again, no doubt, but how could I resist? "I would love to be your maid of honor." I smiled, and I didn't even have to try that hard. Wearing a dress was like taking medicine, but if it was going to make Aunt Rose's special day a better one, then I would do it. There was nothing I wanted more than her to be happy. She had done so much for me.

"Here, take a look at the pictures of the resort. We—or I should say *I*—already started to plan our honeymoon. *Bahamas*!" she shrieked as she bent down to pull something up on her laptop.

"Wow, that place looks amazing," I said, bending over so I could see the pictures more clearly.

We talked for the next hour. She gave me all the details: the way he'd proposed to her at their favorite restaurant, the way she cried when he asked her, and the way the whole restaurant applauded when she said yes. We both decided to call it a night when neither of us could stop yawning. I gave her one last hug and headed upstairs.

"Oh, Meredith," she called, stopping me about halfway up the stairs.

"Yes?"

"We start dress shopping tomorrow."

I nodded and went to the bathroom to get ready for bed. Just as I had finished washing my face and brushing my teeth, there was a faint knock at the bathroom door.

"Meredith?"

"Yes?"

"There is someone at the door for you. He said his name is Blake."

My heart stopped. I looked at my reflection in the mirror and cursed under my breath.

"Um … Okay. Tell him I'll be down in a minute." I tried to keep my voice even, hoping that I hid the excitement and confusion that I knew it held.

I tore the rubber band out of my ponytail and used my hands to comb through my hair. Looking down, I realized that I had already changed into my pajamas, but there was no time to worry about that. I didn't want to leave Aunt Rose and Blake in the same room for long. Who knows what they could be talking about? I tried to remain calm as I skipped down the stairs, my heart fluttering with each step.

"Blake … Hi."

When our eyes met, I couldn't help but smile. I turned to Aunt Rose, and she gave me a questioning look, but I ignored it and looked back toward Blake.

"Let's go outside. I won't be out long, Aunt Rose."

"Take your time," she called after me as I took Blake's arm and pulled him out the front door.

"Hope I didn't get you into any trouble," he said as we walked toward the large tree that was centered in my front yard.

"Um, it's fine," I answered as I leaned back up against the tree facing him. I wondered what he could possibly want that couldn't have waited until tomorrow. "Did you need something?"

He nodded. "You."

A shudder ripped through me, and I didn't know how to respond. My whole body felt weak. "Me?" I asked, holding his eyes.

"It's harder than I thought. I can't get you out of my head, and the desire to be with you is greater than the consequence."

I swallowed hard. "Consequence?"

"It doesn't matter. The only thing that matters right now is you—and me."

So many emotions were swimming around inside me, it was getting more and more difficult to keep my breathing under control. I felt him move forward, closing the small gap that was between us. His eyes never left mine as he inched closer to me, moving slowly, allowing me too much time to think about what was about to happen. I inhaled a large breath, taking in his scent. Then gently, his lips brushed mine. I could feel our bodies meld together, and his weight pushed me back against the tree. It was out of my control. My body took over, and I ran my hands up his chest and around the back of his neck, pulling him closer to me, crushing his lips into mine. I felt his hands graze over my back, then up and around my neck. He began to withdraw and I fought to keep him near me, not wanting the moment to be over, realizing that I had wanted this for a while now.

When he pulled away, he kept his hands around my neck, his thumbs caressing my cheeks as he whispered into my ear, "That couldn't wait until tomorrow."

I breathed in deeply, knowing that I was in big trouble. The feelings in my stomach that burned like fire when he was near could only mean one thing: I was really falling for him. And as much as that thought excited me, I also knew it held dire consequences. *Consequences*. This must be what Blake was talking about. The reality was that we would both be leaving Marblehead in just a few weeks, and we were both stupid to be having these types of feelings.

His eyes found mine, and it took all of my power to keep his gaze and not concentrate on his lips. I wanted to skip the uncomfortable conversation that was about to occur and just keep continuing our previous one.

"About tomorrow," he began. "My family and I would like to invite you over for dinner."

My mind was still swirling from the kiss, and it was difficult to think about anything else. "Dinner? Tomorrow?" I breathed.

"I'll be here at seven."

I nodded. He bent down and lightly pressed his lips to mine again for the briefest moment. Then he was gone.

I walked inside in a daze, not able to wash the smile off my face. Aunt Rose was sitting on the couch, pretending to read a magazine, but I knew the real meaning behind her staying up.

"Blake?" She drew his name out as she raised her eyebrows in interest. "Even though I don't know him very well, I already love him. Anyone that can put that kind of smile on your face is a winner in my book."

"Thanks, Aunt Rose." I blushed.

It was difficult for me to sleep. There were so many emotions running through me. My stomach was coiled up so tight that I feared sleep would never come. But somewhere in between thinking about our kiss and the excitement of knowing I would see him tomorrow, I drifted off into a deep slumber.

Chapter Thirteen

The next morning Aunt Rose woke me early, announcing in a very chipper voice that we would be leaving for our dress-shopping marathon in an hour. I rolled out of bed and headed for the bathroom to get ready. After a quick breakfast, we jumped in the car and drove into town. There were only a few dress shops that would have wedding-type dresses, so I took comfort in knowing that we would be done by six or so. I didn't mention my dinner date to Aunt Rose yet, so she wouldn't feel rushed.

After six long hours of trying on every wedding dress that Marblehead had to offer, we were on our way back home. Aunt Rose had picked out a beautiful silk, cream-colored dress, and I had chosen a very simple, navy blue gown.

“That wasn’t too bad, was it?” she asked as we got into the car and headed home.

“No, not bad at all.” I smiled.

The clock on her dashboard read 4:33 p.m., still plenty of time to get ready for dinner that night. Now I felt it was safe to tell Aunt Rose about my plans.

“Blake invited me over to his house for dinner tonight,” I blurted out.

“Really? Does this mean things are getting serious between you two?”

“I don’t know what it means. It could just be an innocent dinner.” I shrugged.

“Well, I don’t think it’s innocent if a guy comes to your house at ten o’clock at night just to invite you over for dinner.”

My stomach twisted with the memory of the night before and the anticipation of seeing him again soon. I had a difficult time hiding my smile.

“He seems great, but when he left last night I started to think about it some more. I just don’t want you to get so wrapped up in him before you leave. I don’t want to see you getting hurt. Have you thought about that?” she added, glancing in my direction.

Yes, I had thought about the consequences. My brain told me to end it, to not let it go on any longer. Then there was my heart telling me to dive right in and don't hold back. Which one was I going to listen to? That was the question.

It didn't take me long to get ready. I had already applied a little makeup before leaving that morning; so a little touch-up was all that was needed. I decided not to change out of my black capris and pink blouse. Aunt Rose said I looked nice, and I figured, if she approved, then it must be good enough for dinner with the Harpers. The next couple hours flew by as Aunt Rose and I sat at the kitchen table, going over some of the details for the wedding.

Then out of nowhere, something strange happened … A strong sensation came over me, a small fluttering in my stomach. Then Blake's face popped into my head. It was like I could feel him, like he was close or something. And that's when I heard a soft knock at the front door.

"Do you want me to get it?" Aunt Rose asked.

"No." I jumped up, still feeling the weirdness inside me. "I'll get it."

I half-ran to the door, and I wasn't even sure why. When I opened it up, Blake was standing there, looking irresistible in just a simple baby blue T-shirt and jeans. Suddenly, I felt very overdressed.

"Hi." He smiled. "You look lovely."

I swallowed hard before answering. "Thanks." Then I heard Aunt Rose's footsteps behind me, and I hoped that what was about to come would be short and painless.

"Hi, Blake. Nice to see you again."

"You too, Rose."

"Well, you two have fun," Aunt Rose said as she placed her hand on my shoulder, practically pushing me toward him. I'm sure she was over-the-moon excited that I had a date … if that's what it was. I mean, I had had dates before, but they were always forced and ended up being disasters. Something inside told me this was not going to turn out like any of my previous dates, and that both excited and scared me.

"Your aunt seems really nice," Blake said as we walked down the sidewalk toward the street.

"Yeah, she's the best." I smiled.

As we walked, I couldn't help but think about what had happened right before he knocked on the door. It was such an overwhelming feeling, like I could sense him being there. That weird, fluttery thing had happened in my stomach, and then I just knew he was near. But that couldn't be possible, could it? I glanced over at him as I wondered.

"What is it?" he asked.

"Nothing really. Just something really stupid."

"Enlighten me?"

My nerves heightened, wondering what he would think, and still I wanted to tell him. "Well, before you got to my house, my aunt and I were sitting at the kitchen table going over some wedding plans—"

"Wedding plans?" he interrupted.

"Oh yeah, my aunt's boyfriend Jack proposed to her yesterday," I explained.

"Really? That is great news. Sorry to interrupt your story. Continue."

I took in a deep breath. "As we were sitting there going over the plans, I had an overwhelming feeling. I felt like I could sense you, like I knew you were there before you knocked on the door." I braced myself, waiting, almost expecting him to start laughing or to tell me I was strange for feeling that way, but he didn't.

Actually, he didn't say anything for a moment. He took in what I had said and seemed to be pondering it.

"See, it's silly," I said to break the silence between us.

"No, it's not *silly*." He looked over at me, his blues eyes smoldering. "It's very intuitive, and I would be lying if I said I didn't get the same sensation when you are around."

That was definitely not the response I had been expecting. We stared at one another for a long minute, and I was not sure how to interpret what he had just said. What did he mean by *intuitive*? And did he really get the same feeling around me? Could that be possible? I broke his gaze and looked forward, not really knowing what to say next.

We arrived at their estate. The smell of rosemary filled the air as we entered the house. Then the memory of what had happened there just a few days ago sent a shiver down my spine. A flashback of the vision entered my mind: the man who held me in his grasp in a dark, unknown location. I shook the thoughts out of my head and glanced into the living room where the incident had taken place. The room had drastically changed since I had been there last. The walls were painted in the steel blue color, the color I had been experimenting with the moment my vision came. The white Victorian couches were pushed back to their rightful places, and beautiful oil paintings had been hung on the walls.

Abby sat on the couch nearest the fireplace, reading a book. Her head popped up the moment the door shut behind us, and she shoved the book she was reading underneath a pillow on the couch. It seemed weird for her to do that, but my mind was quickly distracted by her cheerful personality as she came over to greet me.

"It's so good to see you again and with some color back in your face!" She smiled timidly.

"Hi, Abby." I swallowed hard, feeling embarrassed. I had hoped she had forgotten about the way I had looked that day.

"Come in, come in. Sit." She pointed to the couches, allowing me to take my pick. I glanced back at Blake. He was wearing that smile that showed off the dimple on the left side of his cheek. My heart sped up.

"After you," he said, placing his hand on the small of my back. His touch sent an electric feeling all throughout my body, making me shiver ever so slightly.

I walked toward the sitting area and sat down on the couch, opposite the one that Abby had been sitting on. She took her same seat, and Blake sat down beside me, sitting close enough that our bodies touched. My rapid heart rate picked up more speed, and I tried to distract myself in order to calm it back down.

"I love how the room turned out. The color looks amazing." I nodded, looking around and admiring how the dark blue walls allowed the beautiful paintings to stand out. "The paintings are beautiful."

"Yes, my brother is very talented," Abby said as she glanced around the room.

"Wow, you painted these?" I asked, looking toward Blake, hoping my mouth was not hanging open as wide as I felt it was.

"He didn't tell you about his many talents? You will have to ask him about those someday," she joked. "My brother is too modest to brag about himself. He needs a little push."

He glanced at me and shrugged like it was no big deal.

"Meredith, so lovely to see you again," Annette said, coming from around the corner to my right.

"Hello, Mrs. Harper. It's nice to see you again, too." And it was. The moment I saw her, her presence put me more at ease.

It was strange that I was nervous with just Blake and Abby around, but they always seemed to talk cryptically when I was nearby and I was never able to crack their codes.

"Oh, please, call me Annette." She smiled. "Dinner is ready. Please join us in the kitchen." She turned and waved us on to follow her.

Abby and Blake stood, and I quickly shadowed their movements. We followed Annette down the long hallway and past the bathroom I had spent recovering in last week. My stomach turned over, remembering the pain from the headache and the terror from the images I had seen. I turned my head forward and pushed the memory from my mind.

We entered the brightly lit kitchen. It had also changed from the last time I had seen it. The pale yellow color that Abby had painted as a sample covered the walls, and there was now a table sitting at the far end of the large room.

"I thought we would eat in here. It seems less formal than that stuffy old dining room," Annette said, taking off her apron and laying it on the island.

Blake pulled out a chair and then glanced at me. Was he pulling out a chair for me? No one had ever done that before. Well, except once, when Roger did it as a joke. I thanked him and allowed him to push it in for me as well. The table was all set with plates, silverware, and a spread of roast beef, potatoes, broccoli, and rolls. It had been years since I had had a dinner like that. Maybe since my parents were alive.

Just then Samuel entered the kitchen, giving me a warm smile. "Meredith, we are so glad you could join us."

He walked over and was the last one to take his seat at the table. Annette asked Abby and Blake about their days, and each of them rambled on as we passed the food around the table. Blake had mostly worked on the yard and had begun re-staining the outside shutters black. Abby had spent her day re-painting her bubblegum pink bedroom to more of a neutral tan. It was nice to sit around a table with more than just me—or occasionally, Aunt Rose—at it. It felt nice to be in a family setting, sitting there and listening to them all discuss their days.

"What about you, Meredith? What did you do today?" Annette asked, glancing in my direction.

"Oh, um, I went dress shopping. My aunt is getting married, and I'm the maid of honor." I smiled.

Annette and Blake shared an awkward glance.

"How nice," Annette said, turning her head back toward me. Then I watched as she shot a quick glance at Abby, who was looking distant as she twirled her fork. Have I said something wrong? I wondered.

We all ate dinner, and the air was full of conversation, mainly between the four of them, though they occasionally asked me a question or two, forcing me from my usual quiet. As dinner ended, Blake invited me outside to the backyard, saying he wanted to show me something. I thanked Annette and Samuel for a wonderful dinner and followed Blake out the back door. We walked across the yard and down a set of stone steps. There at the end of the path sat a wooden bench that opened up to a small clearing. He took a seat, and I sat beside him, leaving a small distance between us.

"It's beautiful out here." I leaned back and looked up toward the stars.

"Yes, it's my favorite spot on the estate."

It was quiet for a moment, and I looked back at Blake, catching him in a fixed stare ... on me.

"Meredith, I need to tell you something, and I'm hoping it's not too soon. I have tried to find the right way to tell you this, but I'm afraid there's no other way than to just say it."

I didn't like where this was going. My throat felt like it was being strangled. I wanted to speak in order to quiet his voice, fearing what he was about to say. I hoped he wasn't about to say anything cheesy, like he had feelings for me. Dread filled my mind, and I closed my eyes, hoping that he would not say what I thought.

"Meredith ..." he began.

"Stop," I choked out, finding my voice again. "Just don't say anything, please." I opened my eyes and found him staring down at his hands, refusing to meet my gaze.

He couldn't tell me he had serious feelings for me. That just couldn't happen. I had plans. Well, I had plans to make plans. And Blake didn't fit into them. In a few weeks, I was leaving and was probably never coming back. Plus, Blake and his family were just in Marblehead temporarily, and they would be leaving soon, too. What did we think was supposed to happen between us? That we'd start a long-distance relationship only after spending a few weeks together that summer? Yeah, like that would really work out. Even though I knew there was something special between us, I had to call it off. It would be better that way, before any real feelings got involved.

"Blake, whatever it is you are about to say, just don't. We both know this isn't going to go anywhere. It's just horrible timing. Soon, we will both go our separate ways. It's just not fair to start something like this."

He glanced up toward me with a mangled expression, confused, almost, like he had no idea what I was talking about.

Oh no, had I just said too much? Was he *not* about to say what I had thought?

Then Blake rearranged his face and opened his mouth to speak. "You're right. It is horrible timing."

With the awkwardness between us, I felt that I should leave. There was nothing left to say. "I think I should go."

"I think that would be a good idea."

"Please thank your parents again for dinner, and tell Abby goodbye for me." My voice broke on the last few words. I stood up to leave and walked around the side of the house to the front yard and down the circular drive. On the way home, I kept wondering why I felt so sad when I had been so sure that that was what I had wanted.

The next week flew by. The wedding plans were overwhelming, but it made the days and nights pass quickly. I couldn't believe when Jack and Aunt Rose actually pulled it off. They were somehow able to plan a wedding and have it go off without a hitch in just a week's time. Aunt Rose was beautiful in her cream silk gown, and Jack cleaned up well, too. The wedding took place on the beach my family and I had used to picnic on in the summer. It was a small ceremony with just a few of their friends and afterward a nice dinner at their favorite restaurant. Soon enough Aunt Rose and Jack were off on their honeymoon, and I had the next few days to myself.

Normally, being alone for that long wouldn't have bothered me, but Ms. Donaldson had shut down the library for a few days due to a convention in Boston, so work would not be there to keep me busy. And I needed to keep busy. Blake was on my mind constantly. Even though I had not seen him since dinner the previous week, I got the weird fluttery feeling in my stomach all day every day, like he was always around me. A part of me wanted to see him, wanted to see how things felt between us. I knew I missed him and yearned to see him again. But even though I knew there was something special between us, I was convinced it would just never work out.

It was clear to me that in order to stop these thoughts of him, I had to find a distraction. So I decided to call up the only person I knew who could get my mind off of things.

"Roger?" I asked. For some reason, it hadn't sounded like him when he had answered. Maybe it was because we hadn't seen or talked to each other much over the past few weeks.

"Hey, Meredith, what's up? Sorry I haven't called."

"Yeah, what's up with that? You promised to call me," I huffed.

"I know, I know. How 'bout I give you one free shot next time you see me? Then we'll call it even."

"Deal." I smiled, already feeling a little more at ease.

"What's going on? Anything crazy happening in Marblehead?"

"Not really. I just wanted to talk for a while. You busy?"

"Just getting ready to go out with some friends," he answered.

"Oh. Well, never mind, then. I won't bother you."

"*Stop*. What's going on with you?" he pressed me. "You sound a little strange."

"It's just, Aunt Rose and Jack left on their honeymoon today, and—"

"*What*?" he shouted into the phone.

"Oh, yeah. Aunt Rose and Jack got married."

"Go, Jack! About time that dude asked her."

"Anyway … They're gone, and Ms. Donaldson shut down the library for the next few days, so I just wanted …" I trailed off, not knowing what I really wanted.

"Why don't you drive up?" he said, as if it were a no-brainer. "We can go out, and I will show you a good time in Rockport."

I sat there for a minute, contemplating my choices. Either I could sit there for the next few days and feel sorry for myself, or I could be in the company of my best friend in under an hour. "Okay, I'm in. But are you sure your dad won't mind me staying there?"

"Not at all. He's always liked you."

"I mean, since I'm a girl."

"Seriously, Meredith, he knows you're my best friend, and it's not like that. Besides, we have a great spare bedroom, so there won't be an issue."

"I will leave here in ten minutes. What's your dad's address?"

I threw some clothes in my backpack then packed up my toiletry bag. It took me just five minutes to be fully packed and downstairs rummaging through the key bowl next to the door. Aunt Rose had told me she had left the keys in case I needed to make a trip to the grocery store. I wasn't sure how she would feel about me going all the way to Rockport, but I didn't care too much. I was desperate. After finding the keys to the Grand Cherokee, I jumped in the car, feeling anxious and excited as I pulled out of the drive, knowing the next few days would not be as horrible as I had expected them to be.

The forty-five minute drive flew by. I turned the radio up loud and tried to think of nothing but the music. Luckily, Roger's dad did not live too far off the highway, leaving me only a couple turns before finding his street. As I pulled up to the house that matched the address I had written down, excitement gripped me. I couldn't wait to see Roger.

"Meredith! Man are you a sight for sore eyes," Roger shouted as he opened the door, yanking me inside and squeezing me so tightly that I felt like my eyes were going to pop out.

"Missed. You. Too," I squeaked out with each small breath I could find.

When he finally let me go, we headed back to his room. He plopped down on his twin-sized bed, and I chuckled when his head hit the headboard. His feet still hung a full foot off the end. Seeing there was no room left for me, I fell down onto the black beanbag next to it and faced him. I leaned back and got comfortable as he spent the next couple hours talking about how much fun he had had so far that summer and how much he had wished I had been there.

I nodded, knowing that he was just saying that to be nice, because he would have not had a chance to hook up with any girls if I were hanging around with him. Because as weird as it sounds and as much as it grossed me out just thinking about it, Roger and I could pull off being a couple. I mean, anytime you see a guy and a girl hanging out together, your first thought is they must be together, right? And it didn't hurt that we were so comfortable around each other and could talk to one another so effortlessly. But if you really paid attention, you would easily hear us making fun of and bashing each other the first chance we got.

For a moment, there was a break in our conversation. I leaned back and stared at the ceiling. My thoughts drifted to Blake. It was strange that I was sitting there with my best friend, and I couldn't get my thoughts away from Blake.

"What is up with you?" Roger asked, his voice teetering on a thin line between curious and worried.

I tilted my head to look at him and saw that his right eyebrow was arched, meaning that he was really stumped. "Nothing. Why?" I quickly answered, sitting up and crossing my legs. He knew me too well. I should've known he was going to see right through me.

"Not buying it. Something is up. You're hiding something. I can see it in your eyes." He nodded his head like he knew he was right.

"Well, look at you, Mr. Observant. Why don't you tell me, if you're so sure?" I snapped back sarcastically, hoping it would make him back off.

"Ha, ha. You are not getting off that easy, Mer. Tell me what's going on," he pressed.

But just as I was about to begin, just as I was about to tell him I was starting to have feelings for Blake, a large thunderclap made us both jump.

"What the heck! I didn't know there was a storm coming tonight." He groaned.

"Ugh, me either. That's just great. I guess we'll be ordering in?" I predicted.

But when I turned to look at him, I didn't like the way he was shaking his head. "No way. I'm taking you out. You aren't scared of a little rain, are you?"

He pulled me up by my hands and then pushed me out the door. Before I knew it, we were in his Mustang and headed into town. It didn't take long for us to drive to the waterfront, where restaurants lined the streets.

Chapter Fourteen

We pulled up to Atlantic Pizza Company, and my mouth began to water the moment we stepped inside. I hadn't eaten all day and hadn't realized how hungry I was until the smell of pizza hit my nose. As we approached the hostess stand to be seated, the brunette on the left winked in Roger's direction. I shook my head, knowing she was probably one of the many girls he had hooked up with in the past few weeks. The hostess on the right, who had red hair and was way too dull to peak Roger's interest, sat us down in a back corner table.

"Man, it's just now dawning on me that you will be leaving town soon. All these years you've been talking about leaving Marblehead, and now it's just a few weeks away," Roger said as we both glanced over the menus.

"It's just now dawning on you, genius? We've known this for months now. And to think you got into Harvard. Man, it speaks volumes for the place," I joked.

He rolled his eyes. "What am I going to do without you next year? You're the only one who gives me crap. I think my ego may double in size without all your sarcastic remarks putting me in place."

"I'm glad I won't be around to see that." I smiled.

"So have you nailed down any plans yet?"

"Um … kinda. But I haven't bought the plane ticket yet," I said, tripping over my words.

"You're not getting cold feet are you?" He looked at me, mouth gaping.

"No," I replied confidently. "Just still trying to decide on all the details. So, what's good here?" I asked, trying to change the subject.

"Well, you can't go wrong with the Classic, but the Supreme is good, too. Depends on what you're in the mood for, though."

"Right now, anything sounds good." My stomach gave a low rumble.

Just then a guy walked up to our table. He and Roger exchanged some sort of strange handshake, fist-bump thing, and I had to stop myself from rolling my eyes.

"Meredith, this is Ethan. Ethan, Meredith."

"Nice to meet you," I said.

"Well, well. Where have you been hiding all summer?" He smiled, and his white teeth sparkled against his dark tan complexion.

This time I couldn't stop myself. I rolled my eyes and looked back toward Roger. He couldn't help but chuckle.

"She's actually my best friend from Marblehead. She's just visiting."

"All right, man. Best friend's a hottie."

They did another handshake, fist-bump thing, and I couldn't stand it any longer. "I have to go to the restroom. Be back in a few," I said, not interested in hearing them fight over which bartender was hotter.

"It's back behind the bar. Hang a left!" Ethan shouted to me as he saw me walking in the wrong direction.

"Thanks!" I yelled back. All of the tables were empty so I began to navigate my way through them toward the back of the restaurant. In the back corner, I saw the sign for the restrooms pointing to a hallway.

Just as I rounded the corner and began my walk down the hall, someone from behind me grabbed my arm. He whipped me around so that my back was up against his chest and began pulling me down the hall. Just a couple seconds passed before I heard him kick open the side door and drag me outside. Before I could think to scream or run, he whispered in my ear, "Keep quiet. No sudden movements, and this will all go a lot smoother. We don't want to involve your friend Roger in this, now do we?"

I swallowed hard, my heart began to pick up speed, and I held my breath. The entire time I was panicking on the inside, trying to search my mind for things to do in a situation like this. But my mind was blank with fear.

"Shh, it's all going to be okay," he whispered again, dragging me out and into the dark alley. I quickly noticed the light rain falling onto my trembling body. I looked down toward the ground, searching for something—a glass bottle, a stick, anything to defend myself with. But nothing but darkness covered the ground. I held my head steady, remembering what he had said about no sudden movements. I reached my eyes right and saw nothing but street lights a few blocks away, a couple dumpsters, and a brick wall with graffiti on it.

My heart stopped. I was having a major case of déjà vu—but even worse. This was the vision I had had at the Harpers' the afternoon I helped Abby choose paint colors.

"Ahh, much better," he said as he whipped me around to face him. Fear gripped me. The moment our eyes locked together, my heart thudded loudly in my ears. I knew that I was in a lot more trouble than I could have ever imagined. It was not some stranger that had pulled me out into the shadows; it was the man that had been haunting me for weeks now. He was there, in the flesh, no longer a figment of my imagination.

"Now that we are all alone, allow me to introduce myself. I think it's about time we were properly introduced, don't you?" His evil eyes narrowed and bore into mine. "My name is Isaac, Isaac Waters."

My arms, legs, and feet felt numb. The only part of my body that seemed to be operating was my brain, and it was only flashing images of my nightmares over and over. I tried my hardest to focus, to try and get my brain to signal to my mouth to scream for help. *Just open your mouth and scream.*

But before my brain got the signal to my mouth, he spoke again. "No need for an introduction on your part. I am well aware of who you are, and I must say it is a pleasure to finally meet you, Meredith Martin. How are you feeling? A little paralyzed, maybe?" He laughed a sinister laugh, tilting his head back slightly while still keeping his eyes fixated on me. "I just can't believe it's working." He marveled at me as he lightly caressed my cheek, his evil smile growing larger.

"You really have no idea how long I have waited for this moment."

My breathing was becoming shallow and rapid. I felt like I was suffocating. I tried to focus on screaming for help. It felt like if I could just open my mouth, the scream would come out. But I was paralyzed, just like he said. I couldn't move my mouth or any other part of my body.

Then slowly I began to feel tingling in my toes, and then the feeling spread up to my legs to my torso and then eventually up my arms and neck. He was still staring at me, caressing my cheek like I was some sort of prize that he had just won.

Then just like a switch had been turned back on, I felt like I could speak again. "H-how do you know my name?" I asked, cold sweat spreading across my hairline.

The two corners of his mouth curved downward, like someone had just snatched his prize out of his hands. Then his face turned to pure anger. "Oh, I know a lot more than just your name. We've been searching for you for a while now, but you were hidden under one big protection spell," he said, twirling a piece of my hair between his fingers. "Oh, the plans we have for you, my dear. Now, I'm not sure how you just broke through that binding spell, but it just means I have to do this quicker than expected." He laughed another sinister laugh that made every hair on my body stand on end.

Then out of nowhere, he stopped laughing and pulled me back toward him, suddenly on guard for something. "Damn! Well this complicates things. But I must say, I was a little disappointed that it was ending so easily. I knew *you* could not go down without a fight." He spit through his teeth as he stared out into the dark alley.

I wondered who he was talking to. He whipped me around, facing me toward the darkness, gripping me even tighter. I searched the dark alley, but saw nothing. My eyesight was adjusting to the darkness, but I was still only able to make out outlines of large objects. Then my eyes caught something moving. The person was still far away, but I watched as he got closer, growing larger and clearer. I let out a silent gasp, realizing who it was: Blake was standing about ten feet in front of me, staring at the man who had me in his grasp.

"Let her go," Blake demanded as he stood with his fists clenched, his eyes focused on Isaac.

The evil laugh that had shot goose bumps all over my body was loud in my ear. "Now why would I do that? All this work, and you just expect me to give it all up? I'm so close. Actually I should give *you* a round of applause for finding her and keeping her safe for so long. But as you see, my hands are full." Isaac squeezed me tighter, and I could feel my breath getting more and more shallow. "That was some protection spell you had on this one. It took me a while to figure out how to break through it. But it would not be much fun if there were no challenge, now, would it?"

I stared at Blake. His eyes darted quickly upward, and I followed their gaze. There on the roof above us stood three statuesque figures. I tried to focus and make out their faces, but it was too dark.

"Does it have to be like this, old friend?" Isaac growled as he gripped me closer to his chest.

"We are nothing to each other, least of all friends," Blake snapped.

"Oh, I'm sorely disappointed to hear that. Alexander will be, too."

"Where is Alex these days?" Blake asked.

"Oh, he's around, *my friend.*"

A small grin spread across Blake's face. "So it seems that you are doing Alexander's dirty work now. He was not brave enough to come here himself, so he sent you?"

Blake's condescending demeanor was making Isaac angrier. I could feel his grip getting tighter with Blake's every word.

"Let her go, and I may just let you live—for now," Blake warned, his voice full of rage.

"You will pay for this, you know. I will have her again. I have to."

He released his grip on me, but I was still too scared to move a muscle.

"Meredith, please walk toward me." Blake spoke calmly as he held out his hand. He kept his eyes focused upon my captor.

I looked into Blake's eyes, not knowing what to do. None of it made sense.

He nodded as if he knew what I was feeling, and I began to walk forward to his outreached hand. As I walked away from Isaac, I could still feel his presence at my back. His eyes were boring holes into me. It felt like at any moment Isaac would grab me and pull me back into his tight grasp. Finally, my hand reached Blake's, and our eyes met for a split second, before he shot his gaze back toward Isaac.

"Meredith, I will explain everything later. I just need you to trust me now," Blake whispered so softly that I could barely hear him.

Trust him? It seemed like a strange request, since I had no idea what was going on. But I had no reason not to trust him. He had just saved me from the crazy person I had thought existed only in my mind.

I nodded my head, and then Blake was shouting at me. “Hang on tight to me and close your eyes. *Now*!”

With only that warning, before I could question or object to what was happening, I was thrown into what felt like a mix between a washing machine and a wind tunnel. The whirling feeling was overwhelming, and my already-mangled stomach began to feel nauseous. The sensation of spinning and whooshing through the air lasted what seemed like a lifetime, but in reality it was probably just a few minutes. Next thing I knew, I was standing on my own two feet again, but my body still felt like it was spinning. I stumbled backward, and then Blake caught me just before I hit the ground.

“Meredith, Meredith, are you okay?” Blake shook me lightly. “Just a few more seconds, and the dizziness should pass. Just breathe,” he encouraged me.

Easy for you to say, I thought to myself. What about the nausea? I felt like asking but was too afraid to open my mouth in fear that it wouldn’t be words to come out. I kept my eyes closed to try and still my spinning head. A few moments passed, and although I couldn’t be sure, it felt as if

Blake had lifted me and was carrying me in his arms. I was too scared to open my eyes to tell.

After a few minutes, I was finally able to open my eyes and focus again. My first sight was Blake's concerned eyes, staring at me. My previous thought had been correct; he was cradling me in his arms.

"What?" was all I could mumble, but I really wanted to scream out, *What the hell is going on?*

"Please, just breathe. I will explain everything once you are feeling better."

I began to look around the dark room. My eyes adjusted just enough to realize we were in a very large, circular room. Squinting, I tried to focus in order to make out more of my surroundings, but I realized it was an impossible task. Blake knelt down and placed me onto something velvety-feeling. I felt him move away from me, and I begin to pat the space around where I was sitting. Beyond the soft material Blake had laid me on, there was a cold, hard surface.

Suddenly, Blake struck a match, and my eyes were drawn to the light. The glow of it shined on Blake's face as he slowly guided the match down to a candle. The flame filled the room with just a faint beam of light, but it was enough for me to see my surroundings a little better. Windows encircled us, and I looked up to see that the ceiling was endless as it rose and faded into the darkness above. Blake crawled toward me and came to a stop a few inches in front of me.

"Are you feeling better?" he asked, his face full of apprehension.

"A little," I lied. But of course I wasn't better! I had just almost been kidnapped, hurt, or even worse by a man who had been stalking me *in my mind*—and who I had previously thought was just a figment of my crazy imagination. Then out of nowhere, Blake, the guy who I was starting to fall for, comes out of the darkness to save me. The words that came to mind to describe how I was were *scared*, *freaked out*, *terrified*, and *confused*. Not *better*.

"What happened? How did we get here? Who was that …?" I rattled off questions as they popped into my head, and it soon proved to be too much. I could feel my chest beginning to constrict and my breathing becoming erratic.

"It's all going to be okay. I won't let anything happen to you," Blake murmured, quickly wrapping his arms around me to comfort me. "I let him get too close. That was never supposed to happen. I'm sorry."

And as confused as I was about all of this, and as much as I wanted to fight Blake off and demand answers, I couldn't find the strength. It was difficult to accept that being in his arms made me feel safe, but just then it did, and that was all that mattered.

I must have fallen asleep, because when I opened my eyes, there was light trickling in from the windows. It took me a minute to realize where I was and remember what had happened the previous night. Soon enough the memories came back to me. Trying to be discreet, I tilted my head down, seeing Blake's arm wrapped around my waist. Swallowing hard, I lifted my left arm and placed it on his arm around my waist, preparing to gently lift it off. But just as my hand made contact, Blake unwound his arm, and I immediately felt the lack of warmth from where it once had been.

"Sorry, I was trying not to wake you." My voice was just above a whisper.

"I've been awake," he answered back in the same soft tone.

"Oh."

"You slept soundly all night." His voice sounded pleased.

"You were up … all night?"

"You must want a hot shower and change of clothes," he offered, totally ignoring my question.

There were so many things I wanted. The main one was answers to the millions of questions that were floating in my head. Like, who the hell was Isaac? And how did he know where I had been? And where were we? And many, many more. But before I asked all those questions, a shower and change of clothes did sound nice. A toothbrush wouldn't hurt, either.

"Yes, that would be nice."

He nodded as he began to gather the candle and matches, pushing them into a brown leather backpack. I stood, picking up what I then could see was a beautiful quilted blanket made of purple velvet fabric.

"Here, let me get that. Why don't you just put your shoes on," he said as he motioned toward the corner behind me.

Shoes? I didn't even remember taking them off. I watched him for a minute as he carefully folded the blanket and placed it in the backpack before fastening it up. When I turned around to put my shoes on, I got a glimpse out the window and nearly fell over. I grabbed onto the bar that was directly below it and pulled myself up on my tiptoes to peer out. Wherever we were, we were really, really high up. I stood there gazing out the window, looking to my right and left and seeing nothing but deep blue water as far as I could see. I wondered where we could be. But then I saw the beach where Aunt Rose and Jack had just married, and it hit me: we were in the lighthouse near the beach.

"How did we get up here? I don't remember climbing up," I said, still peering out the window. Blake chuckled shallowly behind me, and I turned around to see him wiping a grin off his face.

"I carried you," he responded.

"Oh," I whispered. And then I faintly remembered being carried. I remembered leaving Isaac's grasp, walking to Blake, and feeling the wind on my face and a whirling motion. How did we get all the way back here so quickly? It had been no longer than a few minutes. That is what it seemed like, anyway. I had so many unanswered questions.

"Are you ready?" he asked, glancing toward me.

I nodded and began to walk toward the white door on the other side of the room.

The climb down the stairs of the lighthouse was terrifying but bearable, much easier than the silent walk home. Neither of us spoke a word. I mean, what were supposed to say to one another? The only thing I wanted was answers, and the more I thought about answers, the faster I walked. We arrived back at my house, and he offered to wait in the living room while I showered and dressed.

I had never thought I would be so happy that Aunt Rose and Jack were gone, on their honeymoon. But there was no way I would have been able to explain to them what had happened to me.

Chapter Fifteen

After taking an extra-long shower, I dressed quickly, eager to begin the question-and-answer session I was planning to start with Blake downstairs. I believed that he held the key to all the strange things that had been happening to me over the last few weeks. Come to think of it, all the strange things had begun right after the Harpers arrived in town.

After one last look in my full-length mirror, I turned toward the stairs. Just as my right foot hit the first step, I began to feel that familiar, awful pain in the back of my head. The headache that had not shown its ugly head for days had returned with a vengeance. Before I knew it, the pain was more than I could bear, and I found myself screaming in agony. Blake's footsteps were urgent as he flew up the stairs, taking them two at a time.

His arms enveloped me and then the whirling motion came again. This time I appreciated the cool air on my face; it helped to dull the pain. I kept my eyes shut, trying to drown out the pain that pounded in the back of my head. After what seemed like just a few seconds, we came to a sudden halt, and it felt as though we were running—up one, two, three, four steps.

"Hang on, Meredith. Please hang on. The pain will stop soon, I promise," he whispered in my ear. "We are here, just a few more seconds."

The pain was crushing, and I was too afraid to open my eyes, fearing that the pain would escalate to a new level. I heard a door swing open with such force that it hit the wall behind it. Then I was set down on something soft, and I realized that I was no longer being held in Blake's arms. The loss of him sent me into a panic.

Regardless of the pain, I opened my eyes, and even though my vision was blurred, I recognized the somewhat familiar room. The steel-blue painted walls surrounded me, and I realized that I was lying on the bright white Victorian couch in the Harpers' living room.

I tried to prop myself up using my elbows, but the task proved to be too difficult. The searing pain in my head sent me straight back down. Refusing to give up, wanting so badly to find Blake, I opened my eyes again, focusing even harder. Then out of nowhere, two figures began to walk toward me, and it was not until they came within a few inches of my face that I recognized who they were.

Blake came to sit at my feet and Abby knelt down beside me, placing her hand on my forehead. She began to mumble something under her breath. I couldn't understand the exact words, but it sounded as if it was the same few words over and over again. Slowly the pain began to retreat, almost as if someone had stuck a syringe into my head and was slowly drawing out the painful poison.

"Just rest now," Abby said as she brushed the hair out of my face. "All the pain should be gone in just a few minutes."

I did as I was told and lay back down, trying not to think about anything but the pain disappearing. And just like she said, within a few minutes, the pain was gone. My vision came back, and I glanced around the room, seeing Blake, Abby, Annette, and Samuel all huddled near the fireplace across the room. They all wore the same serious expression, as if they were preparing for battle. Even though I was feeling much better, I decided to keep my mouth shut, not knowing what to say. I was more interested in what was being said between them. I had to struggle to hear them as they all spoke in nothing more than whispers.

"Blake, you had your chance. We agreed, you had a certain amount of time, then we would do things my way," Abby's voice was soft but firm.

I could see Blake, breaking apart from the huddle and beginning to pace in front of the large stone fireplace. "Abby, now is not the time," he gritted through his teeth, clenching his fists. "Can't you see she has been through enough already?" He glanced in my direction, his bright blue eyes meeting mine.

I quickly averted his gaze, looking toward Abby and then the ground. The look on Blake's face had been too painful to look at, torn between anger and acceptance, as though he knew that he was fighting a losing battle.

"Meredith," Abby said as she walked across the room in my direction. "I really wanted to go about this all a different way, but I think we are running out of time." She sat beside me on the white couch, taking my hand.

My heart began to pound against my chest again, and I could only fear what Abby was about to say. The way Blake and Abby were speaking to each other made me nervous. Maybe I didn't want to know. Fear consumed me. My stomach began to turn, and I could feel the bile beginning to rise in my throat. I swallowed hard. My eyes floated back toward Blake, and he tried his hardest to comfort me with one look.

But before I could stop it or fight it back, bile crept its way up again, only leaving me seconds before the certain eruption. I lurched forward and ran as fast as I could to the only bathroom I knew in the house. Sprinting down the hall, I held my hand over my mouth, trying to prevent anything from coming out. I found the open door on the right, rushed in, slammed the door behind me, and dove toward the toilet. Just in time.

After I finished getting sick, I rinsed my mouth and leaned back on the wall, sinking down and resting my head in my hands. Deep breath in, deep breath out. In and out, I kept telling myself.

"Dammit, Abby!" I could hear Blake shouting. "Look what you've done to her! You just couldn't keep your mouth shut, could you?"

I closed my eyes and tried to drown out the yelling. But it was no use; their voices were too loud.

"Blake, she has to know. She is ready. She was born for this," Abby countered, her voice calm and sincere. "Blake, I know you care for her, and I do, too. But this is all for her own good, for her own safety."

"No! No! She has been through too much already. She is vulnerable; she is not strong enough yet," Blake shouted.

"Quiet, the both of you," Annette said firmly. "We owe her the right to choose. She deserves the right to know who and what she is, but it will be solely up to her what she wants to do with the information."

"Hmph," Abby said triumphantly.

Samuel spoke up next. "Blake, we knew this day would come. That's why we are here. Now all we can do is try our best to protect her, guide her, and teach her the ways—if that's what she chooses," he added.

Then there was silence until footsteps sounded on the wooden floor, heading in my direction. A faint knock made me flinch, even though I knew it had been coming.

"Meredith, are you all right?" Abby asked, sounding concerned.

"Fine. Be out in just a minute," I answered, trying to keep my voice as even as possible. There was no real explanation as to why I was trying so hard to act tough, like none of this was really getting to me. Who was I fooling? Definitely not myself—I was totally losing it.

"Is there anything you need?"

I couldn't get the taste of puke out of my mouth. I walked over to the door and whispered to her, "I could kill for some mouthwash. Do you have any?"

"Of course."

I leaned up against the door and tried to clear my mind.

Just a few seconds later, Abby's soft voice spoke to me from the other side of the door. "I'm back."

I opened the door just a crack, and she passed the bottle of mouthwash through. "Thank you," I said.

After splashing some water on my face and rinsing my mouth a few times, I opened the door and walked back toward the living room. The second I entered the large room, Blake was at my side, helping me to the couch, not that I really needed it. Though a large part of me felt safe when he was around, but the other part that knew he was hiding something from me—that he and his family were all hiding some dark secret.

Glancing around the room, I saw four sets of eyes staring at me, all with the same pitying look on their faces. I couldn't stand it any longer. I decided to answer their question before any of them asked it. "I'm fine … Just confused as to what all is going on."

"I'm so sorry, Meredith. I did not mean to upset you," Abby said, rushing to my side and sitting down beside me.

"I know you all have information for me, about why all these bizarre things have been happening. So please, just tell me," I pleaded, somehow finding the strength that I had not realized I had inside me.

Abby stared at Blake for a long moment.

He nodded his head and then turned his focus on me. The defeated look in his eyes was clearly painful for him—and for me. It was crazy to think that I could be hurting just because he was hurting. He was the one keeping secrets. He was the one who possessed some supernatural power to get from one place to another at the speed of light. But I knew that he had saved me from Isaac and that he wanted to keep me safe. So for now, that was enough for me.

"Meredith, you know that I would not do anything to put you in harm's way, right?" Blake asked me.

"I think that's pretty obvious." I swallowed hard, anticipating what he was about to tell me. Everything was about to be explained and make sense … I hoped.

"There are things about us that you don't know," he said glancing up to his family and then back to me. "Who we really are, or why we are really here. We are …" He trailed off and then took in a deep breath. "We are here for you. We are here to protect you."

"And teach you," Abby added quickly.

Blake glared at her, and she mouthed the word *sorry* in his direction.

"I … don't … understand," I said, drawing out each word as I tried to process what Blake had just said. They were here for me? Here to protect me? Why? From who? Where did they come from?

But before I could get any of those questions out of my mouth, Blake continued his explanation. "The man that tried to hurt you last night—he is part of what we are trying to protect you from. Our main priority is to keep you safe."

Shock and terror ran through me. "How did you know he was after me? How did you know how to find me?"

"We know a lot more than you think we do," Blake answered.

I tensed up, suddenly feeling violated. Realizing that I couldn't stop there, I had to know morc. "Why arc they—Isaac and Alex—after me? Why is all this happening?" I paused, waiting for the answer. I could feel the fear registering on my face. Until now, all of this had been just in my head. But now it was real, and the Harpers knew about it, and by the sound of it, they knew more than I did.

"They are after you because of what you are, the power you possess."

"*Power?*" I repeated. A part of me wanted to laugh, and a sudden feeling of calm ran through me. This, all of it, was a mistake. I didn't possess any power. "You all have the wrong person. I don't have any *power*."

"Not any power that you know of," Blake corrected me. "But you do possess it, there is no mistake about that."

"What kind of power are you talking about, exactly?" I asked, confused.

"Magical power," Blake said.

I didn't understand any of this, it all sounded made up. How could it be real? That stuff only existed in the movies. It didn't exist in real people, especially not in some small-town girl who lives in Marblehead … and definitely not in me. "Not possible," I muttered to myself. "Where did you all come from?" I clenched my fists together, prepared to hear that they were aliens from some other planet. From what he had just told me, that would not have been too far past crazy.

Blake and Abby looked at each other again with the same tangled expression. Then Blake looked back to me and answered, "We come from a very similar place. Actually, not much different from the world you live in today. We have lived our entire lives in Marblehead—but we live in the year 1905."

I swallowed hard, not knowing how to compute what I had just heard. How could that be possible? I sat there in a daze, taking in what he just had said but not sure if it was registering. “Do you hear yourself?” I asked. “This is absurd. You are talking about me possessing powers and you all traveling from the past to come here and protect me and teach me. It’s crazy talk. You are all crazy.” I stood up, prepared to storm out of there and never look back.

“Please, let us explain,” Samuel pleaded. “The name Emma Watson should be familiar to you ...”

I gasped. My heart ached at the sound of her name. “My mother?”

“Yes, she was known as a very powerful witch. She came from the most powerful lineage in witch history,” Samuel said, speaking about her like she was part of some epic tale.

I fell back toward the couch. “My mother was a-a witch?” I choked, barely getting out each word. “But how do you even know about her …?” I trailed off, deep in thought, not able to continue. I couldn’t make sense of it all in my head, so talking about it out loud sounded even more weird.

“Your mother was one of the most powerful witches to have existed, that is until you. And now she’s part of the Witch’s Council,” Blake said. “They called on us for help and it was your mother who told us what to do. She told us that you needed help."

"Part of the Witch's Council? What? My mother is ..." I stopped, not feeling emotionally strong enough to finish the sentence.

"When I saw you in the cemetery that first day, you looked so much like your mother," Abby explained. "That's why I reacted the way I did."

"Is this too much for you? Would you like to take a break?" Blake asked.

I ignored his question, feeling my eyes widening with what I was thinking. "So what does that make me?" I gasped, all the puzzle pieces finally coming together. "Does that mean that I'm a-a witch, too?" I swallowed hard and turned to Blake for answers.

But the answer was clear on his face. "You hold *the* greatest power inside you, Meredith," Blake said as he touched my arm.

"What? But how? That can't be. I-I don't have any powers," I stuttered.

"Your mother would have passed the powers to you when you were ready, but she died when you were still much too young," Abby spoke softly. "I did not acquire my powers until I was twelve."

"My mom was a witch," I found myself repeating. Strangely, those words became easier and easier each time I spoke them. All these years of not knowing why I felt so different, why I never felt like I fit in, could that be the reason? It was strange, but a feeling of peace washed over me at the thought. Maybe that was the explanation I had been searching for my entire life.

"See, I told you she would be happy about it." Abby chuckled. "What person would not want to be a witch? It is …."

Her voice trailed off, and I looked up just in time to see Blake quieting her with his scowl.

"How are you handling all of this, Meredith?" Samuel asked, and I glanced up to look into his anxious eyes.

"I … I … I'm not sure" was all I could mumble.

"See, I told you. She was not ready for this," Blake said, gritting his teeth together.

"Blake, I know you are only trying to protect her, but your sister is right. This is why we are here. It is better for her that she knows," Annette said.

Then they began arguing again.

I sat quietly, alone with my thoughts, trying to process everything I had just been told. I started to look back into my childhood to see if there was a clue, something I had missed.

How could I not have known that my own mother was a witch? The questions began to pour out, and my mind could not keep up.

"Wait," I interrupted, and everyone stopped talking. I looked up to see four faces staring at me, awaiting my next word. "You … said … my mother came to you and told you about me. But that doesn't make sense. I mean, my mother did not even exist in 1905. She was not even close to existing in that time," I mumbled as I tried to wrap my head around it all. It didn't make sense. Nothing made sense.

"The Witch's Council does not operate in a specific time period," Samuel explained. "There are witches from as early as the 1800s on the council. When your mother died, she took her place on the Council."

Abby spoke next. "Meredith, you should know that that when we came here, we were expecting to find an experienced witch. Your mother never informed us that you were not in tune with your powers. So when we arrived, we were just as confused as you are now." She smiled nervously. "Well, maybe not *that* confused."

"That's enough for tonight. No more," Blake ordered.

"Excuse me," I said in a quiet, but firm voice. "I have spent my entire life wondering why I felt so different from everyone, why I felt so lost. If all of what you say is true and this is who I am and who I was born to be, then I want to know all about it. There is someone or something out there trying to hurt me. And the past few weeks they've been winning, because I'm defenseless against them. The visions, the nightmares, the headaches ... they must all be linked to this magic or the people trying to get to me. I need to know what to do in order to protect myself. I don't want to be the helpless one and just stand by and watch you all get hurt—or even worse." I gulped as I finished talking, not knowing where all of my newfound courage was coming from. I sat there and waited for their reactions.

"Meredith, you don't know what you are asking for here," Blake said sternly.

"Blake, this was a part of my mother. If she sent you to me, then I can only see this as being a good thing. I want to help. I want to be able to protect myself."

Annette spoke up next. "Like I said before, we tell her everything, and then we let her choose. It sounds like she has made her choice," she finished, and a small smile crossed her face.

Everyone's eyes were upon me.

"So where do we begin?" I asked.

"We will start with a summoning spell to link you with your powers bright and early tomorrow morning, once you've had a bit more time to recover and allow some of this to sink in," Abby said. "Once the summoning spell has been cast, then we can begin with the basics. It will be a long process, but I will be with you every step of the way. I'm hoping over the next few months, we will make it to the intermediate stages."

I gasped. "Few months?" My heart began to pound as I realized this was going to mess up my plans for leaving town. Not that I minded; if that was the price for finding all this out, then it was definitely worth it. It was just that I was not sure how to tell Aunt Rose about my change of plans. Aunt Rose knew deep down that I wanted nothing more than to get out of Marblehead as soon as I had enough money saved up. Now I would have to make up a really good excuse for why I would not be leaving.

Chapter Sixteen

Later that evening Blake walked me home, and we spoke very little. I was hoping he understood my silence, as I was still trying to process the information I had learned that day. I wondered what was going on in his head.

"Blake." I finally broke the silence.

"Yes?"

"What are you thinking about?"

He was quiet for a moment, and it was killing me each second he didn't respond.

"I was hoping that we have done the right thing by you. You had your whole life ahead of you and knew no concept of magic or evil. Now that is what your life will become. You welcome it now, but I don't know if you always will." He stopped and turned toward me before continuing. "When I was thirteen and received my powers, I was scared and I didn't want them, but I had no other choice. That was my destiny. You have lived this life outside of magic, and you don't know how much you will miss your old life, once it's gone."

"Isn't this my destiny, too? And don't you think if you would never have come, Isaac or Alex would have gotten to me eventually?" I asked.

"Possibly, but maybe we could have found another way. A way to protect you without bringing you into this world, this life. I fear that this will just bring you even more danger than before."

"But this is why you came here, right?"

"It was different then." He paused. "My feelings toward you have changed."

"Consequences. That is what you were talking about that night, isn't it?"

He nodded. "I knew the closer I got to you, the more it would get in the way of me doing my job. But I soon realized that I couldn't stop thinking about you, and I didn't want to fight my feelings any longer."

I swallowed hard. "Listen to me, Blake. I have lived my entire life wondering why I never fit in, why I always felt so different from everyone and everything, and why I never felt whole. I feel whole now after what you all told me tonight. I feel whole when I am with you."

He took my hand and delicately kissed it before he spoke. "I just want to keep you safe. I don't want anything bad to happen to you. When we came here, it was my job to protect you, and that was it. But now it's much more than that. Keeping you safe means everything to me."

"Blake, I appreciate you and your family coming here and trying to keep me safe. I don't know what would've happen if you hadn't. But one day you are going to have to trust that I can take care of myself. I mean, part of why you all came here was to teach me how to protect myself, right?"

"Yes. And once you begin your training I may let up a bit … but not until then," he said firmly.

We arrived at my house, and I could feel my anxiety as we approached, scared that he would soon disappear.

"I can stay if you'd like. If it would make you feel safer. Of course, either way I will be keeping a closer watch from now on."

I looked into his eyes and saw his love for me and his desire to protect me. And even though I hoped one day soon I would be able to protect myself, the sweetness of his intention overwhelmed me. Without hesitation, I reached up and pulled his head down to mine. Our lips pressed together, and it was clear that he had wanted the kiss as much or maybe even more than me. He pulled me closer toward him and crushed my body against his. The kiss held so much passion and desire that it was almost painful. As we pulled apart, he smiled gently as he tucked my hair behind my ears and then cradled my face between his hands.

"Do you think you can sleep?" he asked, his eyes staring into mine with so much intensity that I felt like I would burst.

"Not a chance," I whispered.

"Let's get you a jacket, and then I would like to show you something."

He followed me inside and waited patiently in the living room while I ran upstairs to get my jacket.

My mind was flying in so many different directions. I had just found out the biggest secret of my life from the guy I was falling for, who had been sent from the past to protect me by my mother, who was supposedly a powerful witch! And as much as that put my head into a tailspin, I wanted nothing more than to go back downstairs and spend more time with Blake, despite the fact his family coming into my life was exactly what brought on all of this craziness.

I threw on my jacket and stopped off in the bathroom to give myself a quick once-over. Although I didn't particularly look terrible, I was not looking my best, either. Knowing there was nothing I could do at that point and not really caring too much about it, I raced downstairs and found Blake standing by the door, looking intently at me.

"All ready?" he asked, his lips breaking into a gentle smile.

"Ready," I responded breathlessly.

We began our walk in silence, like most of our walks in the past. But now we stood much closer to one another. Every few steps, our arms would swing and glide across one another, barely touching. But the touch was enough to make my heart flutter and the nerves in my stomach twist. The next time our hands brushed together, he grabbed my hand, interlocking his fingers with mine.

He glanced toward me, his expression serious. It seemed as if he was having an internal battle, like he knew what he was doing was wrong, like he was breaking some rule.

My hand fit so easily into his, and his grip was gentle but firm. It made me feel safe. I knew now that he *was* really my own personal protector. We continued our walk in silence until we came to the docks and stopped in front of a small white boat. It was not a motorboat or anything that could get us somewhere fast, but a rowboat with two paddles laying on the bottom of it.

"Where are we going?" I asked, a little confused.

"My favorite place. The place where I go to think when I can't sleep."

"Oh," I said, sounding surprised, but not really sure what else I had been expecting.

Clutching my hand tighter, he guided me into the small boat. After I sat down, he climbed in without much effort, looking like he had done this so many times before. He picked up the two oars, and we paddled out into the dark night.

"So, where exactly are we going?" I asked, the anticipation too much for me to bear. Also, I had had my share of wondering those past few weeks.

"Tinkers Island," he responded, not offering up any more details.

I knew Tinkers Island. I had been there once on a school field trip. It was a small island about a mile from the mainland. I thought it was an odd place to go and think, since it was so far away. But then I remembered he could get from one place to the next as fast as he wanted. Then I wondered why he was not using that whooshing, whirling motion-thing now; we had done it together before.

Even though I was eager to get to wherever we were going, I also enjoyed the peaceful noises of the night: the sound of the water crashing upon the bow of the boat as it was gliding through the water and the paddles as they cut through the blackness beneath us. I leaned back, propping my hands on either the side of the boat, and stretched my head upward to the star-filled sky.

Then a thought popped into my head. The night at the Harpers when Blake took me outside on the bench—he was going to tell me about being a witch; it had nothing to do with his feelings. That explained the confused and mangled expression he had worn after my rant. Humiliation filled me. There was no way I could bring that up, not then and probably not ever.

Besides, there were too many other burning questions I wanted to ask. I had to try and glue all the pieces of the puzzle together. "Blake?"

"Yes?"

"You said that you and your family live in Marblehead back in 1905. This is going to sound crazy, but do you all live in the same house … back in 1905, I mean?"

He laughed. "Yes, that has been my home for the last couple years. My father built the house for my mother, and we had just finished putting the final touches on it before coming here to find you."

“What was it like coming here? To the future?” It felt weird asking that question out loud.

“The unknown is always scary. You never know what you are going to get when you cross time. When we performed the time-crossing spell that night, we were fortunate that the house still existed and that no one lived there. We cast the spell on the outside of town, in hopes of not being seen by anyone. When we arrived at our house, my mother cried when she saw the condition of it and Abby screamed when she saw what had been done to her room.” He laughed, remembering the memory.

I echoed his laugh, remembering what Abby had said about her pink room.

He continued and went into more detail about the night they arrived. “That night, we stayed up and formulated a plan. We performed a tracer spell on you and were able to find out where you lived. Our plan was to confront you the next day, see what you knew, and go from there. It was dawn before we all retired for the night. But I couldn’t sleep, so I took a walk outside. That’s when I saw Abby sneaking out and walking toward the cemetery. I almost stopped her, but I figured she needed to be alone. She was having the toughest time out of all of us. It wasn’t until she came home in hysterics that I knew how bad it really was. She had told us that she went to the cemetery and saw our graves. It just didn't make sense to her that we could have died yet been here, in the future. Then she told me she saw you and sensed the energy in you but she was certain that you had not had been linked to your powers. And that's when I decided to follow you in town. It wasn't until the crosswalk that I was able to test your powers—or should I say, lack of powers."

I gulped, remembering Mr. Griffin's car coming to a startling stop just inches from me.

"I turned the light from green to red, making the crosswalk read that it was safe for you to walk. It was a test to see if you could stop the car before it hit you. I wanted to know what we were dealing with. I had never been given a person to protect who knew nothing about who they were. It made me very suspicious of you, and I wasn't sure if we could trust you," he finished.

I thought about what he had said for a moment. "But I didn't stop the car. I saw it slow down and stop just inches from me, but I didn't do it."

"It took just a second for me to realize that you didn't have the power to stop it, so I did."

I swallowed hard, knowing that I could have been roadkill that day, and it would have been at Blake's hand.

"Have you protected many others like me?" I asked.

“The Council has given me a few other assignments but no one quite like you.” He smiled.

A few moments later, the boat hit the banks of Tinkers Island. He got off first, pulling the boat up onto the beach. Then he grabbed my hand and helped me out when we were clear of the water. He didn’t let go of my hand as he led me down the beach. We walked about a hundred yards until we reached a wall of rocks.

Glancing up at the full moon, I saw there were no clouds in the sky to block its bright and crisp glow. It provided just enough light for us to see by. He climbed onto the rock formation, taking a few steps before turning around and holding out his hand for me. I grabbed hold, and he pulled me up to him. We both stood, balancing on a small rock, our bodies touching casually, making me struggle to keep my breathing under control. He turned to walk farther out onto the rocks and finally came to rest a few feet from where the ocean crashed upon them. I could see where it looked like someone had made a bench out of a few long, flat rocks. There was a long rectangular rock that was meant to be the seat and a matching one to be the backrest.

“I couldn’t believe this was still here. A few nights after we arrived, I came out here looking for it. I was thankful to see that it still existed,” he said as he took a seat on the far end. He glanced up at me and patted the open spot next to him.

“This is amazing,” I said, sitting down beside him.

“I built it for myself shortly after I found out what I was. It was a place I could come to think and get away from it all, first by boat then by flying. I thought you could use it. You have a lot to think about after all that’s happened in the past twenty-four hours.” He shrugged.

“So is it flying … that swooshing, tumbling feeling?” I had assumed it was, but had not been totally sure until then.

“Yes, that’s flying. I remember what it felt like when my parents first took me. Taking deep breaths helps to calm the dizziness, and then you eventually get used to it.”

There was something that got me thinking, and even though I was sure of the answer, I wanted to make sure. “You can fly and you have powers docs that make you a witch, too?”

“Yes, but I’m different from you. See, when we come into our destiny and master our craft, we are then given roles by the Council. Each of us is appointed certain responsibilities as the Council sees fit. There are roles to protect future witches, not just from evil but also from themselves. Magic can be very dangerous without even adding evil into the mix. Abby was given the role of a teacher and my parents are guardians … which is really just to make sure we don't mess up."

I nodded and stared at him in amazement. It was hard to get over that I was sitting next to a protector, my own personal one at that. He was sent to the future to keep me safe, enabled with powers that allowed him to fly through the air, stop speeding cars, fight off evil, and who knows what else. And even though there was a lot that I should have been thinking about, mainly that *I* was a witch too, for a minute, I couldn't think about anything but him.

Then before I knew it, all of the unanswered questions consumed me. Why didn't I know anything? How I could have missed it growing up? Why had my parents never told Charlotte and me? The most difficult questions were: Why had my parents changed over the last few weeks of their lives? Were they running from the same thing I was when they had left with me and my sister that night? Did they die trying to protect us and something went wrong? But why would they just leave me to deal with it all on my own, totally unprepared and vulnerable? Blake had been right about the place: in the cool night air, listening to the waves crashing upon the rocks below, I was more able to open my mind and take everything in.

"Blake." I could see in my peripheral vision that he had turned his head in my direction, but I continued to look forward out into the black ocean as I spoke. "You said it was my mom that came to you and told you about me, right? Why did she come specifically to you and your family? Why not just directly to me?"

"As much as she probably wanted to, it would have been impossible for her to contact you. Witches that have crossed to the other side can only contact other witches that are linked with their powers. It's a portal, so to speak. We are all linked, connected in some way. Good, evil, dead, or alive. But why the Council chose me and my family specifically, I'm not sure." He sighed before continuing his explanation. "It's also more complicated than just that. There are rules that the Council has to abide by as well. They can't just contact anyone they want. Imagine how you would have reacted if your mother just showed up one night. As witches, we all have to be careful and not allow the outer world to see us using our magic."

I nodded in agreement, although I was confused as ever. There were rules? This was information overload. It was just becoming clear to me that I was a witch, that there were people after me, and that I would soon have powers. But rules? How was I supposed to absorb all of this? I tried not to dwell too much on all of that. The most important thing was for me to learn who my enemies were and what I had to do in order to protect myself.

"Isaac said that *they* had special plans for me. What did he mean by that?"

"You don't have to worry about that, he will never get that close to you again. That was my mistake. One that I don't plan on making twice."

"What do you mean *your* mistake? And please don't take this the wrong way but I think I deserve to know everything, I have a right to know what I'm up against."

Sighing, Blake leaned back farther into the bench and gazed up towards the star filled sky. "Abby cast a protection spell on you when we realized you had no way to protect yourself. Even though we were still unsure about a lot of things, we knew that Isaac was tracking you, and more than likely Alex was nearby as well. And it was my duty to keep you safe until we could figure it all out. The night you left to see Roger, Isaac was able to break through the spell somehow and find you … or the spell may have had boundaries and you crossed over them. Either way, it was a stupid, careless mistake on my part—one that I may never forgive myself for." He looked over at me with an agonizing expression. "And you're right; you do deserve to know what you're up against. I just don't know how to explain it all to you. But I will tell you anything you want to know, no more secrets."

I stared out into the ocean, not knowing what to say. Just the thought of Isaac gave me flashbacks of my dream, the first one I had had about me running into the forest. There were two men that day standing near the tree line, staring at me. Now I was positive that one had been Isaac, and I could only assume that the other was Alex. There was a large part of me that wanted to know about them … everything I possibly could. But another part of me didn't know if I had the capacity to take all of that in right now. There was already so much information that I felt I hadn't fully processed yet.

"Oh, and don't worry about your friend," Blake said, totally redirecting my thoughts.

"Friend?"

"You know, the guy you met in Rockport."

My heart sank … Roger. For all Roger knew, I had gone to the bathroom and disappeared.

"What do you mean don't worry about him?" I gulped, hoping nothing bad had happened to him.

"After you and I left last night, Abby put a spell on him and his friend. He won't even remember that you went out there. It was the easiest way. Your aunt's car is also safe. My dad got it back safely," he said reassuringly.

I had remembered seeing the Cherokee in the driveway earlier that evening but didn't think anything of it. It looked so normal to be sitting in its rightful place.

"Do you have any more questions for me? I'll tell you anything you want to know," he said, shifting his body so that he was fully facing me.

I turned to look at him. The moon cast a shadow on half of his face, but it was still easy to find his eyes. I stared into them, immediately forgetting the thousand questions I wanted to ask.

"Lots, but I don't think I can handle any more information tonight. I better let some sink in a bit."

Scooting closer to him, I rested my head on his shoulder, and he wrapped both arms around me, holding me in a sweet embrace. An hour or so passed in silence, and I caught myself nodding off. I jerked my head back to an upright position, not wanting to sleep. Not wanting to miss any moment when he was near me.

"I should probably get you to bed. Abby will kill me if you're not ready to go first thing in the morning. Ready to go back?" he asked.

“Not really. I used to love being at home; it was the one place I felt safe. But it doesn’t feel that way now.” I sighed, realizing that nothing was sacred anymore.

“I told you that I wouldn’t let anything happen to you. That one slip-up with Isaac won’t happen again. Don’t you trust me?” he questioned. I couldn’t help but hear a slight sadness in his voice.

It had nothing to do with trusting him. Of course I trusted him. He had saved me from what could have been one of my worst nightmares come to life. Literally. But I knew I couldn’t run from it. I would have to go home one day.

Chapter Seventeen

By the time we got back to my house, I was exhausted. Blake offered to sleep on the couch and promised he would stay until Abby arrived in the morning. After changing into an oversized T-shirt, I washed my face and brushed my teeth then crawled into bed. With Blake downstairs, I felt safe. But even though I was completely exhausted, I couldn't sleep. Lying in bed, I stared at the ceiling, trying to envision what the next day would be like. Abby would perform a summoning spell on me to link me with my powers. Even though I knew all of the typical clichés that went along with witchcraft, I would probably feel like a fool when it was nothing as I had expected.

After tossing and turning for what was probably an hour, I got up and headed downstairs, hoping a glass of milk would help calm me. As I got to the bottom of the stairs, I couldn't help but look around the corner to sneak a peek at Blake. I found him lying on the couch, eyes wide-open, and deep in thought.

"Blake," I whispered.

"Aren't you supposed to be sleeping?"

"Can't sleep." I sighed.

"You have a big day tomorrow, and I will have to answer to my sister if you are not fully rested. She may not look like it, but she can be pretty nasty when she gets angry." He grinned as he adjusted the pillow behind his head in order to get a better look at me.

"I was thinking … about the other night with Isaac." Just the thought of him having me in his grasp sent a shiver down my spine.

Blake's face had turned serious at the mention of Isaac.

"What did he mean when he called you a friend?" I asked.

He let out a loud sigh, and I walked over toward him, taking a seat at the end of the couch, never taking my eyes off his face.

"We used to be friends. It seems like a hundred years ago, but it was just a few years back … in my time, that is."

I gulped too loudly, and he began to explain. I assumed he felt that he owed me an explanation as to how he had been friends with a guy that wanted to hurt or maybe even kill me—the jury was still out on that one.

"Years ago, Isaac and I were like brothers. We trained together when we first found out about our powers so it formed a strong bond between us. My family and his family were all very close. Abby and Isaac were engaged to be married."

"Abby and Isaac?" I gasped. Then I remembered the awkward glance that Annette and Blake had shared at dinner and the distant look Abby had had on her face. When I brought up the wedding between Aunt Rose and Jack, it must have triggered something for her.

"Yes, he was very different back then, before his entire life changed, transforming him into the monster he is today." Blake looked back toward the ceiling, diving deep into his thoughts, back into the past.

"One night, Isaac and I were up late studying some spells. It was around two in the morning when we finally called it quits for the night and he headed home. By all accounts, he saw the fire consuming his house from a few blocks away, but he was too late. When he got to his house, it was engulfed in flames. He tried his hardest to go in and save his family, but the flames had already taken over. Word spread quickly through town, and I found him the next morning, sitting near the embers where his house had once stood. When I approached him, he didn't flinch or speak. For days, he wouldn't respond to me or even Abby. It was so difficult for us not to be able to help him. He stayed at our house for a few weeks without speaking to any of us. He was in a constant daze. It took all of us to just get him to eat and drink something every day. Then one night he disappeared. We didn't see or hear from him for a year. Then one night he returned and he was very upset. He started mentioning Alex, saying Alex told him that if he helped him get what he wanted, then Alex would bring his family back. He said that he and Alex had a plan but it had gone wrong. That everything was all ruined. I tried to calm him down. Abby tried to comfort him, but he stormed off in a rage. He seemed upset that we didn't take him seriously. A few more months passed before we saw him again. He was a totally different person then. There was no soul left in his eyes. He said that he and Alex had another plan, one more chance, and they were confident that it would work this time. We didn't understand anything of what he was saying. And we couldn't understand why he had trusted Alex. Alex had been our biggest enemy for years. He practiced dark magic and would do anything for more power."

“Wait … are you saying that Alex could bring Isaac’s family back … from the dead?” I asked, interrupting his story.

“Yes. Ancient stories have been told that an Astoria—an all-powerful witch—has the power to bring the dead back to life, among other great powers. If a witch were to perform a ritual to take the powers from the Astoria, and then kill them, then that witch would consume their powers. Only every two hundred years does an Astoria exist, so it’s a very rare occurrence. It was prophesied that, at the end of the twentieth century, two Astorias would be born: twins.”

The calculation came up quickly in my mind, and I gasped, knowing that could only mean one thing. Charlotte and I were the two Astorias.

Blake paused, searching my eyes, trying to measure my reaction. But I must not have looked too overwhelmed, because he continued, “When Isaac came back to us that last night, he started to ask specific questions about you. He began to go on and on about a sacrifice that had to be made and then he would have his family back. It was just a few hours after he left that the Witch’s Council called upon us for help.” He finished, his eyes finding mine again.

I sat there stunned, not sure of what to say. As crazy as it was, my thoughts first went to Isaac. The loss of his entire family in one single night had sent him into a tailspin of destruction, and oddly, I felt like I could relate. I didn't agree with what he was doing, but somewhere inside me, I understood how he felt. If there was some way I could bring my family back, I was not sure what I would be capable of doing to make it happen.

Then my thoughts drifted to Abby. I couldn't imagine what she was going through. The man she loved had turned evil. Now she and her family were hunting him and ultimately trying to stop him … all in order to protect me.

"I really think you should be getting some sleep." Blake's voice interrupted my thoughts.

"You're probably right," I agreed. "Would you mind if I slept down here with you? I don't feel like being alone right now."

"Of course." He adjusted himself by turning over on his side, giving me the other half of the couch.

It's not that we hadn't just slept like that the night before. Could that have only been last night? I thought. It seems like it was a lifetime ago. I snuggled up beside him, our bodies barely touching, but it was enough. My heart began to pound against my chest as he pulled me in closer, wrapping his arms around me, forming a protective cage.

When we were finally settled and my heart had calmed, I quickly fell into a deep sleep.

When I woke the next morning, I was alone. There was a faint ray of light coming in from the window, and I knew it must still be early. I glanced around the room and began calling out for Blake, but there was no answer. Then I heard the doorbell.

Who on earth could be here so early? I wondered. I glanced at the clock on the mantle. It was only six-thirty in the morning. I opened the door, and whose face did I see smiling back at me? Abby's.

"Good morning, sunshine. I did say first thing, didn't I?"

"Yes, you did." I laughed, trying to be inconspicuous as I looked around her, searching for Blake. But he was nowhere in sight.

"You can quit looking for him. He already left," she said, entering the house.

"Oh." I frowned.

"No pouting. He really wanted to be here, but he did not want to put too much pressure on you."

"Pressure?" I questioned.

"Yes, learning the craft can be very difficult at first. We still have to do the summoning spell just to get your powers. I need all of your focus, and I think he's quite a distraction for you. But I must say it's been a long time since I've seen my brother this happy. I just hope …" Her voice trailed off before finishing.

"You just hope what?" I questioned, fear running through me.

"Nothing. I'm sure everything will work out just fine. Now, are you ready?" she asked, this time forcing the smile across her face.

I looked down and wondered how she could even ask me that question. I was a total mess. "No, but give me just a few minutes," I said, sprinting up the stairs.

When I was getting dressed, I couldn't ignore what Abby had said about the hoping thing. Was she hoping that Blake and I would work out? Did she know something that I didn't? There was the fact that they came from a different time period, and there was the possibility that one day they would have to leave. I guess I hadn't even thought about that yet. I tried to avoid negative thoughts, hoping, just like Abby, that everything would work out fine.

After throwing on a pair of jeans, an old T-shirt, and tennis shoes, I ran into the bathroom, threw my hair in a ponytail, and brushed my teeth. I bounded back downstairs and found Abby sitting with her legs crossed on the couch, reading from an old brown leather notebook.

"Just trying to catch up on some of the beginner spells. It's been years since I've even looked in this thing," she said as she continued to flip through the pages. "You should eat some breakfast. It's going to be a long day, and I'm not sure we will break for lunch."

She was really taking this seriously. But she was my teacher after all. I walked into the kitchen, pulled out two pieces of bread, and popped them in the toaster. As I stood there waiting, I couldn't help but think of what Abby must be going through. Here she was fighting against a person she once loved or maybe still loved, the man she had been engaged to no less. I couldn't imagine how much that would hurt, to fight against someone you loved.

"Penny for your thoughts." Her voice made me flinch. I had not even noticed her come in. She was sitting at the kitchen table, staring at me intently.

"Um, it's nothing really. I'm just a little nervous about today, that's all," I lied.

Saved by the toaster. After putting a thin layer of peanut butter on each piece, I wrapped them up in plastic wrap and turned toward Abby. "Ready," I said. "I'll just eat on the way. It will save some time."

She laughed. "No, we will wait until after you finish. Rule number one: no flying and eating."

"Flying?" I swallowed hard, remembering what it had been like when Blake flew me away from Isaac and then back to the Harpers'. The nausea slowly started to rear its ugly head. "How does that work anyway?" I took a large bite out of my toast and chewed quickly, hoping to dull the queasiness.

"With magic, of course. It's one of the simplest forms, actually. That is one of the first things we will learn. But we are getting way ahead of ourselves here. Just finish up your breakfast. We will have plenty of magic-talk today. I promise, by the end of the day, you will be begging me to stop."

She made it sound so simple, and I began to feel a little apprehensive. What if the summoning spell didn't work? What if they had it all wrong and I was not the great and powerful Astoria they thought I was? They had quite an expectation of me, and I hoped that I lived up to it in the end.

I stuffed the last bite of toast into my mouth and stood up, ready to go.

"Chew and swallow, I don't want you to choke on the way over there." She laughed, shaking her head.

I chewed and swallowed, opening my mouth to her just to prove it was empty.

All of a sudden, my world as I knew it was spinning, and I had no control. It continued like that for about a minute or so, and then I could feel myself slowing down and then finally coming to a stop. Even though my body had come to a halt, my head continued to go round and round.

"Whew, that is tiring with two people. I forgot how exhausting that is." I heard Abby speak, but I could not focus on her face. "Don't worry; the dizziness—"

"…will fade, just breathe," I interrupted her. "You forget, this is not my first time flying."

It took me a few minutes to gain my bearings back and to realize that I was in a place that I did not recognize.

"Where are we?"

"Steer Swamp." She grinned.

"Wow, that's impressive. You got us all the way over here in just those few seconds?" I asked, astonished.

She smiled proudly. "Yes, it was actually fifty-eight seconds to be exact, but I'm a little rusty. Can you walk? You don't look so good."

"Yeah, I can walk." I stood up, determined to prove it, but the moment I got up, I stumbled forward.

Abby caught me before I collapsed onto the green grass. "Oh, boy. This is going to be fun. Come on, I have us set up over here." She groaned as she lifted my arm over her head.

"Set up?" I questioned.

"What did you think, that I was going to fly over here with you and all the supplies? I'm a teacher, not a miracle worker."

We walked about twenty feet. Behind a large wall of trees, we came into a small open space. We stopped, and she guided me down to a small circle on the ground. It was about three feet in diameter and looked to be made from a mixture of flowers, pine needles, and some type of ash. She sat across from me and asked for my hands. I reached over, placing my hands into hers, mimicking her by crossing my legs into an Indian-style position. Immediately, energy rushed over me. There was a tingling sensation shooting throughout my body, and for the first time, I actually believed that powers did exist somewhere in me.

"Follow my lead. Just relax, let your body open up to the energy and the natural elements. I will take care of everything else."

She closed her eyes, so I did the same. She began to murmur something under her breath, and I tried my hardest not to concentrate on her voice. Instead, I let every bone and muscle in my body relax. It was difficult at first, but slowly it felt like my body was melting into the earth. I was tempted to open my eyes to see what was happening, but I resisted.

Soon I was totally zoned out, feeling like I was having almost an out-of-body experience.

Then there was silence. No wind rustling the leaves in the trees above us, no birds chirping happily, and no more chanting from Abby. I sat there frozen, unable to open my eyes in fear of what I would see if I did.

"Okay, all done," Abby said after just a few minutes. "That went better than I could have expected."

With some hesitation, I opened up my eyes and was shocked at what I saw. Nothing had changed. Absolutely nothing. "That's it?" I asked, curiously.

"*That's it?* Is that your way of saying thank you?" she teased. "I will have you know that that was one of the easiest summoning spells I have ever done. It was like the power was about to erupt out of you any second. All it needed was a little guidance."

"Sorry, I was not trying to insult your work … It's just that I was expecting something a little different."

"Like what? Sparks? Or maybe puffs of smoke?" She laughed. "Just be patient. We will be here every step of the way, but it will take some time."

After a few hours of training, we were finally finished for the day. She was not kidding, either. I felt like I had had a crash course in magic, and I was definitely worn out by the time we were finished. My whole body ached, and we had not even done anything that strenuous—not physically, anyway. The most exciting spell I had learned was how to move a leaf and rock with my mind. I admit that it was awesome the first, second, and third time, but by the fiftieth time I had done it, I was so over it. I wanted to move on to something I could protect myself with.

We began our walk home, and for once I wished she would just fly us there. It would be so much faster, and I could get home and change quicker.

"So, Blake told me he explained the whole Isaac situation to you," Abby said out of the blue.

It shocked me. Firstly, I hadn't thought Blake would tell her that I knew. And secondly, I hadn't thought that Abby would actually bring it up.

"I just wanted to explain it from my side. I can't imagine what you must think of me. You must think I'm crazy for loving someone who is now so troubled," she said.

"Crazy? I think the exact opposite; you're one of the strongest people I know. It's amazing to me that you can fight against someone you once loved. It must be ... difficult." I struggled for the right the word.

She glanced in my direction with a curious expression on her face. "I'm not fighting against him, Meredith. I'm fighting for him. I truly believe I can bring him back to me. It's the only thing that gets me up each morning."

"Oh, Abby, I'm sorry. I just thought …"

"Really, there's no need to explain. I can see where you would think the other way."

I sighed.

"What is it?" she asked.

"It's just that, before I thought you were the strongest person I ever knew, and now I can add bravest to that as well. I just don't know how you do it."

"You should give yourself some credit, too, you know. You lost your family at such a young age, and yet here you are, still functioning, strong, and about to be the most amazing witch. It takes more courage and strength to do what you are doing than what I am," she said.

No pressure, I thought to myself.

"Abby." I paused for a moment. "How does it all work? Contacting the Council and the other witches that have crossed over?" I hadn't forgotten what Blake had said about witches in tune with their powers being connected to other witches. The thought of being able to contact my mother excited me.

"I think I know where you are headed with this and I'm afraid it's not that easy. The council has to have good reason to contact the witches still living. There has to be an immediate danger to the craft or something similar to that. But you may find comfort in knowing that we are all connected and even though you may not be able to see or hear them, they are with us always." She smiled looking over at me.

Chapter Eighteen

As we arrived back at my house, Blake was sitting under the tree in my front yard, engrossed in a book. My heart soared when I saw him. The moment he realized our presence, he glanced up, smiling at me.

“Can I steal her away now?” he asked as we approached, not taking his eyes off of me.

“Sure, but don’t keep her up too late.”

Blake was already at my side, and he scooped me up into his arms.

“She will be at this again first thing in the—” Abby called after us, but her voice faded away before I heard her finish.

We must have been flying again, because my world was spinning again. But that time it was a little different. Blake was either being a little more careful or maybe I was finally starting to get used to it.

Blake took me back to the lighthouse in Fraser Bay. He carried the same backpack as he did the night he rescued me from Isaac. He had packed us a few sandwiches and some fruit for dinner. We ate on the purple velvet blanket and talked about my day of training.

As hard as I tried, I couldn't stop myself from yawning.

"I think it would be best if you got some sleep. Abby would kill me if I brought you to class tomorrow with bags under your eyes." He smiled as he reached for the candle and blew it out.

"We are sleeping here tonight?" I asked.

"Is that okay?"

"Sure," I guessed. "But is there a reason why we keep coming here? Don't get me wrong, I love this place. I'm just curious is all."

"Yes, there is a reason. When we first arrived in your time, my family and I searched for a safe house so to speak. A place where I could take you and no evil, no matter how strong, could get to you. It takes a lot of magic to create such a place so it couldn't be too big. When I saw the lighthouse, I thought it was perfect."

"Oh … that makes sense." It seemed so strange that the Harpers' went to all this trouble for me. It was something I couldn't get over. I had spent so much of my life not feeling that important, always flying under the radar. But now I had these amazing people looking out for *me* and willing to put everything on the line to protect *me*. The feeling was overwhelming.

As much as I wanted to stay up and talk all night, I knew that I needed my rest so I could learn as much as possible the next day. No one knew when Isaac, Alex, or any other dark magic would come for me, and I had to be prepared. I had to be able to protect myself.

Blake and I melded together into one as we lay in the darkness. I laid my head on his chest and got comfortable. Just as I was about to drift off into a deep slumber, I heard a whisper in my ear that made my heart skip a beat and my eyes shoot wide open. I could've sworn that I had just heard Blake whisper "I love you."

I lay there too scared to move, thinking that Blake had said it thinking that I had already fallen asleep, not wanting me to hear him. After a few seconds, I decided to be brave and look up to face him. But I found his eyes were closed, and he looked to be in deep and peaceful sleep. The innocent look on his face made my heart melt, and I whispered back, "I love you, too."

The next morning, Blake and I arrived at the beach late.

Abby was already waiting for us, tapping her foot. "Seriously, I'm going to have to start keeping tighter tabs on you two." She gave us both a pointed look.

"Sorry, won't happen again—promise," Blake said. He kissed me on my cheek then whispered in my ear, "See you this evening."

I swallowed hard and tried my hardest not to blush in front of Abby.

"Okay, lovebirds. It's class time now."

Today would be flying lessons. Great! I mean, how cool would it be to fly? I had never owned a car, never wanted one, and here I was about to learn free and fast transportation. We started the lesson back in Steer Swamp. Abby had set up a few different stations, and they all involved a ladder and a ledge. The first station was the smallest and only looked to be about ten feet high. It didn't look so bad when I stared up at it from the ground, but as I stood on top of it, I was nervous.

"Come on. You can do this," Abby encouraged.

Easy for you to say, I thought. But I tried to push everything out of my mind and concentrate on what Abby had told me: “Think of a feather floating through the air. Slowly. Gracefully. Feel the energy running through your body, and let it all go.” I pictured it. I could see the feather gliding through the air and then the energy came over me and I released it, feeling total freedom come over me. That’s it, I’ve got it! I stepped off the ledge, and for a moment, I felt like I was floating. Then a second later, the feather disappeared from my mind, and I felt myself falling. It was not long before I landed on the hard ground beneath me.

“Ow. Are you okay?” Abby was beside me, helping me up.

“Damn, I had it.” I groaned, looking down at my scraped knees and hands.

“That was excellent! You levitated for an entire six seconds.”

“Excellent?” I questioned.

“Don’t be too hard on yourself, it takes most people days to get to that point.”

Days? I was not going to have any skin left on my knees and hands if I kept this up for days.

“Let’s do it again. This time hold your concentration and focus.”

It took all of my concentration and focus not to glare at her. What did she think I was doing? But I withheld; she was just trying to help me, after all.

Again. And again. I tried it for two hours straight, but could not improve past thirty seconds of levitation. Finally, Abby called it quits for the day. I wanted to keep going, determined to get it right, but she couldn't stand to look at my knees and hands anymore. She was kind enough to fly me back to the lighthouse, seeing as I was a wounded student.

When we arrived, I saw that Blake was holding a small white box in his left hand. As I got closer, I realized that it was a first aid kit. How had he known?

"It happens to the best of us," he whispered to me, and I melted into his embrace.

Abby looked at us for a moment, and I couldn't help but see the agony in her expression. I wondered if she was thinking of Isaac.

Abby turned to head home, but not before telling me that I would have to report for class again after my shift at the library. Work. Ugh. It was just a few days ago that I had been looking forward to going back to work. But that was before I knew my destiny and before I knew that evil was after me. Now all I wanted to do was practice, practice, practice, and learn, learn, learn.

As soon as she was out of sight, Blake lifted me up and sat me on a rock near the water's edge. He knelt down and opened up the first aid kit, taking out some rubbing alcohol, ointment, and a few bandages. Very lightly, he cleaned my wounds, bandaged them up, and kissed each one lightly before pulling me back up into a standing position.

"Better?" he asked.

"A little," I teased.

He narrowed his eyes on me, trying to survey the situation and figure out what it would take for me to feel better. Then he held my face in his hands and kissed me until I felt my knees go weak.

"How about now?"

"Much better," I breathed.

Back in the lighthouse, things were peaceful. I stood on my tiptoes, trying to see the sun setting over the water, the day's events running through my mind. I tried to recite the things Abby had said to me over in my head, trying to engrave them there so I wouldn't forget anything for my next lesson. But the sunset and my thoughts quickly became second place to the person standing behind me.

Blake reached his arm around my waist and pulled me against his chest. Our bodies melded together, and the warmth of his presence set off the butterflies in my stomach. He then used his other hand to move the hair away from the nape of my neck so his warm lips could find a place to land. My heart pounded so hard that it ricocheted down into my ribs.

"How is everything going with the training?" he whispered into my ear as I felt his hand gently raking through my hair.

"Fine," I breathed. "A little frustrating."

"Abby says you are doing wonderfully. She says that you are the quickest study she's ever worked with, and that's saying a lot coming from her."

"I just want to learn something useful." I tried to focus on our conversation and not what his touch was doing to me.

"Patience." He kissed my neck again, and at that moment I forgot everything except for him.

Patience. Fine I would have patience with the whole magic thing, but not with him.

I twirled around and pressed my lips against his. The unforeseen force sent him stumbling backward and me along with him. We stumbled a few steps before he found his balance and used it to steady the both of us. My hands ran up his chest and wrapped themselves around his neck, pulling him closer to me. Just when I felt things were starting to get good, he stopped.

Then he slowly pulled away from me and collapsed down onto the blanket beneath us. It took me a second to come to terms with the fact that he had stopped.

"We can't … I can't do this, Meredith. It's not right. I'm afraid that this might get in the way of my purpose for being here."

"What are you talking about?" I asked, my voice quivering.

Rejection washed over me, and I knew that I was on the verge of tears.

"My job is to protect you."

"I'm safe here with you, aren't I?" I questioned as I sat down beside him.

"Let's just try and get through the next few days, okay?" He whispered softly as he looked into my eyes.

I nodded, knowing his thoughts were rational. As much as I wanted him, I knew it wasn't the smartest thing for me to be distracted like this either. My main priority was to learn my craft and keep the Harpers and myself safe.

But it doesn't mean that it didn't hurt. I'd never wanted someone like I wanted him and the feeling of rejection crushed me. I fell back toward the blanket and rolled over on my side. He gently placed his arm around my waist. We lay there, and somewhere in the silence, I drifted off to sleep.

When I woke, it was still dark in the lighthouse. I guessed that it was in the middle of the night or early morning. Blake's warm arm—that I was expecting and wanting to be holding me so badly—was no longer around my waist. I panicked and then shot up into a sitting position, searching for him.

My eyes found him, sitting across the circular room, staring at me. The few other times I had caught him staring; his eyes were filled with longing and desire. His eyes did not hold either of those two things this time. Those emotions seemed to have been replaced with fear and confusion.

"What's wrong?" I asked, hoping it was not still about how things almost went too far earlier.

A small grin appeared on his face, creating the dimple that I loved so much. But there was something in his eyes that made me feel like something was very wrong. "For right now, it's nothing. But I need to get home to my family so I can talk to them about it," he spoke intently, not releasing the stare he held on me. "You have work this morning, right?"

I nodded.

Before I could question what was going on in his head, he began to gather up the candle and matches, shoving them in his backpack. "We better get going then. Don't want you to be late for work." He glanced back toward me again, still smiling. But the smile was not genuine; it was forced.

"Is everything all right? You said that you would not keep anything from me. That you would answer any questions that I had, remember? I'm tired of being kept in the dark." The distant look in his eyes was beginning to scare me. It was as if the last few days between us had not happened.

He stopped packing and sat with his back against the wall, looking at me. "It's just a theory now, but I have an idea of how Isaac and Alex got here to this time. When my family and I traveled here, we had the power of the Witch's Council with us. So it leads me to question how Isaac and Alex could have crossed time to get here. Then last night when I was watching you sleep, I remembered something I had told you. That witches from the past, present, dead, or alive are all connected to one another. Maybe Isaac and Alex are using my family and me as a portal of some kind. Maybe they are channeling our powers somehow. I'm beginning to think that we brought them here. The last night that Isaac came to our house he was asking questions about you and talking of a sacrifice. The council must have heard what they were planning do. They knew you were the Astoria and had to be protected. Isaac and Alex knew the council would assemble a team to go to you. It was probably only a matter of hours before they figured out we left. I'm sure they began to plan immediately how to follow us and use our powers against us." He stood, glancing out the window. "But like I said, it's just a theory."

I didn't respond. What could I possibly say? He was thinking that he and his family were the reason that Isaac got to me. The main reason Blake and his family were sent to my time was to protect me, but Blake believed that they could have possibly led the enemy right to me. No words worth responding came to me. I reached down to fold up the velvet blanket.

On the walk back to my house, both of us considered what he had just said. Once we were there, Blake assured me that I would be safe that day at work. Abby and Annette had been working on a new protection spell the last couple days. It would deter Isaac and Alex from finding me again … at least for a few days. For the moment, neither of them would be able to step foot inside of Marblehead or anywhere within a hundred miles of it.

The moment Blake told me that I would be safe, I believed him, which was new for me. After my parents, there had not been one person in the world that I trusted with my entire being, until Blake.

I showered slowly, allowing my mind to open up and sift through what had happened the last few days. I knew that Aunt Rose would be home soon and that Jack would be moving in. It would be difficult to hide everything that was going on with me from them, but I had to; it was the only way to keep them safe.

Fear suddenly gripped me. What if Isaac or Alex eventually broke through the new protection spell and got to me … or, worse, to Aunt Rose and Jack, too? That just couldn't happen, not to them. The Harpers and I were going to have to think of a bulletproof plan to keep them safe.

Maybe instead of trying to think of a plan to stay in town longer, I should think of one to leave sooner. Maybe that would protect them. After work, I would have to go see Blake and his family. I would have to know what else could be done to safeguard the few people I had left from Isaac and Alex.

Work dragged on. Every time I glanced at the clock, I hoped it was almost time to go, but each time only a few minutes had passed since my last glance. I was tempted to ask Ms. Donaldson if I could leave early, but a part of me was scared to leave, scared to go to the Harpers' and hear what Blake would tell me about Isaac and Alex, about how he and his family may have been the portal that got them here to this time. Relief ran through me as I remembered that I would be training with Abby after work. That would steal my attention—for a little while, anyway.

I tried to keep myself busy and began to unload a box of stuff that Ms. Donaldson had gotten out of the basement. She explained to me that the boxes were full of antique items from the courthouse that had been donated to the library. Ms. Donaldson wanted to put any important or interesting pieces out on display for the public to see. If you asked me, it seemed a little strange. I guessed it was a part of the town's history, but it just seemed weird to want to keep items like that from the past. Ms. Donaldson had warned me to be careful as I sifted through the boxes, so I wouldn't break anything.

I carefully unveiled a magnifying glass and an old wooden gavel that I envisioned some judge using to order a hanging or something. The items seemed so old, and still I couldn't help but wonder if they existed from the Harpers' time. Then I couldn't help but question, was it really possible that the Harpers had traveled from the past? It was still so difficult to wrap my head around that. There was a part of me, a large part, that did not believe all of this was happening.

But I had proof. I knew the men in my dreams were not just figments of my imagination. They were real, and from what Blake had told me, in order to get my powers, they wanted to kill me. I also knew that Blake and Abby could fly and had powers beyond regular humans. Then there was me. It was just a few days ago when life seemed simple, boring, even—that was before I had known what I was and what power I possessed. But it was true I had magical powers, and Abby had shown me the other day. Sure the spell was simple, but I *had* moved a leaf and rock with my mind. I *had* levitated for thirty seconds. So even though a part of me didn't want to believe all this could be real, it was, and the only thing to do was embrace it.

"Meredith, are you okay?" Ms. Donaldson asked me.

The sound of her voice made me jump. I hadn't even realized I had zoned out. "Fine," I answered, shaking my head back to the present.

She looked skeptical but turned and headed back down toward the basement to retrieve more boxes.

The longest day in my working life thus far ended, and I was eager to begin my training with Abby and see Blake.

But as I walked out of the library, I realized that I would not have to wait long. There he was sitting on the bench, staring off into space. He had not noticed me, and for a minute, I got to stare at him and forget everything about what I had learned the past couple days. Forget that I was a witch, an Astoria to be more exact, and forget that he and his family were sent to protect me and teach me the ways. Oh, yeah, and forget that there was someone out there trying to kill me. For a moment, I pretended that he was just an incredibly good-looking guy waiting to walk me home and nothing else … that he was just a guy that I was falling head over heels in love with. But the moment didn't last for long. His head turned, sensing my presence, no doubt. His eyes met mine, still holding the same fear in them as that morning.

Chapter Nineteen

"Hi," I said as he approached me.

A small smile broke across his face.

"I was not expecting to see you until later. Did you convince Abby to let me have the day off?" I asked, now just hoping for another night alone with him.

"Something like that," he responded.

"I think my knees and hands could use a day off. Plus, I don't think my brain could handle any more information right now anyway. She can cram as much as she wants into my brain tomorrow. I think a night off is just what I need right now." I was rambling, and I realized that I was nervous. It had been a long time since I felt nervous around Blake, but the look in his eyes caused fear to flow through my veins.

And what made me even more nervous was that he was not talking, like he was afraid of what he would have to say.

“Well, what would you like to do? We could go to your house and hang out,” I suggested.

“My house is not a good idea right now. That’s why I had to get out of there. How about your house?” he asked, looking down at the ground as though not wanting to meet my eyes.

I swallowed hard. There was something different between us. I felt like my insides were being torn out. “Sure, Aunt Rose and Jack are still gone. They won’t be home until tomorrow afternoon.”

He nodded. Every part of me wanted to grab him and hold him. I wanted to take away the pain that he was so clearly feeling. Even though I wanted to know what that pain was, hoping that I could help, I was scared to know. Instead, I settled on just being with him.

It was not difficult to notice that our walking had been relegated back to the way it was in the beginning. We walked a foot apart, and when I would try to get close and hold his hand, he would just adjust the distance, not allowing us to touch. A part of me wanted to demand what was going on, why he was acting so different toward me, but I had a feeling that I was going to find out soon enough.

"I talked with my family about my theory," he said once we stepped in the door of my house. "And after much thought, they think I have a point. They believe that our coming here has done nothing but bring more evil into your world. We brought the one thing we were trying to keep away right to your doorstep. If it wasn't for us, none of this would have happened. Isaac would have never gotten so close."

My stomach dropped. "But how can you be so sure? I mean, he would have found a way sooner or later. You all couldn't have known. You all were told to come here by … by my mother. So it couldn't have been wrong, could it?" I swallowed hard, hoping he would agree with my logic.

"No. We believe the Council's intentions were good, just like ours. The Council sensed you were in danger but they didn't know specifics. I don't think anyone could have predicted that Isaac and Alex would be able to penetrate our magic and use it against us. Now it makes a little more sense that Isaac came to my family and I those nights, the way he was going on and on about you. He must have been doing that intentionally, trying to provoke the Council to send someone to help you. He must have known that he couldn't get to you alone. He knew he needed more powerful magic in order to get here." He looked at me with concerned eyes that also held something much deeper, a longing consumed with sadness.

There was only one way I knew to stop the emotions crossing his face. I leaned in and pressed my lips to his. It seemed to be working; I could feel the energy and safety that I had been longing for coming back. I could feel it in the way he kissed me. Then his kiss was more urgent, more passionate than we had ever had before. He wrapped his arms around my waist, pulling me closer to him. Then I felt him beginning to pull away.

When I looked into his eyes, I saw they held even more sadness than before, and I couldn't understand why. I knew he felt guilty for bringing Isaac and Alex to my time, but it was fine. I was fine. More than fine. I had finally figured out the secret of my life. Now I had Abby to teach me, Annette and Samuel to guide me, and … and …

"No!" I gasped. "No, you are not leaving me!" That had to be what he was thinking. That's why his face held so much grief.

"Meredith, please let me—"

"Explain?" I yelled, cutting him off. I had no idea where my anger was coming from, maybe from the many years of holding anger in, anger at the people I loved for leaving me. "No, you can't leave. There's no way I'm letting you. They were going to find a way to get to me. You and your family saved me. If it weren't for you, I would probably be dead by now."

"Don't talk like that, Meredith," he said shaking his head.

Anger rose from deep within in me. It was clear that I was prepared to say whatever I had to in order to get them to stay. "Do you think leaving is going to stop them? No! They are just going to find another way, and then you all won't be here to protect me or teach me how to protect myself. You can all stay. We can all stay here and fight when they find another way in," I said desperately.

But I could read his face, and it said that their minds had already been made up. "We have to leave. It's the only way to keep you safe. The only way to stop them is to go back to our time. They won't be able to remain in this time without our power. Alex and Isaac don't know you have summoned your powers. We can force them back to our time and take care of them there. That is the only way to know for sure that it's done."

My heart felt like it was being ripped out and my entire body as though it was about to crumble at any second.

"We are so sorry. I'm so sorry—"

"Stop," I interrupted him. "Please. Just stop. Don't apologize for coming here. Meeting you was the best thing that has ever happened to me. Don't ever forget that." My voice grew softer with each word.

"Meredith, you are misinterpreting what I'm saying. Do you not understand what danger you are in? What evil is out there tracking you? Of course I don't regret coming here; I would never in a million years regret meeting you. I will always remember this as the best summer of my life. But the only way for you to be truly safe is for us to leave," he finished.

I tried hard to contain my emotions, but it was hopeless. The tears came out so quickly that I could not make out any words.

Blake pulled me in and held me close. I knew that I was fighting a losing battle. I knew that no matter what I said or how hard I begged, there was no changing his mind. It took everything in me, but I composed myself. I had to ask the question that I knew no matter what the answer was, it would be devastating to hear. "When do you have to leave?"

"Soon. Before the sun rises," he whispered. "You know that I would never leave you unless it was a matter of life and death. You know that I would stay with you if I could.

But my family needs me right now, they can't do this without me."

I pulled myself together before answering. It was selfish of me to continue this guilt trip I was putting him through. It's not like I wanted him to feel bad for leaving, but there was no controlling my emotions now.

"Of course, I know that they need you," I said in between sobs. "It's just … that I need you, too. I need all of you." I could feel myself getting angry. Not angry at Blake, but angry at the world, at the universe, at magic, at evil. I had already had so many people I loved taken away from me. Hadn't I suffered enough? Was wanting Blake too much to ask for?

"Please, Meredith, look at me. I can't stand this pain I am feeling and knowing the pain I have caused you. You have to believe me, when I came here, I had no intention of finding someone like you and certainly not falling in love."

He grabbed my chin and pulled it up in order to look me in the eyes. That was the first time he had said it when I was meant to hear it, the first time he had said he loved me.

"Coming here *was* the best thing that has ever happened to me. I will find a way for us to be together again. Time will not keep us apart, I promise you that."

“Blake, please don’t make a promise you can’t keep. It will just make it worse.” I tried to shove back the tears. “I don’t want to spend our last hours—maybe ever—talking about empty promises. Can we please talk about something else?” The tears that I had so masterfully held back began to pour out again, and this time I could not suppress them for anything in the world.

Then a crazy thought popped into my head. Even though I knew it was a long shot, I tried, anyway. “Blake, please take me with you. I can help.” My voice rose with each word.

“If I thought it was the best thing for you, of course I would take you—but it’s not the right decision.” His voice was firm. “You just started your training, and it would put you in too much danger. It would be a risk for you and us to have you there.”

I couldn’t speak; all I could do was hold on as tight as possible.

We lay on my couch all evening, just holding each other. I knew the feeling of safety from being in his arms would soon be gone, and I wanted to enjoy it while I could.

I felt Blake take in a deep breath and let out a sigh before he began to speak. “Meredith, I have to go.”

At that moment, I knew he was really leaving, and I felt an overwhelming hunger to know as much as possible about what would become of him, even though deep down I knew I was just delaying the inevitable.

"What are you all planning to do? You have to tell me something, I have to know something …" I said, standing myself and following him to the door as he got up to leave.

"Shh." He held his finger up to my lips in order to quiet them.

He wiped the tears from my cheek and moved the hair out of my eyes as he lightly traced the curvature of my face, beginning at my temple and all the way down to my chin, ending at my lips. Then he kissed me, gently at first, then more urgently. I felt the burning desire start in my stomach and work its way up all the way to my lips. After being so exhausted from the last few hours of crying, it was as though my heart was revived as it began to beat again at full speed, so fast that it almost burst out of my chest. He pulled back and held me in a tight embrace.

After a few deep breaths, I was finally able to look him in the face. Somehow I was able to control the stream of tears that so badly wanted to escape again. "What am I supposed to do without you?" I spoke, my voice raspy from crying.

"I will be back for you soon," he promised.

Soon? Was that all he could give me? I guess it was a lot to ask for a specific date and time … but *soon* seemed so indefinite.

"The days apart from you will be the hardest days of my life." I sighed, placing my forehead on his chest. "You have no idea how much I will miss you."

"Oh, I think I will have somewhat of an idea," he spoke softly in my ear.

"Promise me something?"

"Anything."

"Promise me that you will never forget me." I spoke as clearly as I could. "No matter what."

"That is definitely a promise I can keep."

"Tell Abby, Annette, and Samuel thank you—for everything." I choked back my tears.

After one last kiss, he opened the door and turned to walk away. Not able to move, I stood there in the doorway, watching his figure slip deep into the shadows of the night. I couldn't help but hope that he would come back for one last kiss, one last goodbye. But as much as I wanted it, I knew it would just be more painful if he did.

When I finally dragged myself back inside, I was too tired to wash my face or brush my teeth. I just crawled into bed and curled up into a ball, holding myself as tightly as possible. The emptiness, the solitude, and the pain were overwhelming. I lay in bed staring at the ceiling, hoping that Blake, Abby, Samuel, and Annette would find their way back to their time safely. What if something went wrong on the way back and they never made it? What if this was all just a trap? What if Alex and Isaac had planned this all along? What if they were waiting for them to leave so they could have me all to themselves? Were there more witches out there? Now that my powers had been summoned, would they try to get to me? I wondered if magic was a part of my time like it was in their time. Did other witches exist around me?

I lay there thinking of a million questions, knowing they would probably all go unanswered. The only people in the world who knew anything about me, the real me, were not just in some other city or state. They were in an entirely different century. As much as I tried to fight it, I knew the reality. There were so many things that could go wrong and keep him from ever coming back. I tried to not think those thoughts. Instead I tried to focus on the positive one: that he could come back … He had promised me that he would.

The hours after he left were torturous and allowed me no sleep. So I stared at the ceiling, and my thoughts drifted to

Blake, Abby, Annette, and Samuel. I thought about what they were risking to save me. Why? I wondered. I am no one. They say that I am this all-powerful Astoria, the most powerful witch to exist in two hundred years, but all I can do is move a leaf and a rock with my mind. I can't fly or say the simplest of spells without difficulty. Abby, who was supposed to my teacher, left after only three days into my training. How am I supposed to be this great and powerful witch and help save the people who now mean so much to me?

Light was beginning to break through my bedroom window, and I knew that it was the start of a new day, even though I hadn't slept. But the day felt different. I knew that Blake and his family were gone.

I also knew that Aunt Rose and Jack would be back from their honeymoon that day, and I would have to explain myself if I couldn't dry my tears. My alarm rang out, startling me back into reality, letting me know it was time to get up and go to work.

Chapter Twenty

I performed the bare minimum morning ritual, brushing my teeth, washing my face, and changing my clothes. I just didn't have enough energy in me to do much else. When I opened the front door, a part of me hoped to see Blake there, leaning against my tree, waiting to walk me to work. But of course he wasn't. He was in some other time, some other century trying to fight some evil to save my life. Ugh, it was just so difficult to wrap my head around.

Ms. Donaldson eyed me suspiciously all day, but she didn't ask me any questions. Regrettably, work flew by. Deep down, I knew why—because I had spent the whole day worrying about what I would do when Aunt Rose and Jack came home. They would be back from their honeymoon, expecting me to be the same girl they had left a few days ago, the same girl who was still planning on leaving soon to go to London. But I wasn't that girl anymore. My plans for London were definitely on hold. I mean, how I could leave when Blake had promised me he was going to come back for me? I had to at least give him a chance to keep his promise. Plus, I had this whole new life that I had not known about before. It made sense to stay until I got it figured out. Now I just had to find a way to explain that to Aunt Rose and Jack.

After work I was still not ready to face going home. I still had no idea of what I was going to say. So instead I went for a walk that led me to the docks and the small white boat Blake and I had gone to Tinkers Island in just a few days ago. I stepped in, and the boat rocked right and left under my weight, and I wished Blake were there to balance me. I grabbed the two oars and began to sweep myself out over the ocean. The afternoon sun was straight above me, and it only took a few minutes until I was dripping in sweat. Turning my head, I looked to see how far I was from the other shoreline. It still looked far enough to be a daunting task, but desperation pushed me onward. I wanted so badly to get to the place Blake and I had been the other night, to help me feel close to him again.

A few minutes later, I had to let go of the oars and let my burning arms rest. I wondered how Blake had made it all the way over without stopping and breathing heavy like I was just then. Just thinking of him sent fresh determination pulsing through my veins. I picked the oars up and began to paddle harder, faster. This would be so much easier if I had just learned how to fly, I thought to myself. I would have been there twenty minutes ago.

As I got closer to the beach, my heart began to ache. It took just about all of my remaining strength to pull the boat up onto the shore, enough so it would not get swept back into the ocean. After taking my shoes off, I walked along the beach until I came upon the wall of rocks. Without Blake's help, I was relegated to crawling in order to ensure that I wouldn't fall and break something. When I reached the bench, I collapsed down onto it, breathing heavily for a moment and feeling as though I had just completed a triathlon. The physical and emotional exhaustion, coupled with not sleeping the night before, put me right to sleep.

I dreamt of Blake, a quiet dream where we didn't talk. It was just the two of us, sitting next to each other in the very spot I was sleeping. We smiled occasionally at one another and looked happy, fulfilled, even, like we didn't have a care in the world: no sadness, no fear, no pain.

I woke up crying again, and the streaming tears burnt my already red and swollen eyes. I told myself it would just be temporary, that I would see him again and then nothing would ever keep us apart. Sitting up, I peeled my drenched shirt away from my burning hot skin. My hair was plastered to the left side of my face and the nape of my neck.

Eventually, I made it back to the beach, and I scooped up some water, rubbing it up and down my arms and around my neck, trying to rinse off the sweat. Then I pushed the boat off the sandy bank and jumped into it just when it was floating on enough water, mimicking what I saw Blake do.

I knew that Aunt Rose and Jack were probably already home, wondering where on earth I was. Guilt filled me, but I still couldn't find it within me to face them. My selfish demeanor shocked me. How could I do this to them?

After yet more difficult rowing, finally the boat smashed into the wooden dock. I jumped onto it, not even bothering to tie the boat off, knowing it would be gone in the currents in no time, but I didn't care. I found myself running as fast as I could back to town. But I was not running to my house, I was running to the Harper Estate. I had to see they were gone with my own eyes. My head already knew the truth, but my heart was telling me to prove it. I hated when my heart and head disagreed; it only made it that much harder to deal with things.

By the time I got to Estate Lane, my lungs were on fire. I bent over and rested my hands on my knees, trying to catch my breath. When my breathing began to even out, I continued on. The Harper Estate had changed so much since the first time I'd come there. From the outside, the large stone home was still as beautiful and peaceful as I remembered it. They had done wonders in restoring it, restoring it back to their home from their time. But as I walked up the stone circular drive, my heart began to ache. I was sure that the inside was going to be different ... the house would be empty. It was as if I could hear the emptiness, echoing throughout the house. This time Blake would not be on the other side of the door with a smiling face and open arms to welcome me.

Maybe it was too soon; maybe I was not ready for this. For a long minute, I hesitated as to what I should do. Taking a deep breath, I pushed all thoughts away and focused on turning the large gold knob. There was no use in knocking; I knew all too well that no one was home. The desolation was spilling out of every crack and crevice of the old house.

Gone were the books that lined the floor to ceiling bookshelves, as were the paintings that Blake had painted over the summer. A small smile broke across my face as I visualized Abby reading a disappearing spell in order to erase any evidence of their lives there in that time. I walked down the long hallway and stood in the kitchen, seeing nothing but a small stack of books lying on the island: *Beginners Guide to Witchcraft* and Abby's personal spell book! I was shocked that she had left it. She had said that she never went anywhere without it. I opened it up and read the words she left for me:

Dear Meredith,

I leave these for you to practice becoming a strong and wise witch. Don't give up on your destiny, and don't give up on us. We will see each other again, one day.

Love,

Abby

I sighed, fighting off the tears, gripping the books close to my chest. I walked through the rest of the house, finding one empty room after the next. I left Blake's room for last, knowing it would be the most difficult. As I sat on the foot of his bed, I noticed an envelope lying on his pillow with my name on it.

Meredith,

I am hoping this letter will find you. I am sure your heart is breaking, and I will never be able to explain to you how sorry I am for that. When we came here to this time, I was not expecting this. It was for your safety that I came here and for your safety that I left. You must know that leaving you was the hardest decision I've ever had to make. We will meet again.

Forever and always,

Blake

That was it. There was no way to hold back the tears any longer. I curled up on his bed, burying my head in his pillow and breathing in the scent that he had left behind. The tears I cried were not tears of sadness, but tears of joy. The letter had helped me feel close to him again; being in his room and reading the letter had made me feel like what we had was real. He loved me, and he was hurting, too. Somewhere in some other time and place, he was missing me. It was horrible to admit to myself that him hurting was a positive thing, but in some twisted way, it gave me comfort. For a few hours, I stayed curled up on his bed, thinking about the time we had spent together, hoping that he would keep his promise and we would see each other again.

When I got back to my house, I was exhausted from an emotional day and the trip out to Tinkers Island. My body felt like it was going to collapse at any moment. Just as I was turning my key in the lock on the door, the porch light came on and Jack flung open the door.

"Meredith!" Jack screamed. "Where have you been?" He gave me a once-over.

I stood silent, not sure what to say. At that point, I had no energy left and too little brainpower to think of a good enough lie. I just stood there in the doorway and closed my eyes. I was about to collapse when Jack grabbed me. As he carried me inside, I glanced around the room, seeing Aunt Rose coming out of the kitchen, holding a phone up to her ear.

"Oh!" Aunt Rose shrieked. "Get her in here right now. Lay her on the couch," she shouted to Jack. "She just got home … thank you, officer."

I really could not deal with this just then. Even though I was barely conscious, I could tell by the panic in my aunt's voice that I looked pretty bad. The moment Jack laid me down, I sat back up and opened my eyes, trying to show them I was not as bad off as I seemed.

"What happened to you, Meredith?" Aunt Rose asked, shaking her head in disbelief. "We have been worried sick about you! Where have you been? Are you okay?"

She kept firing question after question until Jack finally cut in. "Rose, let the girl relax. She looks like she has been through enough already." His voice was stern.

"No, don't worry. I am fi—"

“Please don’t tell me that you were about to say you are fine,” Aunt Rose interrupted me.

“Please stop,” I begged. “I-I slipped and fell, no big deal.”

“It’s two o’clock in the morning. You expect me to believe that you slipped and fell and it took you all this time to get home? You had us both so worried I couldn’t think straight the last few hours,” Aunt Rose said, panic filling each word. “Does this have anything to do with Blake? Do I need to call his parents?”

Just hearing his name crushed my already wounded heart. I didn’t respond.

“We are just glad that you are all right. Are you hurt, or did someone hurt you?” Jack asked.

Did anyone hurt me? How was I supposed to answer that question? Yes, the love of my life—who just so happens to be my protector—had hurt me by leaving to travel back in time to keep me safe. And I can’t forget about Abby, Annette, and Samuel. *Hurt* didn’t quite do my feelings justice.

“I’m sorry you all had to come home from your honeymoon like this. Really, it won’t happen again, promise,” I said, exhausted. “By the way, how was the honeymoon?”

I heard Aunt Rose scoff in frustration. Apparently, I had done it this time. I had never seen her that distraught before.

"Let the girl get some rest, and we can finish talking in the morning," Jack said, looking at Aunt Rose.

I hated that I was causing all this drama. Aunt Rose and Jack had just gotten married; this was the last thing they needed to deal with. And the last thing I wanted was to cause them any pain or give them any reason to argue with each other. This was my problem, my battle. But I was thankful that Jack had stepped in. The thing I needed most just then was some sleep. It was clear that my brain needed some time to think in order to get myself out of this mess. I began to sit up from the couch, and Jack reached out his hand to help.

"Thanks," I croaked, my voice was still hoarse from crying.

I gave Aunt Rose a hug and told her that I would see her in the morning. It was clear that she was not satisfied with my answers and that she would have a lot more questions for me then. I dragged my tired body upstairs and went immediately to the bathroom to shower off the tears and sweat from the day. When I looked in the mirror, it was clear why Aunt Rose and Jack had reacted the way they did. I looked awful. My hair was a rat's nest, my eyes were puffy, and my cheeks were a glowing red from wiping away tears. I got in the shower and showered slowly, trying not to think about anything but the hot water running over my body. The warm water stung my raw cheeks, but the pain was a welcome distraction. After drying off, I threw on an oversized T-shirt, hopped into bed, and buried myself under the covers.

My alarm clock rang, and I fumbled around trying to shut it off. I lay there and tried to process the last few days. Aunt Rose and Uncle Jack were probably already up and discussing the millions of questions to ask me at breakfast.

There was not a doubt in my mind that I had failed miserably at hiding my crying last night; even stuffing my head into my pillow couldn't have muffled the sobs. I had to be prepared to answer questions and to come up with a good story for why the Harpers had had to leave town so suddenly, should their name come up. Which I'm sure it would. Aunt Rose had already implicated Blake last night, so I was sure I had not heard the end of it.

Maybe I would say they had an ill family member, and they had had to rush off in a hurry to be the caretakers. That was believable. It would explain why they left so suddenly and why they would not be back for a few weeks. Or maybe an excuse was not needed at all. Wasn't just saying that he was gone, that his whole family was gone, enough?

There were also more in-depths answers required as to where I had been all day the day before and why my eyes were so red and swollen. I was still not sure what lie I would come up with for those questions. *Everything* I was about to say was going to be a lie. It was not something I was proud of, but it was necessary. There was nothing I wouldn't do to prevent the Harpers' secret—newly my secret—from getting out. And there was no way that Aunt Rose could find out that I was a witch; she would surely have me committed. All of this lying was also for their safety. The less they knew, the better.

With that determination in mind, I got up with eagerness, prepared to get it all over with. Before I headed downstairs, I checked myself in the bathroom mirror. Just as I suspected, I still looked like hell. "Here we go," I whispered to my reflection, dragging a brush through my tangled mess of hair, trying to make it look a little more presentable. It was no use. I gave up and walked downstairs, prepared as I would ever be.

Chapter Twenty-One

"Good morning, Meredith." Aunt Rose smiled as she looked up for a moment from the eggs she was scrambling.

"Good morning," I spoke softly. "Need help with anything?"

"No, I think I have it covered. Why don't you sit down? Breakfast is almost ready." She pointed to the table, which had a large carafe of OJ, a few condiments, and three place settings already on it.

I pulled out my usual chair by the window and sat, anticipating that at any moment the questions would begin. But for a long while, there was only the sound of the spatula against the frying pan. I looked around and saw no signs of Jack. I hoped they had not argued and it had caused him to leave or something. But there were three place settings, so someone else was expected to be joining us for breakfast.

“Where’s Jack?” I asked curiously.

“Oh, he just ran out to pick up some donuts.” She looked at me and smiled.

Okay. What was going on? She was cooking breakfast like we were celebrating someone’s birthday or something. Eggs, fresh OJ, and my favorite—donuts. It had been years since we had a spread like this. Did she develop a serious case of amnesia during the night? The last time I had seen Aunt Rose, she was practically spitting fire at me.

“Why the big commotion over breakfast this morning?” I asked.

“Aren’t you hungry?” she questioned.

“Starving, actually.” I couldn’t remember the last time I had eaten.

“Good,” she responded, looking satisfied. “Well, Jack and I were up talking last night, and we feel that we have not been paying close enough attention to you, the last month or so. We were so focused on us—you know, getting married—and you were so busy with graduation and work that we hardly saw you.”

Just then the front door slammed and Jack yelled, “Donuts!”

"Great, we can start," she said as she finished putting all the scrambled eggs in a large bowl, placing them on the table.

Here it comes. Their questions, my lies.

"Did you sleep well, Mer? You still look exhausted," Jack said as he sat down.

"Fine, I slept just fine." And I actually had slept fine, after all the crying I had done that day and night, it eventually put me to sleep.

"Meredith." My aunt spoke with seriousness now. "We wanted to sit down with you and talk to you about a few things. I came off a little harsh last night, and I'm sorry about that, but we were just worried about you." She paused, grabbing my hand. "We just want to make sure you still plan on taking the path you have been talking about the last few months. We know that you met someone, and we are thrilled that Blake is making you happy, but we want to make sure you have thought about your future."

I decided to interrupt her before she dove in any deeper. "The Harpers left." I really didn't mean for it to come out that blunt, but it escaped me without too much thought. "They had to leave town unexpectedly … something about one of their family members falling ill. So—Blake's gone." I have always thought the less details, the better, when telling a lie. I took a deep breath, uncoiled my hand from Aunt Rose's grasp and reached for the eggs.

"Oh, I'm so sorry, Meredith. I know how much you cared about him," Jack said, sounding sincere.

"So, that's where I was yesterday. I was upset … about Blake … so I went to the beach." I was only half-lying with that—that was not so bad. It did not seem right to let them know that I went to the Harpers' house. One, they just wouldn't understand, and two, they would think I was a crazed stalker girlfriend.

"Oh, Meredith, I'm so sorry. Why didn't you tell us last night? I wouldn't have acted the way I did. I feel awful." She covered her face with her hands.

No one spoke for the next few minutes as we each piled food onto our plates. I was starving, so I piled mine high.

"Have you thought about what you are going to do next?" Aunt Rose asked, guilt covering her face. "I don't want you to feel rushed or anything, but I was just hoping you had at least been thinking about it."

"I am going to stick around here for a little while longer." I winced as I finished, expecting the questioning to begin again.

"Okay, if more time is what you need, then you should take it," Jack spoke slowly, drawing out each word as he glanced in my aunt's direction.

Apparently, they had discussed a lot last night, and Jack seemed to be in favor of leaving me alone to figure out what I wanted to do, no badgering.

We finished up with breakfast, and I offered to help clean the kitchen, but it was made pretty clear they wanted me out of there so they could talk more—about me, no doubt.

I thanked them again for a wonderful breakfast and walked upstairs. Part of me wanted to sit on the steps like a child and eavesdrop, and the other part of me wanted to go back to bed. But neither of those would be possible. It was a work day.

I took my time getting dressed for work. There was no rush, since I had plenty of time. I was also not looking forward to facing Aunt Rose and Jack again. Even though my door was shut and they were trying to whisper, I could hear them arguing over what was the best thing for me.

I had never known Jack cared for me like that. I mean, I knew we had grown close over the last few years, but he was down there defending me and talking about me like he was my father or something. I felt so awful for causing all of this arguing between them. This was all my fault. If I had just come home yesterday and pretended to be happy instead of staying out until two in the morning, none of this would be happening. I felt like I was eight years old again, listening to my parents argue.

Then it seemed suddenly clear: those few weeks before the accident, my parents must have been arguing about how to keep my sister and me safe. They must have known what we were and what was potentially coming for us. How hard that must have been for them.

Even though I was not in the mood, I put on some makeup after being frightened by seeing my reflection in the mirror. There was no need to scare the patrons.

I went downstairs and told Aunt Rose and Jack goodbye; both were still sitting at the kitchen table, sipping their coffee. Each of them gave me a smile, but it was clear they held different meanings.

The walk to work was peaceful, and it allowed me to put my thoughts in order as to how I was going to get through the day.

"Good morning, dear," Ms. Donaldson said as I walked through the double glass doors.

“Morning.” There is nothing good about it, I thought to myself. I walked over to the counter and threw my purse and backpack underneath it.

“Are you feeling alright?” Ms. Donaldson asked as she looked me up and down, eyeing me suspiciously.

“Just a little tired,” I lied.

“Well, if you need to go home early, just let me know. I will be down in the basement again today. The courthouse brought more boxes over for us to go through.” She turned around, heading toward the back of the library.

“Um—Ms. Donaldson—do you think I could work in the basement today? I’m not really up for working with people right now.”

“Okay, if you’re up for it. But it’s covered in dust down there.”

“Sure.” I tried not to look too anxious as I walked toward the back of the library. It was such a relief knowing that I was not going to have to deal with anyone face to face.

Ms. Donaldson was not kidding when she said it was dusty down there. But she had left out the part about it being dark and putrid-smelling. I stuck my nose in the corner of my right elbow and used my other hand to sift through the first box. It was full of magazines and newspapers. All of them were about Marblehead and dated back from the early to mid 1900s.

Then I thought of something. Maybe one of the magazines or newspapers would give me a sign that the Harpers had made it back in time. If it would just mention one of their names, then I would know they had made it back safely. I began to dig, desperate to find anything that alluded to the fact that they had survived after crossing back in time. But as I reached the bottom of the box, I had found nothing of the sort.

What was I expecting to find? Was I really just hoping to find something to prove that they were alive and well? Would that really make me feel any better, knowing that they were there and I was here, separated by over a hundred years of time? Giving up, I pushed the box out of the way and sat back against the wall.

Then something drew my eyes downward. It was an old newspaper, lying on the ground beneath a box. I couldn't explain it, but I knew that it held some meaning without even reading it. I reached down and pulled the paper close to my face in order to see it better. Everything in my world stopped. A tingling sensation spread throughout my body like wildfire. Then I began to shake, and I could do nothing to halt it. My breathing became rapid, and I was overcome by the yearning to get away as fast as possible.

I ran up the basement stairs, tripping over the first few, but finally making it back to the main floor. From the corner of my eye, I could see Ms. Donaldson, staring at me with her mouth hanging open. I would probably have stared too if I had seen me running like a crazy person toward the front door.

"Meredith, is everything all right?" I heard her shout to me just as I reached the double glass doors.

I didn't answer. I pushed open the doors and continued running, not even bothering to look before I crossed streets or to stop when I saw people staring and beginning to whisper. I just ran, a part of me wanting to believe that if I just pretended to not have seen what I had, then it wouldn't be true.

I didn't stop running until I reached the front lawn of my house. My legs ached all over. My lungs burned. My heart pounded against my chest. I bent over and gasped for air, wanting the words I had just read to disappear, even though the words were engraved into my head forever:

Harper Family Perishes in Church Fire

Services will be held at Waterside Cemetery – July 1, 1905

The article said the fire had happened June 27, 1905. That was it; I had lost them forever. I had lost Blake forever. All the people who I had come to love were all going to be killed. My body went limp, and I fell to the ground.

"Meredith, Meredith? Sweetie? Wake up. Are you okay? What happened?" When I came to, Jack's frantic face was staring down at me. He was shaking me and calling out my name. "Meredith, Meredith!"

I couldn't concentrate, and I found it difficult to speak. "I-I must have passed out."

With Jack's help, I pulled myself up into a standing position. "Sweetie, you are not taking care of yourself. I know Blake leaving was hard, but—"

"Please, stop right there." I breathed. He had no idea what he was saying and how much those words hurt. Just the hearing his name was too much.

"Ms. Donaldson called the house and said you ran out of the library in a hurry. She wanted to make sure you were all right. Are you—all right?" he asked, his eyes as wide as silver dollars.

"I'm fine," I said just above a whisper. "I just ran home too hard. I was in the basement at the library and—I started to feel sick." I knew without even looking at his face that he didn't believe a word I had just said. But it didn't matter now. Nothing mattered.

Jack helped me to my room and sat me on the bed. "Please, get some rest. Your aunt just left for work, and she is going to flip out when she hears that I found you passed out in the front yard."

"Please don't tell her. She will just worry more than she already does." But I could tell there was no changing his mind.

"Just try and get some rest. We can talk about it later," he said as he shut the door behind him.

I walked toward the window and pushed it open, allowing some fresh air in. I melted toward the ground and began to search my brain, trying to think of something I could do. Supposedly, I was this all-powerful witch that could bring people back from the dead. There had to be a way for me to prevent them from perishing in the fire. All I had to do was somehow get a message to them. I leaned my head back against the wall, trying to calm down so I could think more clearly.

No, no, no … *Please* don't let that be Aunt Rose's car pulling up, I thought when I heard the noise of an engine outside. As I glanced down to the driveway, I saw her getting out of the Grand Cherokee. Jack must have called her.

Leaving the window open, I leaped toward the mirror. I shuddered when I realized what a complete and utter mess I was. Hearing her footsteps coming up the stairs already, I dove toward the bed and laid down.

"Meredith." I jumped at the sound of the voice coming from the other side of my door.

"Come in," I mumbled.

She opened the door just a crack at first, but then swung it all the way open. She was wearing a worried look on her face. "Oh, Meredith. Jack called and told me what happened."

I sighed. "I told him not to. I knew you would just worry."

"Of course I am going to worry about you. You have been a completely different person the last couple days. Is there something that happened when we were out of town?" she asked.

I swallowed hard. "No, nothing out of the ordinary."

She exhaled loudly and sat down beside me on the bed. "If there is anything you want to talk about, please know that I am here for you. I want you to come to me if you are hurt, angry, or confused about something."

I sat there, contemplating telling her everything, imagining feeling the weight lifting off my shoulders. But I couldn't do it. "I'm fine, really. I just passed out … no big deal." It was tough looking into her eyes and telling her that everything was all right when in reality I was having the toughest time in my life.

"No big deal? Listen to yourself, Meredith. Have you taken a look at yourself? You are a mess." She took in a deep breath. "But if you are not ready to talk to me, I will just have to accept that. Just please know that whatever it is you are feeling at this moment, it will change. It will get better."

"I know." I pressed my quivering lips together, fighting back the tears, knowing that it would not get better, knowing that it was only going to get worse, way worse.

"By the way, Jack told Ms. Donaldson that you are sick and at home resting. But I think you owe her more of an explanation, when you're up to it."

I nodded.

"Would you like me to bring you up something to eat? It may help you feel better."

"Sounds great." I forced a smile.

She patted my arm and walked out the door, closing it behind her.

I am a horrible person, I told myself. Look at what I am putting them through! They don't deserve this. If I could just find a way to warn the Harpers and let them know to avoid the church on June 27 ...

Then it came to me. The spell books Abby had left for me, maybe they would tell me how to get them a message or something. It was a long shot, but worth a try.

I jumped off my bed and began to search my room for my backpack. When I had left the Harpers' yesterday, I had put the letters from Abby and Blake and both spell books in there. I threw the covers off my bed, checked in my closet, and under my desk. Then I gasped, realizing the last place I had seen my backpack: It was sitting next to my purse under the counter at the library.

Dammit, I thought. Somehow I have to get out of the house and get to it. But how can I? Not right now. Aunt Rose will definitely be on guard for the rest of the day. There was no way she would let me out of here without demanding to go with me.

As I sat on my bed, I formulated my plan. Just then, there was another knock at my door.

"Come in."

Aunt Rose entered with a tray full of food. Her eyes were red, and it looked as though she had been crying. She set the tray on my desk and made her way over to my bed. I felt horrible that I was causing her all this pain.

"Aunt Rose, I'm sorry for how I've been acting and—"

But she cut me off by putting her hand up. "Please, Meredith." She fought back her tears. "Jack was cleaning out the closet to make room for his stuff and … and … he found something."

She was still talking nonsense as she pulled out a folded-up piece of pink paper. My heart stopped as my mind flashed back to my father waking me up in the middle of the night. My sister and I had met in the hallway and then walked down the stairs to see my mother scribbling a note on her favorite pink stationary before she hid the note in the spice cabinet.

"My mother …" I wanted to say something more, but nothing came out.

"Yes, your mother left this note for me." She began to unfold the crumpled piece of paper that my mom had left all those years ago.

She handed it over to me, and I began to scan the page.

Rose,

Thank you for your friendship over the years. Thank you for always being there for me and for the girls. I'm sorry I had to leave without saying goodbye, but there is one last favor I have to ask of you. Please take care of the girls and keep them safe. Again, I'm sorry.

Love,

Emma

I sat there, unable to speak. If I had read those words a few weeks ago, they would have just added to my confusion as to what was going on that night. But since I had found out who I really was and what my parents were possibly running from, it made all the sense in the world. My mother and father had not expected to live through whatever or whoever they were running from that night. My mother had made plans for who was going to take care of us before we even left the house. Folding the letter back up, I placed it down on the bed.

Aunt Rose closed her eyes, trying to keep the tears from coming again. "Meredith, I know that things have been a little crazy lately. But I just want you to be happy. That is all your mom would have wanted, too. So ... do whatever you need to do in order to figure out what that is. You are more than welcome to stay here as long as you want. It is your house, after all." She took in a deep breath and looked me in the eyes.

It was painful for me to see the hurt and despair in her face, like she had failed me, failed my mother whose last request was to keep me safe. I wanted to make her feel better. I wanted to tell her it was all okay and that she had nothing to be sorry for, but the words never made it out.

Aunt Rose got up and began to walk toward my door.

I couldn't let her leave. Not without saying something. "Aunt Rose," I breathed out.

She stopped and turned toward me.

"Thank you. Thank you for everything." I smiled, hoping that she could understand what I was trying to say.

She smiled and walked out.

When she left, I reread the letter. *Take care of the girls*, it said. Then I wondered, was Charlotte supposed to survive, too? Whatever my mom and dad had known was coming for us, had they expected to die and hoped both my sister and I would survive? I wished I could remember more of that night. If there was only a way to see what had happened to cause my dad to swerve the way the police had said he did. He must have seen something.

After finishing the food Aunt Rose had brought up for me, I patiently waited until they went to sleep before sneaking out. Before I left, I contemplated leaving a note, just in case she woke up and found me missing. But I decided against it, because what would I have said? But there was one person who I felt I owed a phone call to … a phone call that was long overdue.

"Roger?"

"Mer, hey what's up?"

I smiled. It seemed as though I had woken him up.

"I just wanted to say hi and see how things were going," I said.

"Things are good … you know girls, sun, and summer. Can't get much better than that. I do miss you though. When are you going to come see me?"

My stomach turned and I couldn't believe it. He really had no memory of me being there last week.

"Soon. I promise." I sighed. "Get some sleep and I'll call you in a few days."

I hung up the phone and fought off the tears. There was no time for emotions right now. Time was running out and I had to get to the library for the spell books.

Chapter Twenty-Two

There were no lights on in the library, but a faint glow was coming from Ms. Donaldson's apartment upstairs. I pulled out the key from my pants pocket, thankful that I hadn't kept it in my backpack. I inserted the key into the lock and gently turned it to the right. It made a popping noise that I had never heard before that night. But I guess there had not been any other time where I had actually made a point to listen. I opened the door just enough for me to slip through, hoping to avoid the screeching noise when it closed. I crept toward the counter, my heart pounding, my mouth dry, and my body shaking.

I turned on the small lamp that sat at the end of the counter and pulled out my purse first, then my backpack. I sat down with my back up against the counter and pulled out the spell books. As I flipped the first book open to the index page, I scanned down it, quickly realizing there was nothing even close to what I needed. I pulled out the next book and tore through each page, desperate to find something.

There was no point, anyway. Who was I kidding? I was still too young in my powers to even come close to helping them. I set the books down and pulled my knees to my chest. I began rocking, trying to stop the pain and the tears from coming. Was there nothing left? Was this it? Was this how it was going to end? They were going to die?

Suddenly, a light flicked on behind me. I swallowed hard and stopped my breathing. Footsteps were coming toward me, and there was nothing I could do about it. There was no way I was going to get out of there without Ms. Donaldson seeing me. So I just waited.

"Meredith?" she asked, looking around the counter, squinting her eyes in my direction.

I had no idea how I was going to get myself out of this one. Truthfully, now that I had already been caught, I didn't care. "Hi, Ms. Donaldson," I said, trying to keep my voice even. "Sorry to wake you. I just forgot my backpack and needed to get something out of it."

"Well, stand up, dear. There is no need for you to hide down there. Is everything okay? You sure ran out of here fast this afternoon."

For a split second, I wanted to answer no. I wanted to tell her that everything was not okay, that everything was falling apart, and I didn't know how much longer I could hang on. But I couldn't, knowing that she would think I was crazy and probably call Aunt Rose or maybe even the police. She began to walk toward me, eyeing the books that lay at my feet.

"I'll just grab my stuff and be on my way." I fumbled the books, trying to stuff everything back into my bag before she had a chance to see them clearer.

"I know the burden you bear, my dear," she said sympathetically.

Gripping my backpack in my hands, I replied, "I ... don't know what you are talking about. What burden?"

"The books that are in your bag, I know the power they speak of. I know it can be a lot to handle at first." She smiled, trying to put me at ease.

"H-how do you know about the books I have in my bag?" I asked curiously.

"Hmmm ... Well, let's just say that I had a book similar to that many years ago. So did your mother."

My mother. She knew about my mother. I wondered what else she knew. I stood up and began to back away, not knowing if she was someone I could trust.

"Don't be afraid of me. I was once like you, although I don't practice anymore. After your mother died, I couldn't bear to use magic anymore."

"What do you know about my mother?" I asked.

"Ah, well, I was her teacher, you see. We are all given one at one point or another. I had one when I was about your age, and then when I grew into my powers, I was given a student. Your mother was the most powerful witch I had ever seen. She had possessed powers and qualities that I had never witnessed in all my life. Her life as a witch was so promising, but she quit practicing after she had you and your sister. She wanted to shield you girls from magic until she thought you were ready. She wanted you both to have a magic-free childhood. Unfortunately, she became distant to me toward the end. See, your mother had the ability to sense things before they happened; it was a quality I had never seen before. I knew she was in trouble, but she was very secretive and I never knew who or what she was running from. But your father was her protector, and I trusted that he would do the right thing if it came down to it. I know he tried his hardest that night to get you all away from here. I just wished they would have come to me. Maybe I could have helped." She sighed, looking away from me, staring into the dark library.

I felt my eyes grow wide with shock. Ms. Donaldson had been my mother's teacher. My father had been my mother's protector. Just like Abby and Blake were to me. My mind was swimming. Ms. Donaldson had known about me all along.

"I'm assuming that something is going on since you had to come all the way over here this late at night," she said, staring at me with curious eyes.

I was careful about how I answered, still not knowing if I could fully trust her. "Yes. I'm trying to help someone."

"But you're not in any trouble?" She questioned.

I shook my head, not wanting to tell her what I had been trying to do.

"I'm just curious because I've sensed a change in you over the last few weeks. When the accident happened, it was almost like you were wearing some type of armor, I couldn't sense any energy from you. I assumed it was your mother's work; it had her name written all over it." She smiled proudly at that comment before continuing. "That's all she ever wanted for you two girls, to grow up without all of this magic, and when the time came she would tell you about it and let you make the choice to follow your destiny or not. But I also knew that no spell lasted forever. That the spell she had placed in order to protect you would eventually fade and you would be left vulnerable. I know she tried her hardest that night and did the only thing she could. That's why I asked Rose about you a few weeks ago. I knew your 18th birthday had just passed, and I wondered if maybe that was the day when the spell would finally lift. Sure enough, the first day you walked into the library, I could sense the energy inside you. It was magnificent. Now, I can feel an even more amazing energy from you, which leads me to believe that you have summoned your powers. You have chosen to follow your destiny."

I felt my eyes grow wide. How did she know about the summoning of my powers?

"Don't look so alarmed, dear. We are connected now by an even deeper bond, one that can never be broken."

And it was in that moment that it all came together. I knew what I had to do. A part of me wanted to stay and talk to Ms. Donaldson about all the things she had just told me. But I was running out of time. If I had any chance of saving the Harpers, I had to act now. I hugged Ms. Donaldson goodbye, promising her that we would talk again soon, and thanking her for everything that she had just told me.

I ran out the double glass doors and didn't stop. The more I ran, the more confident I felt. It was going to work; it had to work. Blake had said himself that all witches were connected … dead or alive, good or evil. And I know Abby said the Council only intervened if the craft was in jeopardy but it was, wasn't it? I was apparently going to be a powerful witch but my protector, teacher, and guardians were all in danger of dying. I was not sure if this qualified as a major threat in their eyes but I had to at least try. I ran faster, pushing through the pain in my lungs and legs.

I turned the corner onto Shore Drive, and I waited for the pain in my stomach to appear like it had so many times before. But it never came. The gates to the cemetery were closed, so I threw my backpack over and started to climb. I pulled myself up and over the top of the gate and jumped down to the other side. After grabbing my backpack, I raced down the familiar path, passing right by the Harper graves and on to my family's.

When I arrived at the gravesite, I collapsed down to it, gasping for air. About a minute passed, and I felt like I was ready for what I had come there to do. This was the one place I felt the closest to her, it was the only place I could think to ask for her help. I wanted to travel back to 1905 in order to warn the Harpers about the fire. It was the only way to make sure they were safe. Sure I could try and get a message to them, but then I would always wonder if they got it and if it worked.

"Mom." I paused for a moment, not knowing quite how to say what I needed to say or if she was even going to get the message. "I need your help. I know you are out there somewhere, and I'm hoping you can hear me. The Harpers need me. They are all in danger, and I need to get back to 1905 in order to warn them. Please."

I sat there waiting. Waiting for something, anything to happen. But there was nothing. No sounds, no magical lights, no ghostly spirit of her. Ten, twenty, thirty minutes passed with still no sign of her. No sign that I would be getting the help that I had asked for. The way Abby and Blake explained it to me, the Witch's Council had asked them for help. Maybe it was just wishful thinking that I could somchow contact them. Maybe this wasn't going to work like I had originally thought.

I sat with my back up against the gravestone and tried to think of anything else I could do. Another hour passed, and I pulled myself up from the ground. Half of me was in a daze as I walked out of the cemetery. I didn't think I could make it all the way back home that night; I didn't have enough strength left. The only place I really wanted to be was at the

Harpers', anyway. The sun would be up in a few hours, and I knew that I would have to answer to Aunt Rose when I got home, but it just didn't matter.

As I approached the estate's tall wooden gates, my heart began to ache, knowing that I had failed them, knowing that it was for certain I would never see them again. I unlatched the lock and pushed open the gate. Standing there, I stared at the large, empty, dark house. My knees almost buckled under me, but I found the strength to continue moving. The comfort of Blake's bed and his scent that I hoped still lingered on his sheets lured me forward. Once inside, I dragged myself up the winding staircase and curled up onto Blake's pillow. It was not long before exhaustion took over, and I quickly fell asleep.

At first, my sleep gave me relief from the pain. Then came his voice. He sounded so close, almost as if he were in the next room, just a few steps away from me. But as much as I wanted it to be true, I knew that it was just my cruel dreams, torturing me ruthlessly. But I didn't care, so I listened as hard as possible, wanting to hear his voice, even though it was agonizing to hear.

Next, I heard a door swing open and a loud gasp.

"*Meredith*!" He called.

More than anything, I wished I had the power to answer him. Tell him what was going to happen to him and his family. Tell him that I loved him. Tell him that no matter what happened that I would never give up on us. But I couldn't. There was nothing I could do to quiet the alarm in his voice. And there was nothing I wouldn't do just to be able to touch him again, and save him from the terrible tragedy ahead.

His voice spoke up again. This time it was no higher than a whisper, right into my ear. "Meredith, please open your eyes."

No, I thought. If I open my eyes, then his voice will disappear and no telling how long, if ever, it will take for me to hear it again. *No,* I would rather sleep forever.

But then I wondered if he was trying to give me a message or a warning. Maybe he had found a way to communicate with me through my dreams.

"Please, please open your eyes," he whispered to me.

Then I swear I felt his touch, brushing my hair back across my head. The one touch sent chills over my body, and I yearned for it again. Then, as if a miracle had occurred, I felt his lips brush upon mine. His lips were gentle, and I couldn't stop myself from enjoying the moment. It felt real, too real. I wondered if this was some kind of punishment. Was some higher power trying to torture me to death?

Then he pulled back, leaving me desperate for more. I was too afraid to move a muscle, not knowing what would happen if I did, scared that the dream would go away. And even though I knew eventually my eyes would have to open and I would be heartbroken all over again, it was worth the price.

"Now do you believe me?" he asked.

Did I believe him? What was that supposed to mean? But I could tell his voice held a smile in it, and it warmed my insides. This is how I wanted to remember him: sweet, happy, smiling, and alive. There was a part of me that wanted to live in that moment forever, never wanting to open my eyes and see the emptiness of his room. But then I realized that I wanted to lock the moment in my mind forever and be able to look back and remember him just like this.

Chapter Twenty-Three

With much internal conflict, I opened my eyes and saw two sparkling blue eyes staring back at me. I opened and shut my eyes again, trying to wake myself from the dream before anything bad happened, ruining my memory of him forever. But each time I opened them, he was still there. I wrenched forward in bed, realizing I was not dreaming. I was awake.

I gasped. "Blake? Is it really you?"

"It's me." He took my hand and placed it on his cheek, allowing me to feel the warmth of his skin. "See, I'm real."

"Are you back ... or did I go back in …" My mind was so jumbled from being there with Blake that I couldn't get the right words out.

"You're here, back in my time."

"It worked. I can't believe it! My mother, she must have done this," I cried.

"But I don't understand. Why didn't you just wait for me to come back for you? I told you I would."

"The church, you and your family …" I trailed off, not able to finish my sentence. My mind was still spinning at the fact that I had traveled back in time and that my mother had helped me do it.

"It's all going to be fine, Meredith. Isaac has agreed to meet with us. He said he's willing to help us defeat Alex."

"What? Isaac is going to help?" I asked, confused.

"Yes, he contacted Abby, and we are meeting him at the church on the outside of town. Don't worry, we are all going and will be prepared if things go wrong."

"No! That's why I came here. Things go wrong, horribly wrong. I saw it in the papers. You die, you all die in the fire at the church. Somehow you all get trapped inside and can't get out. Please, don't go," I screamed.

Blake's door swung open, and Abby stood there staring at me, much like she had the first day we met.

"How did—you—get here?" she asked.

I couldn't help but smile, just seeing her made it all the more real. "My mother, I think."

She ran toward me, pushed Blake out of the way, and hugged me. "I was scared I would never see you again."

"Me, too," I said, feeling tears welling up in my eyes.

"Abby," Blake said, picking himself up off the floor. "Meredith has come here for a reason. She saw something. She saw that we were going to die in a church fire."

"What?" Abby looked at me with a tortured expression. "No, he said he wanted to help. He wouldn't do that to us … to me." She shook her head and gazed down at the floor.

"It's a trap, Abby. Isaac is luring us there to kill us," Blake said. I was thankful he was the one who told her, so I wouldn't have to.

She continued to shake her head. "I don't believe it."

"I saw it, Abby," I said. "In the newspaper, it said that you all were trapped inside, unable to get out. It only makes sense if they were trapping you in there with magic."

She sat next to me on the bed and stared down at the floor for a long minute. "Well, if that's the case, we know what has to be done, don't we?" She held her head high and stood up. "I have spent the last couple of years loving him and fighting for him but I won't do it anymore, especially not at the expense of losing my family."

I looked toward Blake, and by the expression on his face I knew what he was thinking. Then my heart broke as I looked into Abby's tortured eyes. The pain she must be going through right now must be unbearable, I thought. She was left with choosing the man she loves and her family.

"Let's go. He is expecting us there by sunrise, and if we're late, he will start suspecting something," Abby said, standing and walking toward the door.

Blake stood up and faced me. "Meredith, you're staying here."

"The hell I am!" I said, jumping off the bed. "There is no way. I have come this far to make sure you all don't die out there, and there's no way I'm stopping now," I said with irritation.

"Understood. Let's go and get this over with," he said, not even bothering to put up an argument.

We all went downstairs and found Annette and Samuel in the kitchen.

"Meredith?" Annette gasped.

"Meredith came here to warn us. We don't have much time, I'll explain when we get there." Blake said as he scooped me up in his arms. "Close your eyes, it's probably going to be a bumpy ride."

I obeyed, and before I knew it, we were flying through the air. It was the fastest he had ever flown with me, and it took every part of me to fight back the nausea. The trip didn't last long, and when I opened my eyes, we were standing in front of the church. Blake quickly filled in Samuel and Annette when we arrived.

"Let's finish talking over there," Abby said, pointing toward the large pine tree in the distance. "Isaac should arrive any minute now."

We all followed her and gathered together, out of sight from the church.

"We will somehow have to get Isaac, Alex, and whoever else comes with them inside the church before we enter. Then we will have to combine our powers to seal the doors and ... start ... the fire," Abby said, barely choking out the last few words.

"Are you sure about this, Abby?" Samuel asked. "We can think of another way."

"No. We will always be running from them. This may be our only chance," she answered.

"And here I thought you loved me." A voice from behind us spoke.

"*Loved* you is correct," Abby snapped, whirling around to face him. "How could you do this? Plan to kill us all?" Her bottom lip quivered and it was clear she was suffering terribly.

The five of us stood facing Isaac, the man I knew from my dreams as Alex, and four unidentified men. We were outnumbered.

My eyes scanned the group and stopped on Alex, the last one to the left. Alex was the oldest of the group, whereas all the others were closer to my age. This was the first time I had ever come face-to-face with him in real life. His eyes were locked onto mine. Blake stepped in front of me to shield me from the glare Alex directed at me.

"It was the price I had to pay." Isaac's words drew my attention back to him. "Lose a family to gain a family." He shrugged. "But this is an unexpected surprise," Isaac said, pointing to me. "After all that work in trying to get you all to the future so we could use your powers … and yet here she is."

So it was true then. They had used the Harpers in order to get to me.

"What happened to you?" Abby asked Isaac, forcing back tears.

"What happened? Do I really need to go into details with you?" His voice was full of anger and frustration.

"I just can't believe it," she paused. "You! You did this to him," Abby shouted toward Alex, lunging toward him. Samuel grabbed her by the shoulders and held her back.

Alex turned toward her and smiled. He was smiling the same evil smile that I had seen in the woods that afternoon, the last day my family was alive. That memory made me question how he got to my time all those years ago. Whose power did he and Isaac use to cross time? Could they have somehow channeled my mother's power? Then all the puzzle pieces in my head began to fall into place. Then another memory flashed into my mind.

I saw Alex standing in the middle of the road, on the outside of town. It was *him* that had caused my dad to swerve the night of the accident. My body shook with rage. The longer I stared at him the more I remembered from that night. All the memories that I had blocked out because of the pain, began to come back to me. I remembered my mother surviving the initial impact of the accident. She was awake and speaking coherently. She was saying something over and over again … a chant of some sort … or now that I knew she was a witch, it was probably a spell. I couldn't remember the exact words but I do remember seeing Alex approaching the car but stopping a few feet shy of it. He met my gaze and new that I was still alive. But he looked confused and irritated that he couldn't get any closer to me. It all made sense now. Before my mom died, she *had* said some sort of spell in order to protect me from him. But the spell went far beyond just that night; it had protected me until my 18th birthday.

I felt an indescribable feeling come over me. Anger ripped through me and a craving of revenge twisted all around me. Before I knew it, I felt an overwhelming feeling of power coursing through my veins.

Just then the church doors flew open. Alex, Isaac, and the rest of their group focused their eyes on me. Blake still stood in front of me, but I pulled my head around and focused on them. I focused on pushing them toward the open doors. It took all the courage inside me, but I tried to focus on using the one spell I had learned. It was a simple spell and I had only been able to move a leaf and rock but now my focus was on all the men before me. I could sense resistance, almost as if they were all combining their powers and pushing against me. I was not sure how much longer I could keep this up, the power I felt inside me felt strong but I wasn't sure if I could possibly lose it all at any second. My eyes remained focused on Alex and I slowly began to see all the men before me move toward the opened church doors. I closed my eyes in order to concentrate. I breathed deeply, seeing them moving in my mind, toward the open church.

I could hear yelling in the background, someone screaming to "Make it stop," and I thought it sounded like

Isaac. It was strange, because I didn't know where all this power was coming from. Maybe it was from the anger that I felt toward Alex, knowing that he was responsible for my family dying that night in the accident. Or, maybe it was the fear that he would take away the people standing beside me, the people that I now cared about deeply. I squeezed my eyes tighter, forcing myself to push out every thought, allowing my mind to concentrate. Then I heard a loud slamming noise. I saw the church doors crashing shut in my mind.

"Meredith, let us take it from here," Samuel said, placing his hand on my arm. I kept my eyes closed, afraid that if I opened, they would find a way to escape. "Meredith, please," he asked again.

I opened my eyes and saw Samuel's pleading eyes staring me.

He then turned to Blake and Abby, nodding his head. "We will finish this. Take Meredith back to the house."

Blake scooped me up in his arms, and then we were flying. He was much gentler with me that time than on the way over. I leaned back to feel the cold air on my face. My body felt weak and exhausted. I wondered if this is what it felt like to use the type of magic I had just performed.

It was not long until we were standing on the front porch of the Harper Estate. My heart ached for Abby. I hoped that one day she would be able to forgive me.

"Where's Abby?" I glanced around, searching for her, my voice cracking.

"She needs to be alone right now. But she'll be okay," Blake answered.

It was a couple hours later when Samuel and Annette got home. Their expressions held both relief and sadness, relief that it was over and sadness that Abby was suffering. No one spoke about what had happened back at the church after Blake, Abby, and I had left. I knew deep down what had happened.

I waited up all night until Abby finally came home. There was no way I could sleep until I looked into her eyes and saw forgiveness. I was lying in Blake's arms when I heard her footsteps walk past his door.

Without even having to ask, Blake lifted his arm. "Take all the time you need."

I crept slowly toward the closed door at the end of the hall, not knowing if this was the right time or not. But I had to at least try and talk to her.

I knocked lightly and heard a faint voice telling me to come in. "Abby," I said as I entered the room. "I just wanted to say I'm sorry. I can't imagine how you feel toward me right now."

She looked at me with a curious expression. "Meredith, you saved my life, my family's life. I will forever be in your debt."

"But Isaac ..." I whispered.

"It was difficult for me to see past my love for him, but I realized long ago that I had lost him. It just took me until today to see it. He was too far gone for me to bring back." She sighed, looking blankly at the wall. "You did amazingly today. You should be proud."

"It was nothing, really." I shrugged. "I just closed my eyes and did what you taught me that day in Steer Swamp. But I had this overwhelming feeling within me. I can't explain it."

"Well, it's clear that you have amazing power within you, and you've just scraped the surface of it today." She smiled. "Get some rest. We can talk more in the morning."

I put my arms around her and held her for a long while. When she finally drifted off to sleep, I slowly walked back down the hall to Blake's room. The door was cracked open, and I pushed on it gently, hoping not to wake him. But once I got close enough, it was clear he was still awake.

"You didn't have to wait up," I said.

“I would wait forever for you.”

I melted back into his protective embrace. The warmth of his body and smell of his skin sent me into a peaceful trance at once. His warm lips pressed upon my forehead, which sent a shockwave of pleasure through me.

“It’s all going to be all right now.” He sighed.

I lay there, exhausted from the day. It was just over twenty-four hours ago that I had read the paper and seen that the Harpers were going to be killed. Now I was back in 1905 and had stopped it all from happening. Relief washed over me, knowing that the people that I had come to love were all safe. It should’ve given me the desire to sleep, to let my body rest and recover. But I was scared to close my eyes, scared that when I woke up, Blake would not be there, holding me in his arms. What would happen when I woke up? Would I be still be in 1905, or would my mom or the Council transport me back to my time? Just the thought of being separated from him again sent a shiver of fear through me, causing me to wrap my arms around him as tight as I possibly could, wanting to be as close to him as possible.

“Are you okay?” he asked.

“As long as I have you,” I raised my head and pressed my lips to his.

THE END

Meredith's story doesn't end here. . . .

Check out the author's website for updates on the next book.

www.heatherlondon.com

20. 97, 102, 103, 180, 195, 278, 332, 335

14363466R10200

Made in the USA
Charleston, SC
08 September 2012